'THURSDAY'

G.Davies

THURSDAY
Copyright © G.Davies 2006

All Rights Reserved

First Published May 2006

Printed in Great Britain by www.fast-print.net

°THURSDAY°

To my gorgeous girls –
Fiona and Lara
who keep me going.

PREFACE

Without weather, life on Earth as we know it could not exist. It would be a barren, inhospitable desert, unbearably hot in low latitudes and impossibly cold elsewhere.

Our world and its atmosphere can be regarded as an engine. Its fuel is power from the sun, and its output is the life of every living creature and plant.

Weather has an important place in the lives of us all. It affects agriculture, transport, commerce and industry. It influences our housing, dress, food, leisure and holidays! We cannot tame it, but we can observe and measure it, forecast and use it, and where necessary, take precautions against it...

...and pray that we are wrapped up safe at home when the worst of it hits, because 'if gravity had its way... everything would fall down!'

CHAPTER 1

After the initial loud, innocuous bang outside, a clap of thunder beyond the windows coincided noisily with the sound of a following explosion. The building shook on its foundations as though hit by an earthquake, the shudder both noticeable and frightening to the structure's occupants.

At first, there were just the disdainful raised eyebrows and reserved wariness as the people *still* queued to pay for their goods on each floor of the department store, unwilling to lose their position in their lines. The realization that something worse had happened only dawned as flumes of black smoke and debris billowed up through the stair well, knocking various ascending shoppers to the treads as though a steam engine was sat below them. Screams started at the back of the store, and rippled through the foot traffic like Chinese whispers as people turned towards the noise and smell. People fell unwillingly to their knees as the shuddering floor suddenly took their balance. Windows at the far end of each storey shattered; shards of glass exploded to cover the many people stood beneath them and the glistening wet street outside.

Coughing! Choking! Crippling! The harsh taste of smoke and dust was inhaled by all, hurting like fire in their lungs, irrespective of normal respiratory health, clogging the nostrils with its foul stench.

Instinct started to take over. As they ducked to the ground, men grabbed their wives with protective arms and tried to cover their own mouths. Sparks flew from dislodged electrical circuits; whole banks of ceiling strip lighting blacked out; escalators ground to a halt. Children wailed as they saw the panic around the store, their faces already streaming with tears. Cashiers, their mouths open in the moment of fear, ducked behind their tills as they saw the tidal wave of soot and blown masonry rushing towards them, money and credit cards *now* forgotten on the counters in the desire for self-preservation.

The force of the blast smashed goods from the shelves and threw them noisily to the floor. Heavier items of household equipment teetered precariously as they shuddered on their spots. The detonation reached its worst intensity and rained even more airborne dirt on the crouching public, before diminishing as quickly as it had started, receding back down the stair well, leaving the floor covered with the blackened dirtied bodies of the shoppers. On one floor, a ruptured water pipe in the ceiling created a cascading waterfall that ran down between the aisles of clothes ending in a muddy pool around a till island.

That wasn't the end of it. Almost immediately, an extremely loud, rushing, gushing sound filled the room as the glass atrium at the top of the building suddenly imploded, bringing tonnes of brick, masonry, glass and steel crashing down into the centre of the store. More soot and dirt billowed through into each floor as the quantity of destruction descended the height of the store at high velocity. Polystyrene composite material rained from the false ceiling above as

7

the explosion punched through scores of holes, though the structural metal struts remained intact. Those beneath the vast quantity of building materials on the motionless escalators screamed as they became aware that those split seconds were the last of their lives.

As the people sat on each floor, the doubt, wonder and amazement at what had just happened pervaded them. Still coughing, they were looking up and around the gondolas which were still stocked with goods, though now completely undesired; the children's previous cries now quiet sobbing in fear.

Through the high set windows, the dark sky outside lit up with a flash of lightning which forked across the sky, followed a few seconds later with a close sounding rumble of thunder through the broken windows.

It was at this moment that the power cut out, and every strip light across the ceiling of every sales floor went dark, causing more screams and cries from the shoppers as they sank as low as they could to the relative safety of the ground. When nothing more happened though, these petered out as they sat in the darkness waiting to see what would happen next.

The eerie silence lasted about fifteen seconds, as the people shifted their weight on the sooty floor, hugged their legs and counted their blessings. Couples gripped each others' hands and rested against the shelving. Mothers hugged their children and all anyone could hear, was the force of the rain pebble dashing the remaining windows above their heads.

Heads poked above the till islands as one by one, the staff, comforted by their vantage point of safety, lifted up to see the devastation around them by the dim gloom of the street lighting outside. Convinced that nothing further was to happen, they stood and peered into the gloom that was now their work place.

On the fifth floor there was as much panic as on any of the others – made worse with the distant rubble of thunder.

'Doreen!' cried a man's voice in the darkness, 'Doreen. Are you all right?' Pleading. Earnest.

Heads started rising in the gloom as they turned towards the voice. Confidence building back in their hearts; people wanted to see what had happened. No flames were visible. No fire. That was something at least.

'Doreen!' Now more urgent. 'Doreen! Where are you?'

Mass shuffling now as people started getting to their feet, clutching around them to hold themselves up on the rubbish splattered floor. The pitiful voice was drowned out by the started conversation around the fifth floor.

Another...

'Andy. Andy. Help me Andy!' cried a tearful woman resting against the ruins of an electrical goods display, her blackened and bloodied hands holding her cheeks while slight cuts on her arms and legs oozed from the impact of sharp edges; and bruises slowly formed.

'I'm here, Helen!' her husband responded from the other side of the aisle as he clattered towards her sound. Toasters fell crashing to the floor as he stumbled in the darkness.

9

'DOREEN!' The voice was shouting above the growing cacophony of sound in the shopping area. It was unheeded as everyone around on the floor started down the road to self-preservation. Voices called across the darkness as everyone became more desperate to regroup into their families.

'DOREEN!' the man shouted as he tripped over the prostrate body of his wife and landed on his knees beside her in the wreckage of pottery. Realizing that it was his wife from the distinct smell of her perfume and quantity of shopping bags around her, he peered close to her face to make sure. His wife had been knocked out after being hit from behind by a display of twenty-four assorted sizes of dinner plate, the remnants of which was now creating gashes in the man's trousers and hands as he groped around in desperation. His hands wet with blood from the wounds, he hugged her close despite the lack of response from his unmoving wife. The man sat on the floor and sobbed, his sound adding to that in the aisle.

'Is everyone all right?' shouted a weak but almost authoritative sounding voice from the side of the room, as a security guard, who had previously been cowering down the store's decorating supplies aisle had now ventured into the vast darkness that was once the scene of his work. 'Can everyone stay still until...?' his voice tailed off as he tripped over a bent metal shelving strut.

At this, pandemonium broke out. Despite the gloom and inability of anyone to walk more than two steps without falling over, a sudden desire to leave the scene overtook many. Raised voices. Bickering. Sobbing. Screaming. Commanding. Everyone had a plan to get out and everyone had to get there first. The guard's repeated instructions went unnoticed as a display of microwaves near the stairs collapsed causing more hysteria and disabling fleeing young women in high heels.

The first to the stairs realized the problem before anyone else. The main stair-well which ran up the centre of the building from the ground floor up to the atrium on seventh had collapsed under the weight of rubble from above, rendering it useless as an escape route. Those that got to the fire escape in the corner realised a similar problem; the shaft clogged completely with impassable matter.

Unfortunately, some of these people were too slow in communicating this problem as they were pushed from behind by the jostling of others who had followed them towards the faintly luminescent central green EXIT sign. They tripped over, landing heavily on the rubble, twisting one woman's legs and ripping another's hands to shreds, creating more screams of pain, and ensuing obligatory sobbing.

More people were reaching the area at the top of the stairs now and able to realize that there was no further forward movement despite not being able to see properly. The crushing of the almost dozen people abated as common sense prevailed a little though the noise didn't as they all started clamouring to know what anyone else could see.

'Calm down. Please calm down!' the security guard's voice above all else's. 'Calm!' he repeated as indeed some shoppers did begin to do as he asked.

Outside, thunder could again be heard, rumbling in the distance as the wind whipped the rain against the remaining glass in the windows making it sound as though gravel were being thrown rather than the rain, making a synchronized whooshing and cracking sound.

At close range, thunder is a startling loud crack rather than a rumble, as the sound is less distorted over a shorter path. Thunderstorms are simply showers accompanied by thunder and lightning. They only occur with deep convective clouds called cumulonimbus, which often extend to 10 km from the ground and contain a mix of water droplets, ice crystals and hailstones of different sizes. Because of the weight differences, they are consequently lifted by, or fall through, up-draughts in the cloud at different speeds causing strong up and down currents, producing the quantity and frequency of normal thunder and lightning, and of the unprecedented velocity and volume that Wolverhampton was currently experiencing.

On the fifth floor, calmness was a pleasant relief after the preceding moment's mayhem. Cigarette lighters were being flicked into life as intelligence started to reclaim the panicked people and a yearning to see the true extent of the problem took over. As the lights were held up, the shoppers could see that the stairwell, despite being over ten metres wide, was completely impassable. The central escalator was still, quiet, hidden and impenetrable, almost indistinguishable under the mountain of twisted and broken steel, glass and stone. And what was more, the rubble looked very shiny, and as the men holding the lighters moved closer, they could see that water was trickling from above through the rubble.

'Ruptured a water pipe,' exclaimed one man.

'Rain water from above!' said another.

Bert Simmonds held his lighter closer to the miscellany that was once a route out of the store. He was a tall, darkish skinned man with the current trials and tribulations of his life etched on his face below the close cropped hair style of the recently balding. In the glow of his lighter, his eyes betrayed his fear, and a trickle of blood ran a meandering course from above an eyebrow down to his cheek. A grimy and shaky hand shimmered the light slightly, evident to all around.

'If it is a ruptured water pipe,' he said slowly and carefully, 'then the explosion might also have took out the gas as well as the electric! We'd better be careful!' No one failed to notice the shake in his voice.

Both Bert and another man nervously sniffed the air for any traces of gas, and, after looking at each other, simultaneously flicked back the hoods over their lighters plunging the area back into darkness.

'What happened?' asked the soft voice of a woman sat on the floor resting against a microwave. 'Was that the storm... or a bomb...or...?' Her voice faltered to silence as it became apparent that she wasn't the only person wondering. In the gloom from her position on the floor, she could see the people stood around her looking at each other in a silent plea of explanation. She looked back down into her lap at the damaged flowery dress that until that morning had been brand new. A shower of dust cascaded from her now lank, dirty blonde hair over her hands. She coughed quietly, feeling a pressure on her lungs which were now under the strain of trying to draw oxygen from the sooty air.

There was a loud crash as the security guard made his way down the aisle towards the group, and knocked a stainless steel tea urn from the shelf with his tentatively feeling hands. The guard had only just started his eight thirty till eleven work shift, which had, until five minutes previously, seemed a reasonable alternative to being a steel worker from which he had been recently laid off.

Dave Thompson had decided that this job, though with no obvious career prospects, did mean he went home clean every night and provided a reasonable subsidized canteen meal, alleviating a little pressure from his increasingly more frantic wife. How incongruous that at this moment in time, he would have given anything to be sweating, toiling and aching in the steel mill where he knew his job inside out, rather than clambering through this assault course of bodies and white goods with absolutely no idea of what to do next.

Dave coughed slightly as he said, 'I work here!'

'The stair well is blocked! Is there any other way out?' Bert's voice held a quaver, but otherwise quite firm.

The people around him quietly watched the dark shape that was obviously a man who was remaining calm despite the problems, and listened for a reply from the struggling dark shape that was in the process of tripping over someone's bag of food cans.

'Yes. Yes! The store has freight and customer lifts… no power though!' said Dave, his panting cutting some of his words into over stressed syllables. 'But I think maybe…' he slowed his breathing and rested before he trod on the woman on the floor, 'that we should stay still. Someone will come for us!'

'Where's the fire escape?' came another grumpy male voice in the darkness. 'Which way do we go?'

'There's only one… but it's completely blocked,' Dave shook his head with frustration.

'You are joking!' exclaimed Bert disbelievingly. "Only one!"

No one saw Dave shake his head in the darkness, but everyone heard the other, unseen man, tut and sigh loudly before descending into barely audible swearing and promises of retribution against everyone concerned with the oversight at only providing one fire escape.

The gathering of people swelled slightly as other shoppers from around the fifth floor of the store made their way towards them. No one spoke for a second. A flash of lightning illuminated the sky beyond the window, and provided a glimpse of the store on this fateful evening. Bert could see a cashier at the end of an aisle sat looking mournful at a cash register; a family huddled together on the floor, and an old man cradling his wife's head in what looked like a mass of glass. Beyond them were various grey, indistinct shapes that had collapsed where they were, either knocked out cold by flying debris, or fainted from the stress of the occurrence. He himself was nursing a headache from where the force of the blast had tripped him into a display of vital kitchen aids that, according to the promotional material around it, said: 'no home should be without'.

Reflecting on his current predicament, he cursed the reason he was here. His wife had needed a complete set of steak knives as a gift for a recently divorced friend, and, of course, it was no problem to send him for them. Any other Thursday evening, he would have been sat in his favourite arm chair, cradling his little companion, Tyrone, a terrier, and watching some mindless calming rubbish on television, whilst waiting for Sandra to come home from stacking shelves at the local supermarket. Instead, he was stood here, in near darkness at the top of a blocked stairwell, covered in blood, looking at carnage around, and listening to the distant cries and wails of people on the floors above, below and around him, all worried and in various conditions and states of health.

'Well,' said Bert rationally, 'if there isn't a useable fire escape – there isn't a useable fire escape. We'll have to find another way!'

'I can't smell gas!' said the blonde woman on the floor suddenly breaking his reverie. 'Can't we have some light?' She shifted her weight uncomfortably against the microwave, scrubbing her finger nervously against the feeling of dust on her legs. 'There are candles on a stand over there!'

''Ang on!' said a jaunty voice belonging to a smallish dark shape, 'I jus' passed some of them!' The male voice sounded almost happy, as though having fun – odd, and different from everyone else's in its timbre.

There was a scrabbling sound as though trying to find his feet, a clattering as another tray of cutlery hit the floor, and then he was there again; his hands just about visible in the gloom, clutching a tubular item.

Bert looked back at the stairs and sniffed again for gas. Deciding that they were safe, he reached for the proffered candle and lit it with his lighter.

Within a second or two, the heat gathered in the wick and the flame stabilized, casting a warming glow over the scared and dirty faces of the people stood around whom were all staring with worried faces towards him. In the distance the sounds of sirens could be heard, though at that moment in time, the most welcome sound was the quiet crackling of the wax as it warmed. Across the sales floor, the remaining people were looking towards the group waiting for direction. Even Dave, the security guard was looking. All were almost hypnotized by the comfort of the dancing flame.

'I shouldn't be here!' Bert then voiced the question in everyone's mind. 'What are we going to do now without an escape route?'

In another part of the store, there was initial panic caused by the explosion. They listened in horror as the rush of sound encompassed and shook their small space like an imagined tidal wave or crashing airplane. It was followed almost immediately by complete electricity failure. The lift shuddered and stopped dead between two floors; the interior lights extinguished with a faint 'pop'. The two

17

occupants fell to the floor and clung to each other in the dark, suddenly fearful for their safety. They listened for any follow up sounds to explain the previous ones – totally unnerved because of not knowing – locked in their restricted space.

Nothing!

The lift was pretty well insulated and they could hear nothing but a vague crackling sound through the wall. The man groped for the main control panel and pressed anything he could touch in the dark. Nothing from that either. Ah well. He fumbled for his communication radio and pressed the side button - shouting for help into the mouthpiece.

Nothing but static answered him.

He reached for the other warm and fleshy female body stood quivering in the lift and they clung together for security unnerved by the sudden dark. When nothing further occurred and no other noises resulted, they clung together for other reasons – confident it was just a momentary unusual power failure and not knowing how long they would be there before the power came back on again. However, it was a god send that they were here now and intended to make the best use of the time.

They were soon chuckling and giggling together – not believing their luck. There were plenty of things they could be doing with the time.

Hands fumbled at a belt and it dropped to the floor with a clang and clatter. Heart rates racing, the couple made the best of their location.

CHAPTER 2   *Jealousy*

That Thursday morning, Alison Turner had woken alone in her own bed. She barely remembered the previous evening due to the amount of alcohol she had consumed. She patted the covers around her double bed in a half-hearted attempt to find a missing body.

'Damn him!' she grumbled to herself, 'why isn't he still here?' She absentmindedly chewed phlegm back into an extremely dry mouth and smacked her lips as she tried to recover some feeling back into her mouth. Her eyes opened blearily and she yawned loudly, her mouth opened as wide as possible.

Lifting her tousled hair from the pillow, she tried to sit up, coughing now with the effort and rested her back against the pillow before looking around the bomb site that was her bedroom.

The late morning light was filtering in through the thin, cheap cotton curtains and showed the dust in the air. Sat on the rickety, chipped white bedside cupboard was an ashtray bearing the neglect of more than a week, a selection of cigarette butts stamped out in the blackened basin and the smell hanging obviously in the air!

Alison lifted a breast and scratched at the sweaty patch beneath before reaching across to touch the Marlboro Light box beside the ash tray in order to seek the first white stick of the day. The box slid across the top and fell to the floor, the opening gaping wide betraying its empty interior. The blue plastic lighter that had been lying on top of the box flicked beneath the bed. Grumpily coughing to herself, Alison lifted the duvet and slid her naked form from the bed

19

and padded across the obstacle strewn floor in search of the new pack she knew she had in her handbag.

She must have had a good evening. Last night's clothes had joined previous evenings' on the floor in sweaty smelly piles, half full stained mugs contained the discarded remnants of sugary tea which now languished on the floor as little time bombs for the hapless room occupant. Legs clenched together against the cold, she found her hand bag on a decrepit chair, yanked it open and rummaged around in the murky depths for that new packet, her lank blonde hair cascaded down around her mascara smeared face as the concentration showed in her grimace. It wasn't there.

'That asshole!' she exclaimed to herself as she up ended the bag in frustration all over the floor. Resting down on her knees, her hands picked through the selection of objects… old lipstick, new lipstick, tissues, lighters, slips of paper with hastily scrawled phone numbers and dusty coins to name but a few. With a sudden thought, Alison snatched up her cyan blue purse and unzipped it. A thumb went through the various compartments and suddenly… 'I'll kill him!'

Her previous evenings' discovery had taken the fifty pounds rent money for the flat and, to add insult to injury, her new packet of fags. Boy, could she pick them? She slumped back dejectedly onto her heels and covered her mouth with her hand to think.

Suddenly she jumped up and went to the bathroom, determined that life must go on despite the setback. She decided she'd have to get out the flat quickly this morning before old Mr. Smith upstairs got up. He'd be knocking on her door in a moment for this week's rent, and she couldn't stand him at the best of times. Racing through her ablutions, she passed her toothbrush quickly across her teeth before searching through the floor for her basic make-up.

With a squirt of deodorant, she pulled her work clothes from the pile over a threadbare settee in the living area and started to pull them on, hopping from one foot to the other on the dusty, dirty carpet as she fed the tights up her legs.

Flicking her head back, she pulled an elastic band around her hair and knotted it twice.

Kicking a carrier bag containing the packaging from a previous Indian take-away to one side, she pulled on a grey skirt showing many hideous purple crescents. Sniffing the armpit of a purple blouse, she shrugged and stuffed her limbs down the rolled up arms. Slinging a grey jacket with similar purple detailing around her shoulders, she smoothed everything down with the misguided belief that it would clear the creases. Pushing her feet into a pair of low heeled black court shoes, she admired the effect in a grubby mirror hanging on the back of the living room door.

Her flat wasn't the most expensive. She resided in a poor part of Wolverhampton in an aging terrace. The brick facade was getting blacker with the soot and smog from the cars that passed outside less than a metre from the front doors. The windows in the house had been replaced with cheap brown plastic double glazing by Mr. Smith, who obviously had no taste. The windows had long since passed their second birthday without ever having been cleaned. The effect on the property was one of darkness and neglect. A chipped stone step led up directly from the patchwork pavement to a battered and chipped brown wooden front door. A cheap and scratched Japanese lock was the only thing that stood between Alison's meagre belongings and passing thugs and jobless wanderers.

However, the two storey building looked exactly like its immediate neighbour, and the one next to that, and so on. Alison's house had the dubious honour of being on the end of the row, so the windowless side of the building was host to a massive advertising hording board that currently sang the praises of a local building society's investment rates and promised a wonderful service to anyone who could invest a minimum of one thousand pounds every month. The house owner, Mr. Smith, had lived there for at least thirty years before having the brainwave of bricking up the hallway, creating two living areas, and thus being able to rent out the poorly equipped ground floor. A couple of poor foreign exchange students had occupied the created three room flat for a couple of months, before the worry of seeing large rodents every morning from the vantage point of the peeling kitchen proved too much, and they left, not before being fleeced of their deposit for a contrived incident of damage.

Alison was a god send to Smith. She held down a job in a local store and didn't appear to notice or care that the overgrown rear garden was the home to various undesired pests and a selection of shopping baskets and trolleys. It was true that her living standards fell below even below Smith's, but as long as the week's money was forthcoming every Thursday morning, then he was quite happy. The fact was that he loved collecting it, because Alison's general chaos in finding the money from her bag usually gave him plenty of opportunity to stare down her blouse at the soft white outline of her breasts.

Smith heard the sounds of activity downstairs, and pulled on his grubby green dressing gown, slipped his feet into his slippers and made his way down the stairs in the quest to meet his quarry on her way out of the house.

Fortunately for Alison, her speed and general silence had given her the advantage. She made it out of the flat through the back door, jumped the cracked slab that had often tripped her, twisted past the damaged metal frame of a council refuse bin that had once ripped her jacket, avoided next door's ginger tabby cat that was lying in wait for its breakfast, and was through the feeble garden gate before Smith could get to her. It wasn't the first time she had had to take avoiding action.

Smith stood at the front door, his dishevelled greying hair standing up on end and his robe clenched around his feeble old body, sniffing with apprehension and wondering why she wasn't joining him. As his brain clicked over to realize that she had gone the other way, Alison was striding quickly up the side street towards a local car dealership that was situated on the corner. The car dealership was a nuisance to the local populace due to the fact that it drew opportunist thieves to the area. They walked back and forth looking for untended cars left in the side streets by visiting clientele in the hope of spying unattended mobile phones, loose change, or the grand prize... a laptop on the passenger seat.

Once spotted, the lookout would generally hide in a doorway, a grubby yellowing hand holding a cigarette to his face while he watched out for his friend who was usually in the process of jimmying a drivers' door, or in some cases, just lobbing a brick through the window to gain access to the precious cargo within. Small change would buy more cigarettes... an expensive phone would yield a few grams of cocaine, and a lap top would provide a whole week's retirement to the secluded quiet of the current local squat.

Though Alison was worldly wise, with more than one or two minor law infringements under her belt, she detested walking these streets and always swore to herself that the following year would be the time to move to better premises. However, she paid minimum money to her landlord, whom, she had quite quickly realized would let her off the occasional ten pounds if she asked nicely enough while dressed in her most provocative lacy blouse. She was more than aware of his way of staring at her, and although she found it uncomfortable, used it to her best advantage. Though not a size ten supermodel, her womanly curves often gave her an advantage over the weak will of men.

She made it to the main arterial route and slowed her pace, coming to a rest at a battered green bus shelter decorated with the mindless scribbling of several youths, all who had demonstrated their love for each other, or proclaimed that so-and-so had dubious sexual preferences across the clear-plastic structure.

Above her, dark clouds were beginning to gather. The grey sunless sky was getting darker and the temperature was dropping a

24

little more. As a particularly large Scandinavian lorry passed the shelter, the back draft caught and whipped around her. She was sure she could feel moisture in the air and it triggered a memory of the previous evenings' events. It had rained then as well.

Her 'pulling blouse' had been soaked running from her friend's car to the club that they'd gone to. The effect on her nipples had attracted many panting males on heat, and meant that a full evening of drinking cost nothing at all. She remembered throwing up on a seat somewhere and being taken home in an aging Ford Escort by one of the young men before the bouncer had found out. Half hearted refusal of entry to her flat had resulted in him staying and her subsequent pleasure and pain.

She needed a cigarette. The bastard! Fancy nicking them? Trouble was… she couldn't remember what he looked like. Too many orange flavoured vodka drinks resulted in every man looking desirable, if not all the same, especially when they had bought them.

The bus was late. She looked up and down the road in an effort to see its approach and was rewarded with the loud honking of car horn as a car load of youths slowed down to gawp at her legs. 'Get lost!' she thought. It was half past ten in the morning and the last thing she was thinking about was flirting. If she was late again to work, her boss would have a fit. She was on dodgy ground already due to previous run-ins with him concerning allegations of theft and laziness.

Alison's friend was already at work. The efficient metro system had dropped Sian Williamson right outside the Lexington's Superstore in the heart of the town. She checked her watch, and entered the grand foyer determined to sit in the staff canteen for half an hour and have a coffee before starting her shift at eleven.

Thursday was always a long day. Her lunch hour couldn't come quickly enough at three, and the hours always dragged. Sian started the climb to the sixth floor up the endless escalator system, marvelling at the quantity of enticing stock around the entrance. She wondered if Alison was all right.

Sian's husband had dropped them off at a party at a club in the town and only returned to pick up Sian a little after midnight. Alison had been downing Alco pops and shots surrounded by the worst elements possible, refusing to ignore them, and leaving Sian to chat with the rest of the hen night crowd without her. She was a little disgusted with Alison for her attitude, and more than a little jealous of her life-style. Though the same age, Alison seemed to have a lot more fun with the boys. Several times she had almost removed the band of gold from her finger and join in the fun, but always bottled out at the last minute. Her attitude to monogamy was one of.... 'do unto others...' and she was positive that he shared her viewpoint, and couldn't bring herself to spoil the trust. Sian wished that Larry was more spontaneous with demonstrations of love... bunches of flowers, a box of strawberry truffles occasionally, or bottle of expensive champagne on occasions other than just Valentine's Day or her birthday, but he was a good man who showed it in other ways. There weren't many who would get up in the middle of the night to fetch his wife from a party... and one to which he had not been invited!

Sian had witnessed Alison's retching during the evening and displayed a maternal worry when she was carried out by two young builders to a car. Alison's drunken slurring, 'piss off' when confronted was enough to make her back down and leave her to it. It wasn't the first time it had happened, and it certainly wasn't going to be the last. She just hoped that Alison had the sense to use protection. She tried to be a good friend, but refused to get involved in Alison's continual flirty behaviour.

She nodded hello to another two girls descending on the opposite escalator having finished their shifts. The lifts weren't open to the staff, and though the climb didn't require much exertion, it did become tedious doing it day-in and day-out. Her floor was the Household Supplies, where she was in charge of the Kitchen Needs for the rest of the afternoon. It was going to be a long day and she was already looking forward to a lunch break at half past three as a chance to get away from the seemingly mindless sheep that crawled through her floor more than as an opportunity to eat. Still, she had tomorrow off. Four day weeks weren't too bad and it fitted better at the moment with her home life.

She loosened her coat buckle as the heat of the store permeated to her body and released the buttons down the front. She bore the familiar uniform of the store, required wearing, despite its obvious lack of taste. A little hungry now, she decided to eat quickly before she had to be in the store room of the seventh floor for the shift staff meeting.

Glancing around, she noticed the store wasn't busy yet. It would be later.

'Hi Babe!' she called across to another close friend as she joined her on the escalator to finish the final leg of the journey. 'Enjoy last night?'

Her friend, Sally Phillips, was soon to be married, and although as excited as anything, the thought of settling down was still a tentative proposition... or so she had said last night, when the booze was flowing easily, and the drunken hug had spoken more than the words that had followed.

'What a night? What happened to Alison?' asked Sally, her blood-shot panda eyes betraying the lack of sleep and too much alcohol.

'She went home with one of them lads! I haven't seen her yet... Tart!' Sian grimaced, though with a twinkle in her eye.

They stepped onto the final floor, confronted with various doors. The customer toilets, staff and stock rooms led off the extremely light hallway. Above the store, the midday sky was boiling and bubbling with clouds of varying grey intensity, the central glass dome a perfect observatory position for sky gazers. No further escalator led from this point; the store room floor only accessible through the staff quarters.

Sian keyed in the latest staff code into the silver, round button push pad that accepted the number with the welcome click of the room door release. Sian swung it forward, and the two girls entered, both with the intention of collecting food from the self serve buffet as quickly as possible.

All around them, other staff members were already there. Some stood at their lockers, others at the floor to ceiling windows, gazing across at the world outside. This was a brand new building and one of the tallest in the town. From here they could see the meandering route of the canal... the sprawling shopping malls and the vast car parks containing a myriad of coloured cars. The windows surrounded the whole of the floor, giving all round visibility. Tables, chairs and comfortable couches gave enough seating, and there were enough nooks and partitions to create privacy as required. Both Sian and Sally threw their coats on a settee that would provide a vantage point over the bus station, and crossed to the food counter with Bain Maries and plastic sneeze guards.

The time was approaching eleven when Sian started nervously glancing at her watch. Alison had not arrived. The boss would be furious. It could mean the sack. She and Sally looked at each other, then stood up to clock on and join the group on the next floor up a short staircase for their starting pep talk.

As they reached the top floor, Sally winked at a smart, well built guard who had just exited the purpose built security room, and now stood lounging against the door jam, a cap pushed back on his head, though immaculately dressed in every other way, his shiny black shoes gleaming in the electric lights. As he smiled back, she looked coyly away, feeling suddenly a lot better.

'What on earth has happened to her?' Sian continued the conversation in an undertone, unaware of her friend's change in mood.

Sally could guess. She hadn't the same regard for Alison as Sian had. Probably sat in bed somewhere with her legs still open! Sally wouldn't miss her at all. She wasn't as pretty as Alison. Sally had her own way of getting through the day... Sian never knew, and Alison would definitely have been jealous.

On the Birmingham New Road, a Midland Red bus sat in an extensive traffic jam, trapped behind a brand new blue and yellow Metro tram which languished on the rails in the tunnel beneath a railway track.

In Wolverhampton, the trams ran down rails set in the tarmac along with other vehicles. In places they had their own lane governed by a separate signalling system, but the majority of the distance between towns was along well populated road routes.

Inside the bus, Alison sat sweating with frustration. Desperate for a cigarette, she was almost climbing out of the windows. Her watch now said 11:09 which meant that she'd now have to plead to keep her job. It just wasn't fair! It wasn't her fault that the bloody tram had broken down. Banging her head on the window in an effort to see ahead, she could see various people alighting from the tram and scratching their heads. Cars on the opposite carriageway were slowing down to watch. Traffic lights changed, and the mild annoyance caused by an unknown lack of power, now resulted in mass chaos and mayhem as cars on side streets desperately tried to join the throng of traffic.

She saw many of the ex-passengers drifting around nomadically, wondering what to do... all except one tall dark figure who dashed from the tram in front, across the road without looking left or right, down a side street and out of sight. Alison watched him go with curious fascination.

CHAPTER 3 *Professional*

There is something almost redundant about Wolverhampton. To the casual observer, it appears a bustling metropolis of creed, colour and sound. However, the casual observer is usually by-passing the town centre via the wide ring of tarmac; dual carriageways and islands carrying them around its heart in pursuit of an arterial route towards Birmingham, Dudley or a neighbouring motorway. The casual observer shouldn't take the unassuming side turnings to enter the sprawling area of mish-mash desolation within. As well as disproportionate numbers of Indian, Chinese, Thai and Caribbean fast food establishments and restaurants, the once great historic town illustrates its poor maintenance with rotting, boarded up facades and the constantly crumbling and degrading modern affronts to architecture. The inhabitants of Wolverhampton accept their surroundings with little concern, more enthusiastic about the progress of their local football team in yet another league than the 'too-little-too-late' efforts at area rejuvenation. Indeed, the countless sporting venues offer the gambling minority brief respites from thinking about their decaying habitat; the speedway, horses or dog track revenues doing very well.

The bizarrely over-subscribed university nightly sheds hundreds of students hoping for part-time work in the more well-known retail outlets, while the less lucky assist in the plentiful less reputable businesses. The thousands of daily visiting octogenarian shoppers hunt for bargains in the discrete and hidden alleyway shops, populate the malls, then meet for a healthy grumble in cafes about the good old times, long since past.

The casual observer wouldn't fail to become aware of the many local radio stations, blaring out an assortment of styled music from every open passing car window and shop doorway – the tracks linked with the manic incoherent ramblings of a twenty-something disc jockey – obviously paid by the uttered word – their eye firmly fixed on the bigger picture, perhaps of television fame and fortune.

The countless nightclubs attract the bored youth of the town most weekends, when the average age of the female in the street plummets in the evening; pointless street brawls ensue after a skin full of alcohol before visits to a takeaway that had avoided the council appointed health inspector.

The casual traveller would do well to follow the sign posts towards their destination and avoid stopping. Wolverhampton is a town that they would either love or hate.

William Monkham had lived in Wolverhampton all his life. He loved the local radio stations and was a regular visitor to the restaurants now professing a mixture of food styles now called 'fusion'. Just before two o'clock that Thursday afternoon, he steered his large, brand new, two-tone black and silver four-by-four Toyota Land Cruiser into the narrow space between two other, smaller cars before cutting the engine. The sound of music inside the cab died as he removed the ignition key and jumped out to look up at the gathering clouds. 'Monk' was just starting his watch at Newbury Fire Station but would have preferred to be still on paternal leave, nursing his newborn son with his wife. A large man, his gruff and normally unfriendly exterior had eroded completely over the last week whilst tending to his family. His own family said the birth had changed him completely.

'Y'all right mate!' shouted Bob Tannen from across the car park, wringing a chamois leather of the last few drops of water.

'Aye!' returned Monk as his pressed his remote to simultaneously lock the car and flash the hazard warning lights. He pushed the little black key fob back into his pockets and strode towards his colleagues.

'How is she?' asked a third, Luke Smith, coming through the open mouth of the building that housed the fire tenders upon hearing Monk's arrival..

'She's great!' smiled Monk, 'one in a million!'

'Congrats mate!' exclaimed Tannen as he reached Monk and clapped him on the back. 'So now you're a daddy!'

'Aye!' Monk's shiny bald head almost bounced with pleasure as his face twisted into a grin, the skin rippling slightly at the back of his neck, his hand reaching to clasp his friend's. The two gave a brief manly hug and then parted to continue into the building.

'Welcome back pal!'

They joined Smith at the front of the large, bright red fire fighting unit and all three walked towards the staff room for their start of shift pep talk with the station commander as call sign Red Two.

Above, the afternoon sky gave a low warning grumble of the bad weather destined to come. The sky dimmed and across the road, lights started springing to life as their owners flicked them on, disturbed by the sudden reduction in visibility.

Inside the fire station, the six men on the two till ten watch completed the briefing and started the general duties which included looking after the tools of their trade. They were totally unaware of the forthcoming events for their evening that would effect and devastate the town for many months ahead.

The tall and powerfully built Smith started checking the basic mechanics of the engine, wiping his hands frequently on a dirty, oily rag whilst other members of the team were rebinding hoses, sweeping the area and completing an assortment of other necessary obligations about the place.

Half an hour into the watch, the klaxon sounded and as one, the team pulled their jackets on and collected their helmets. Moments later, the engine was out of the garage, through the lights and speeding to a house fire in the back streets of Bushbury, weaving through the traffic like a guided missile, the siren warbling above them, air horns blaring loudly, on another desperate mission.

The driver, Smith, loved this part; the power above all else on the road; the movement of cars out of his path; the natural caution at lights as he nudged his way through the junctions a necessity. It felt heroic.

At the home of a stressed working mother, one of her teenage off-spring had attempted to make toast for the little sister following their return from school. The toaster was attached to its electrical socket via an adapter plug already bearing five other appliances and pulling away from the wall quite naturally with the weight. Cue sparks and the resulting fire that flashed on a discarded kitchen roll.

Before the young girl could do anything, the fire had spread up from the socket and kitchen roll to the new wooden wall-mounted units, and swept through the kitchen across the oily worktop and started melting the plastic surface on the five year old Electrolux fridge-freezer – quickly peeling away the veneer.

The ensuing black smoke was crippling, and both sisters collapsed to the floor coughing uncontrollably. Like a mini atomic bomb, fire burst into life on every surface and unit. The black smoke curled up to the ceiling, spreading across the artex, flickering over the cheap spot light that hung above. The fire was steadily stripping the wall paper from the walls and spreading interminably towards the light switches.

Fortunately, the older sister had had the presence of mind to close the thin door between the hallway and the cramped kitchen, and the fire was momentarily quite self-contained.

Monk had been first out of the tender, closely followed by his colleagues. Lights still flashing, the tender had been parked across the muddy grass verge. The men were swift and efficient at effecting entry through the rear garden, a swift kick at the cheap wooden screen door being all that stood between them and saving lives.

The children's crawling exit was later a relief to their arriving emotional mother, even though the subsequent soaking wet charcoal look to the room was not one she had wanted.

Monk, Smith, Tannen and the others left the cul-de-sac with relief that no one had died having imparted many words of advice and returned to Newbury in good spirits, headlights visible on all the surrounding vehicles, rain a lot heavier now on the roof of the cab requiring raised voices in order to be heard.

A minor diversion to a warden patrolled home because of a malfunctioning smoke alarm didn't dampen their spirits, even if the weather did try desperately to. Other residents in neighbouring flats raised their eyes in frustration as again it seemed safer than sorry to check the eighty-six year olds' home for indications of problems before continuing their journey back to the station for afternoon food.

Laughing jovially about 'who the daddy was', the fire-fighting team grabbed food from the self-service counter in the mess and sat in the brightly lit dining room to eat, quite happily, the provided healthy three course lunch of: soup, Lasagne with salad and chocolate mousse with custard.

A pre-arranged visit to a semi-detached home in the middle income housing district to give fire safety advice took a chunk of the afternoon tedium... a necessary chore they all bore with good grace on a pre-determined rota.

Monk was in good morale. Years of debate about the financial implications with his wife had ended with an accidental event the previous Christmas time. Nine months with an emotional yo-yo of a wife had ended with the happy event, and although he had always dreaded the sight of his gorgeous wife ballooning to immense

37

proportions, the joy of what she contained negated many worries. Monk couldn't wait to get home and help watch over his family.

His friends couldn't believe he was the same Bill Monkham they'd been on call, and drinking copiously with, for the last four years. They had been through many highs and lows with him in the past, and all had trusted their lives to him at some time. None were displeased with the new version; the job would either make or break you. Monk had had his hard drinking moments but his new family gave him a far more healthy respite from his work day.

Looking through the window the weather was now a lot worse. Rain was lashing the windows in the gathering wind and none of the group wanted a call out tonight. Across the road at the ASDA on the opposite corner, they could see the Thursday night shoppers haring from their cars to the entrance, coats pulled over their heads, husbands resolutely fiddling with shopping trolleys as they found pound coins in the recesses of their trouser pockets to facilitate their release and pushed them towards their waiting wives.

'Look at 'im!' shouted Monk, tapping a finger on the glass indicating the shuffling gate of an elderly man who had just stepped ankle high into a pool of water on the ASDA car park, and was currently hopping on one leg whilst shaking the other as furiously as he could, whilst obviously cursing, his walking stick brandishing angrily at anyone in a surrounding circle who dared to snigger.

'Should have brought ya' trunks mate!' yelled Tannen, screaming with laughter at the unhearing and quite unfortunate man.

'And her...' called Smith pointing towards a lady fighting an inside out umbrella that was in the process of pulling her towards the zebra crossing. As they watched, she bravely stood her ground, her handbag swinging as she forced the canopy back down into a folded position and clenched it beneath her arm, continuing the journey with her head bent low and face twisted in concentration.

An unwatched television high in the corner of the room blared out the signature theme of another pointless soap opera. There was more interest in watching the comings and goings of the traffic passing outside on their repetitive journeys to and from their places of work. The murderous, frustrated, bored and annoyed faces of the commuters were amusing to the watchers, as was the honking of horns by the faster drivers at the slower ones off the mark at the lights. The rain was so heavy it had started to obliterate views through windscreens.

The station commander left them to it. They were loud and raucous when they were playing, but a honed, fit and absolutely committed team when called to duty. He was in his office taking and making calls, assessing the state of the drains in the area and their ability to cope with the increased rain fall.

Watching from the front of the station, the firemen were as interested in the few girls who passed, as the girls were in the firemen, with their quick glances towards them. Many memorable one night stands and future jovial conversations and teasing had resulted from a hot summer's day and the mutual interest between many a warm mini-skirt clad girl and a fireman hosing down the engines.

A hoax call out to the housing estate in the poorer area of Newbury near the dog racing track at seven o'clock provided an annoyance. Racing the tender through slippery wet streets in the driving rain under the illusion of saving people from a house fire was not a nice or safe excursion, they looked in resolute disgust at each other as they realized the pointlessness of it. Parked in the street with curious stares from passing pedestrians and twitching curtains, they looked for any possible culprit. Finding nothing, they restarted the vehicle, and more sedately this time, returned to the warm haven of their station, swearing about the idiocy of the inherently stupid.

It was spot on eight thirty that the main call came.

With the minimum of fuss and trouble, they again slid down the central silver column to the ground floor, grabbed their jackets and helmets and jumped aboard the hefty vehicle on another mission of mercy, this time to the centre of Wolverhampton. Smith ripped the information sheet from the spitting computer that detailed the location and brief resume of the problem, as received by the 999 staff at headquarters. Professionalism beyond everything else, he jumped quickly aboard and passed the information on.

They'd then had to have the station supervisor repeat the call information twice across the communication system to confirm what they thought they'd read.

Monk temporarily put his plump healthy new child and waiting, radiant wife to the back of his mind. This was more important at the moment. They had a job to do; an unusual job; a strange job; possibly a horrific job. A job they'd never forget.

The whole district was on alert. All services and crews from other districts had been called for assistance. All hospitals were on stand by. An incident commander had been requested who would control the various services and ensure cooperation between the different departments. They knew the police and paramedics were en route.

The tender sped through another red light; siren and horns blaring to warn other traffic; the giant wheels creating a tidal wave of gutter water that flooded across the pavement.

A bright yellow mini pulled over and mounted two wheels on the footpath ahead of them, unable to continue with the headlamps blazing in his rear view mirror and the on-coming crocodile of cars slowed to give Smith space to pass round it.

The other drivers had no idea of the fire engine's destination as they silently pulled out of the way, but the officers inside were just as silent.

Not one of them could believe what had happened.

CHAPTER 4

Robert Simmonds wondered what had happened. Half an hour ago, he had been fighting his way into Wolverhampton on the congested Birmingham New Street cursing the thankless task ahead of him... avoiding being broadsided by badly driven white vans and finding a parking space in the increasingly appalling weather conditions, before splashing through rain puddles on the pot holed pavement to the new Lexington's Super Store in the centre.

His day had started pretty badly as well. His job as caretaker to a community centre club was not the most demanding of occupations, but beginning the morning sweeping up from the previous night's celebratory festivities made it just a little bit worse. The surprises that always waited for the unsuspecting tidier made him wonder at people's level of hygiene. Who on earth would have such little manners, that they'd through up over the seats? The stain and smell would never fully leave the upholstery!

He spent the rest of the day running around after the centre manager and putting endless layers of wax on the floor. The tasks would have broken the spirit of the most positive of people, but kept him reasonably fit.

During his childhood, he had been nicknamed Bert by class companions because of his dated view of the world, and the name had stuck. Now, at thirty-nine, he felt that he had never realized his full potential in life and wondered if he ever would now that he was reaching the big '4' 'O'. A lifetime of humiliation and worry had changed his former teenage positive outlook on life to one of extreme pessimism as he seemed to consistently make incorrect life choices. Hindsight was always a wonderful thing.

One area of worry was his wife. Sandra had been the best thing that had happened to him. However, as time had gone on, he felt he was seeing less and less of her.

He wished he could turn the clock back and had taken the option to settle out of the area, away from the people he had grown up with and had the money to whisk her off her feet. Still, he felt he'd done his best. Though his income barely sustained the household bills, her added earnings benefited her wardrobe and cosmetics. There had never been the economic opportunity to have children, but Tyrone had filled the space in their lives.

Sandra had built up a network of friends through work, and always had somewhere else to be, rather than at home with Bert which grated on his nerves and caused more than a few arguments. In the end he always felt it easier to agree with her and recede into his own thoughts and world than to fight to make his opinion matter.

Still, when she needed something, he was always there to oblige. Like today, when he had travelled on one of the worst days for weather that he could remember for quite a while. His trouser legs were soaked from rain water, and a cold trickle of water had found its way down past his collar, into his shirt, soaking his back as he gratefully entered the Lexington's building, lingering briefly under the giant entrance heaters that hung above the door, waiting for the trickle of wet to either dry out or pass his shoulder blades on its relentless journey south.

He turned to look back at the street. Other shops were also still open, the neon name lights shining brightly as they publicized the conglomerates they were part of. All had swarms of people scurrying towards them from the neighbouring car parks. Like bullets from a gun, once their cars were parked, they shot towards the stores in a misguided attempt at keeping dry. Bert shook the remaining droplets free from his grey, threadbare overcoat, wiped his hand over his face, freeing the sticky feeling of dampness and made his way towards the staircase at the centre of the store. Sandra had said that he needed either the fourth or fifth floor… she couldn't remember which.

He passed a family on his way. A harassed looking woman with a miserable, grumpy looking man lingering to one side, were trying to keep two impish boys close by. The boys, who had on identical coats, jeans and the latest logo laden white pumps, were not giving in without a fight. Cue loud words and wails of belligerent demands for attention, sweets and the trappings of modern day junk food junkies. The husband, holding the latest high tech mobile phone to his ear, was trying to keep his distance whilst engaged in an obviously disagreeable conversation. His wife was shooting looks of anger towards him as she tried to cope unsuccessfully with the fruits of their love.

'No Jules!' Bert heard her say as he sidestepped them. 'Just because… Vernon put that down.' Joyce Grenfell, eat your heart out.

Bert grimaced to himself as dirty little fingers clawed at goods on a nearby shelf. Vernon's face turned to look up at him as he passed by, the cunning grin of the intrinsically evil playing around the lips and features of the prepubescent youth. Bert shuddered and hurried on towards a display of cosmetics, beyond which he could quite clearly see the stairs.

Three heavily made-up sales assistants were stood in close formation ahead, like sentries on guard to their domain. The layers of foundation were countable on their faces, their identical suits of purple squiggles on a grey background, worn like badges of honour, their hair wrapped in identical buns. None had hair for eyebrows – instead the briefest of lines had been pencilled in above their eyes.

'Christmas shopping is getting earlier every year,' Bert thought, as he worried about this year's presents. He had not had a pay rise for some time, and his diminishing savings were testament to the rising cost of living under a money-grabbing council. Sandra wouldn't be happy with only a token gift, and he had had more subtle indications of her preferred choice of gift this year than he usually had by this time.

Chatting together, their hands clenched around the latest over priced perfumes, they totally ignored Bert's progress towards them. Engaged in the latest gossip and controversy, Bert was forced to squeeze through a tight gap in-between a pillar and a counter to continue his advancement through the store, coughing at the heavy scent in the air.

A thought struck him and he turned back to the three immaculate clones. None of them noticed his turn so he coughed the 'excuse me cough', a hand held to his mouth more out of nervousness than politeness.

One of the girls eyed him belligerently for a second, totally unimpressed with his visage and the other two twisted to see what she was looking at. All three then gave immediate false smiles that barely cracked the corners of their mouths.

'Can I help you, Sir?' the nearest said; the last word spoken with distaste – almost as though a struggle to impart.

'Err… yes please, love. I'm looking for a perfume for my wife… and…err… I don't know what to get?' Bert felt a little intimidated by the three girls. He had never been a particularly social able animal and never felt comfortable on anyone else's turf especially talking about a topic about which he had no idea.

'Well, what type of scent does *she* normally like?'

All Sandra's perfumes smelt exactly the same. To Bert, there was no more than a slight discernable difference between them. Not blessed with any interest in things that made him choke, there was no way he could answer this question.

'I don't know!'

'Which brand does she normally buy?'

Bert cast his eyes over the nearest counter filled with almost identical boxes of designer stock for inspiration. Silver, gold and a hundred other colours embossed with fancy names whirled in his mind, confusing him.

'I don't know!' he said again. All he had wanted to know was how much the new perfumes were and if he could afford them or not. Was it like buying tyres for the car? You had to know what style or size had come off, so as you knew what to put back on again?

The three girls looked at each other again. The glances spoke the words of patronizing hilarity. Their purpose of their lives *was* the various over-priced scents. There was no doubt that they could discern the differences between them and had no comprehension that there were other people on the planet that didn't have the same interest in this particular subject. Still – he was just a man – what would he know?

'Do you normally buy her perfume?' another of the girls asked. More glances between them with barely concealed mirth.

'No!' Bert must have committed a mortal sin paramount to murder or little old lady mugging judging by the raised painted eyebrows and looks to heaven. He was feeling more and more uncomfortable. Watching the adverts on television for the latest perfumes on the market, he could never understand the sales slogans and advertising gimmicks which all seemed so unsuitable to the product. Did they mean that if you bought this type of smell it could give you unlimited confidence and attract the rich and beautiful? He could not relate logically to this ideology, but the adverts obviously meant something to these girls.

'So, which sort of scent do you prefer?'

Bert rarely used aftershave. He rolled on a deodorant in a morning, but he couldn't remember the last time he had sprayed anything else on himself. He had a bottle of something in his bottom drawer. In the early days of his relationship with Sandra he had been bought something which he had used – it had given him a headache but he had persevered with it – until Sandra had stopped wanting to have an evening out with him. He couldn't remember its name.

'I can't remember!' Bert decided he had had enough. He felt stupid enough most days without asking for someone to make it worse. 'Never mind, love,' he said, 'I'll ask her what she likes and come back. OK?' His lips twitched into a weak smile and he turned from the girls whom he knew were smirking at him.

His heart dropped. Some surprise Christmas present if he had to ask her what she liked. Maybe he could look through her dressing table drawers and see if he could spot any names?

An elderly lady was being served by another of the young sentries. A minute bottle of perfume wrapped in a bag that was five sizes too big, was handed to her as though part of the official Olympic torch ceremony in exchange for four digits pressed in rapid succession on a tiny black key pad, her over used credit card, warm from its excursion resting momentarily in the slot.

He pushed the thought deeper into the recesses of his mind and struggled on through the mine field that was the shop floor.

Everywhere there were signs of people succumbing to the high pressure sales force. False smiles abound as their targets bowed to the realization that lives could be changed for the better once their faces had another layer of lip gloss or eye liner. The clatter of noise was quite deafening, and Bert swayed slightly under the raucous clamouring of packs of little old ladies and the calling of couples across the aisles, his senses befuddled with the heady sweet smell of a mixture of perfumes and various body odours.

Nearing his target, his spirits were again almost shattered as his advancement was blocked by a large woman with the strangest pushchair Bert had ever seen.

The chair looked like a gigantic bubble car on three wheels made from stainless steel with flaps of bright red and clear plastic. The occupant lay inside like a mummy in a mausoleum. The covering bubble dripped rain water, and the futuristic silver wheels betrayed streaks of mud from the gutter outside. The child within was obviously the most precious thing that its mother had ever had; judging by the way she cooed over it and messed continually with the clear plastic casing as though desperate to cut off any hope of fresh air to the passenger within.

Bert couldn't help but look at the expansive backside of the woman as she bent over the baby bubble before quickly tearing his eyes to a display of handbags of various sizes and colours. The plumpness of her legs wasn't a pleasant sight as the hem of her dress lifted beyond her calves. He bypassed the pram, and a quick look within the skin confirming a baby as plump as its mother.

He was at the stairs. A quick glance round and he noticed the painted ladies had jumped on an unsuspecting young mother as she passed, hand-in-hand with her child, reminding Bert of film footage of lions on an African plain jumping on a gazelle with its newborn.

49

Bert gave a low chuckle as he saw the artificial smiles glisten as they tried to persuade the pretty blonde that the latest smell would suit her and fail as she swept past without noticing.

He turned and grasped the handrail before looking up at the expansive void that was the access the upper floors. High above he saw the sculpture of dubiously twists of metal beams and glass that had been an architect's dream vision of the future of shopping design. Through the glass he saw nothing but the darkness of the night sky, but even from the bottom floor, he could hear the pattering of rain.

One last look round confirmed that there was no immediate evidence of a lift, and the crawling escalator already contained a number of people, all preferring to travel slowly rather than use any effort physically climbing the steps. Bert couldn't be bothered to join the surging mass of bodies desperate to save their legs at the foot of the escalator, so with a sigh, he heaved himself up the first few steps, before getting into a rhythm and climbing steadily, zigzagging his way up the store towards his goal.

Looking across, he couldn't help but notice the people around him. All creeds, colours and nationalities, he could hear the throng of people speaking a variety of languages. On each floor he could hear different music being played to entice the passing public.

Men's wear!

Bert looked down at his shabby overcoat, faded blue jeans and soaking wet black boots. He needed a new wardrobe of clothes and a brand new image, but finance was always a problem. He had often seen the look of disgust on Sandra's face as she looked him up and down before he left the house but he was used to it.

His boots squelched on the tiled floor at the top of one flight of stairs and another look down confirmed that Bert had managed to step into a rapidly growing pool of lotion that had previously been dropped, and broken open. Bert sighed. He took another step and looked back at the boot print in the viscous liquid. Shaking his head, he ignored it and continued his climb up the mountain of steps.

Women's wear!

A sea of heads and by far the most popular floor; he could see mild scuffles going on by the many gondola end displays. Summer apparently was back in Wolverhampton. Despite the atrocious weather and rapidly closing Christmas... the impeding winter snow and miserable temperatures, spring fashion was here already in the store. Flighty dresses and sandals were prevalent on the size eight mannequin models in an effort to attract all sizes of woman to them. Patterned mini skirts and wide brimmed straw hats bedecked the female replicas as the latest style to hit Britain's shores. To Bert, they looked exactly the same as last year's. However, because some overpaid and over-hyped designer – who had obviously never done an honest day's toil in his life – said that this design was going to be the next 'in-thing', and some anorexic so-called celebrity concurred by wearing it, then all the public were going to go mad for it.

Bert despaired to himself, and as he grasped the hand rail to swing round to the next zag on the way up, he felt as though he was the only person to think it.

51

CHAPTER 5 *Individual*

Across the second floor sales area however, Brenda Evans was thinking something very similar to Bert. She looked aghast at the prices of the thin cotton dresses hanging on the rail. The mock-up above the section showed a perfect summer scene. If you wore these goods, you too could look perfect and be idolized by all around. As she flicked her fingers through the rail to find her size, she sighed to herself. Pulling out the size fourteen, she held it up and compared it to the perfect looking point of sale. Why did this one look like a tent? …And for how much?

Brenda pushed it back onto the bar crushing it in-between the sizes twelve. They couldn't be selling because there were still so many left. Maybe they hadn't got the best known designer label?

She grimaced to herself, and for the hundredth time, she promised a diet in the new-year to lose those few extra pounds of weight. Subconsciously she held her stomach with one hand, as the other heaved up the Sainsbury's carrier bags of food and trailed back across the floor towards another stand.

Around her, scrawny teenage girls were giggling with each other while looking at a sales-stand showing an almost indecent low cut black top that also seemed to show most of the midriff, coupled with a ripped black denim mini skirt. All three were chewing gum and imperceptibly nodding their heads to tinny music pouring from a shared Ipod with the lengths of earphone trailing across between them.

One of the girls held up the ensemble against her body, stuck out a thin leg and struck a pose, a massive grin on her face. Her two friends nodded appreciatively.

Brenda recalled her own youth when she too had been that size. How the time flies when you're having fun. A dismal relationship in her twenties had claimed most of her figure, though her pretty, blonde, shoulder length hair had never changed, for which she was grateful. She still tried to dress nicely, though covering an expanding midriff was always of prime concern. Lifting her eyes to the three girls, all blissfully unaware of what was waiting for them in life; she noticed that all three were showing their bellies.

All three girls had rings through their belly buttons. One of the girls had a sparkly encrusted dolphin hanging from hers. All three looked very similar in height and dress sense. Why do all the young people copy each other these days? Brenda recalled her own youth when individuality was encouraged. She couldn't remember there being any main stars of the television screen that she had wanted to be or dress like. Mind you, she thought - though the eighties was the decade that taste forgot, it had encouraged uniqueness.

Brenda wanted a belly button ring. She always had. But it looked painful, and it would mean showing her stomach in high cut blouses, and who would want to look at her midriff?

The girls thrust the outfit back on the nearest rail and sauntered off through the store leaving Brenda temporarily alone again. She looked at the discarded garment and thought that her current boyfriend, James would have liked to see her in it. He liked that sort of thing on girls. Well, he spent enough time looking at them, even when she was with him. Insensitive bugger! One day she'd show him. She'd lose that weight. She'd dress in all that revealing stuff he liked so much, and then she'd dump his ass. Hah! Brenda smiled to herself with the confirmed self belief that this scene would happen one day. 'Please God!' she appealed under her breath.

Brenda carried on the meandering journey to the stairs, and as she got closer to the central feature of the store, she could hear the lashing of the rain against the upper windows, which was so loud it almost echoed, and with reluctance, joined the crowd on the escalator to ride up to the subsequent floors, the next one being Home Furnishings.

Home Furnishings wasn't currently as well populated as other floors. The endless rows of suites, chairs and occasional furniture held a few bored husbands whilst their wives sorted through much draped fabric hanging against the walls in a seemingly endless (and pointless) quest to match colour. Some tried to take an interest and have a viewpoint on the thankless task, others stared into the distance or tried to calculate the length of the sales floor based on their pace length. One older man struggled to keep up behind his beloved wife.

'So what do you think of this one Sydney?' asked the woman in a shrill bird-like voice. 'But this would go nicely with the settee!' She brushed her hand appreciably up and down the satin finish of the curtains, but before Sydney could reply, she had jumped to the next. 'This would look good with the wallpaper!'

'Yes dear!' replied Sydney Jones, a long suffering gentleman, with good grace.

Sydney was used to his wife by now. Twenty-five years of marriage through thick and thin meant he had built up a great deal of tolerance for the fads that his wife started. The fads never lasted. Doreen was a window shopper who loved to look and envision. Their home would never be the height of fashion, but clean and tidy, and when their pensions could cope; they did buy new and improve. The years had taken their course with the couple, who still kissed each other before rolling over to sleep every night. Sydney's girth had decreased at the same rate that Doreen's had increased, and when out, they gave the impression of Laurel and Hardy, with their stumbling and shuffling gate and constant pausing for musing. Doreen's heavy tweed check skirt prevented rapid movement, and her tendency to collect shopping bags of cheap 'pound-shop' plastic meant that the mental picture of her movement through any shop was like watching a large refuse collection lorry crawling along the gutter causing inconvenience to all other traffic at the busiest times of the day.

Sydney was thick-skinned. He heard the mutterings of other people, but they rarely bothered him. He had had a good life with his wife. He knew her foibles, and she his. He had one golden rule which had got him through marriage... 'never complain about anything unless it is important!' On many occasions he had had to bite his tongue in order to keep the peace. Doreen, god bless her, was never aware.

Doreen gripped her precious cargo of: draining board plate rack, kitchen clock and 'five scourers for a pound' with one hand and reached for her husband's hand as she neared him, more than aware of his rapidly impending, and poorly contained boredom. Her matching tweed handbag bouncing slightly from the shoulder strap onto her ample chest, she crawled past him en route to the central staircase. She liked the flight of stairs that joined the floors. She thought they gave a unique feature to a store that would otherwise look like any other... similar to a mini mall. The steel and glass design looked very futuristic, but though nothing like it had been around when she was young, she could appreciate the architectural and building advancements of recent years.

Sydney hated it. Bloody unnecessary rubbish! In his day stairs were stairs. It was like walking up a large birdcage, with the metal bars and beams creating the impression of a cell. What was it they called it these days? An atrium? All these over paid architects did was make up fancy names for a scribble on a page and get paid too much money for doing it... it was only a light tube down the middle of the building. A few more decent sized windows and they wouldn't have needed it at all. Humph!

With relief he realized that they were leaving the floor and slowly followed his wife, a wizened hand brushing over his almost bald cranium, before plucking his metal rimmed glasses from his face, and absentmindedly cleaning them with his handkerchief before replacing them with a sniff, his white moustache bristling beneath his nose.

Hearing the loud conversation of a young couple climbing the stairs past this floor, he looked up with envy at their youth.

Andy and Helen Yates were in their early thirties. He was a very tall, fair haired man with a sarcastic smile playing almost persistently on his face. The last five years as an over paid computer programmer had created a sardonic, scornful persona from his original, quite decent husk. The years of scrimping and saving long gone, but not forgotten, Andy was determined to have everything that he'd ever wanted. Today, that meant the latest forty-two inch plasma-screen; twin Dolby stereo system with in built sub woofers. At least, that was all Helen had heard about for the last five days.

Helen was a realist. She too had had a difficult upbringing with money extremely tight. A previous marriage with, what turned out to be a complete lout, had created a girl, who was now a teenager prone to tantrums and currently confined to the house for a minor misdemeanour the prior evening. Helen never took anything for granted, least of all money. But, though her job as clerk for an insurance agency didn't pay a vast deal, her new husband provided a decent and well-equipped home, for which she was grateful.

Andy had the latest clothes and shoes. He never went out without the latest designer names covering his body, from the jacket down to his socks. Helen was more frugal with her purchases, much to Andy's chagrin. He wanted the designer wife to go with his newly found lifestyle, and it frustrated him that she wouldn't make the most of her figure with trendy, revealing clothes. It caused frequent arguments. Helen dressed for comfort unless they were patronizing a

57

very posh restaurant, when she brought forth her one and only posh frock.

Despite only being married for three years, unknown to Helen, Andy was flirting quite openly with a girl in his office across town at I.T SOLUTION. The object of his fancy was an eighteen year old college flunk out who worked on the company's telephone reception. Bad teenage facial skin was hidden beneath several layers of foundation and an appallingly small vocabulary left people trying to communicate with her wondering at her level of education. Andy saw neither of these flaws, but was attracted by the tongue piercing and short skirt. He had yet to find the 'chicken fillet' enhancements that padded out an under-developed bust and to have a conversation with her that consisted of anything more robust and demanding than sexual innuendo.

The girl was more attracted to Andy's top-of-the-range company deep purple Vauxhall Vectra and obvious monthly remuneration than his personality or bad breath. Still... she was intelligent enough to know the path her life was taking, and the fact that if she boosted his ego every morning with a well placed comment, that he'd take her to lunch several times a week in his high speed car to a nicer public house than the one she was used to every evening and buy her the occasional trinket.

Andy was blind to the obvious. He was a man who had grown up through many hard times and troubles. He had always persevered with his career path despite many set backs in his youth with his constantly changing life game plan. Andy was a man who had to make his own mistakes and deliberately avoided any advice offered, seeing it as an attempt to control and belittle him, rather than aid and abet.

Helen knew Andy's history, and still she married him, seeing it as more welcome than continuing the life of a divorcee with a growing child and crippling credit card debt from the idiot she had once thought to be the love of her life. Andy had helped her back from the brink of bankruptcy and shown her care and attention. She intended to be able, once again, to stand proud and tall on her own two feet as she was worried at her new husband's tendency for the expensive and extreme and determined never again to be so silly with a man.

'Entertainment,' Andy was saying, 'is on the next floor!' His hand gripped his wife's as he helped her up the stairs. 'I've been here three times already this week to look at this plasma TV. I'm trying to knock them down on price, because the model BX10 is going to be out classed by the BL12 in about three months time, according to What TV!'

Helen smiled benignly, having no idea what any of the serial numbers meant, pleased in a small way that he had his hobby and grateful that the same expectation was not asked of her.

As they stepped out onto the Entertainment floor, she heard the simultaneous noise pollution that must have been a selection of stereo hi-fi's being tested by spotty youths in grey and black hooded tops and torn, soaking wet jeans that seemed to show most of the wearer's back sides. Fingers were prodding and stroking the metallic silver facades as the volumes were increased and decreased, toothy smiles wide on their furry faces. 'Bum fluff' Helen's father had used to call it on adolescent boys. 'Makes them look like kids!' he said. 'Learn to have a proper shave!'

Helen missed her father. Despite the funeral having been five years previously, not a day went by without a thought about him and desperate desire to have his comfort and security.

An off-duty security guard was stood in front of the latest CCTV technology against the far wall. Helen watched him lifting and lowering his arms to a miniscule camera that was relaying the black and white image to a television before him. As he did so, his coat splattered the floor with the loosening drops of rainwater, and his peaked cap tilted back on his head.

Andy was already dragging her across the floor towards the biggest display on the floor. A mammoth, almost paper thin screen was standing in the centre of the television section. It had already created a lot of interest, and lonely men stood about it, arms folded, heads crocked to one side in wishful desire. A self-important sales assistant in a purple shirt was stood talking knowledgeably to the assembled crowd. His arms waved back and forth earnestly, a sales information pack wafting around like a fan in his hand, the group of five men nodded eagerly to every morsel of information bestowed upon them, the glint of hope in their eyes, and his at a possible sale.

Andy let go of Helen's hand as they neared the display and nodded towards the assistant, who responded with what Helen could only discern as apprehension, the mouth twitching behind a bushy beard, and a dreading look of 'here we go again' in his eyes. Andy must have been driving the sales team nuts with his constant badgering for a deal. If he worked on commission, then either Helen's husband was this week's bonus, or a complete and unwanted tease.

As Andy speeded up, Helen looked around the store. The noise of the rain on the window above was steadfastly drowning out the conversations near her. The spotty youths were moving on. The security guard was already ambling towards the stairs after them. She saw a nice, white-haired old couple who looked like 'little and large' come into view on the escalator, the youths appeared to be casing them, jostling each other as they got closer, perhaps thinking about the possibility of upsetting them. The tallest lad looked around, saw the security guard and nudged his friend. Within seconds all three lads had noticed that they were being watched, laughed loudly and shouted an obscenity before rushing past the couple riding the escalator and down the stairs out of view.

The couple looked at each other in obvious disgust at the lack of manners and poor attitude from the modern day youth, shook their heads and rounded from one escalator to the next to continue their journey upwards. The youths could be heard over the rain as they ran boisterously down the stairs towards the exit of the building.

Helen folded her arms and continued her perusal of the store floor. Another purple attired assistant had rushed to reset the volume controls of the chained radios. The bearded one was now in deep conversation with Andy, who was totally oblivious to her. She noticed a stand of DVD's on sale, and started across the short expanse of shop floor to look for a slushy, girly movie. The Danielle Steele books that Helen loved were being gradually recreated as movies. Andy, of course, was extremely dismissive of anything remotely like these, but Helen had always longed for a romance that emulated those she had read of in these books.

Another girl at the stand shared her viewpoint. She was in her early twenties, extremely pretty with cascading ruffled brunette hair and a microscopic waist emphasized with tight black and light grey striped skirt and three inch heels. Clutched in one hand was a dripping wet umbrella, the other worrying a stray strand of hair that refused to sit neatly behind an ear as she looked over the collection, a faint smile playing on her immaculate face as she lost herself in other fictional worlds.

Helen looked enviously at her, wishing that her own appearance could have been similar and simultaneously wondering if men had the same feelings of inadequacy when confronted with images of muscular hero types with untameable jet black hair and silk shirts that all adorned the fronts of her favourite books before they rescued the damsels in distress within.

Andy was leaving the plasma screen again. From her vantage point she could see him weaving his way from the bearded man towards the stairwell. Raising her eyes momentarily, before Andy did indeed turn to look for her, she replaced the cellophane wrapped DVD on the stand in the correct place and walked towards his now waiting form. Out of the corner of her eye she noticed the sales assistants talking together, with side glances and confirmatory nods and possibly aggressive smiles towards the back of their current nightmare customer.

'They still won't budge on price!' he exclaimed as Helen neared, 'but they've said that they will compete. If I can find a similar model for a lower price, they said they'd look at it!' He opened the brochure that he had obtained and poured over it as though it contained the cure to cancer or information pertaining to alien landings.

'Yes dear!' Helen smiled disinterestedly, as she steered Andy towards the climbing escalator, knowing full well that he had forgotten all about needing that new toaster, Andy's head filled with his own self important problems in obtaining the new electricity and money drain at the lowest possible price.

She had pointed out the fact the previous Wednesday morning that their old toaster wouldn't take the new 'Square Cut, Thick Slice, Best of Both Worlds' bread that they had purchased from the local convenience store, but it hadn't stopped his attempt to squash two slices in, resulting in the hallway smoke alarm beeping annoyingly for over five minutes and Andy consequently jamming a butter knife into the workings in an attempt to free the cremating two. The only result from this unfortunate sequence of events was that the smoke alarm had been ripped maliciously from the ceiling, leaving an unpainted and tatty area of wallpaper behind, sparks flying dangerously from the toaster because Andy hadn't unplugged before surgically operating on it, and Helen's tattered nerves taking another little kick as the whole house fused suddenly and scarily into silent darkness.

Helen was getting used to it. Andy liked to find these things out for himself. Now he had to buy a new toaster and a new smoke alarm as a result of a momentary temper tantrum that ended the life of the West Midlands Fire Service gift.

Ah well.

They stepped onto the stairs and climbed the flight to the fifth floor… Household Supplies.

Lara Lowingstein turned from the Danielle Steele movies and followed them. She stepped on to the escalator; her heels weren't the most practical ones for climbing stairs and she wasn't really with it today. A tedious day working in a local primary school as classroom assistant; helping the children to design Halloween costumes had proved unfulfilling and once again she wished she had the arms of a lover to collapse into to make everything all right. Dreaming lazily, she imagined him sweeping her off her feet as she came through the front door; presenting bouquets of flowers; smothering her with strong passionate kisses and taking her for a beautiful candlelit Italian meal to help her forget her endlessly screaming charges. As much as she liked children, she wished once again that she had made a different decision on her career path. She trickled her hand along the hard black plastic of the moving handrail, and imagined the unidentified and faceless man's hands holding her face, just like on the covers of the books whilst he kissed her… a naked hairy chest… heart beating ardently – just for her. She remembered one such candidate for her affections, last year – a previous life... one night of pleasure and lust... a man she had unfortunately left behind... *had* to leave behind.

The fifth floor came into view and once again she fervently wished she hadn't agreed to fetch supplies for the school. To be out of her shoes and be tucked up cosily in bed on a night like this would be more than enough of a pleasure for now. 'I'll grab the stuff and get out of here,' she thought. She wanted to be home for the latest slice of TV reality – more celebrity wannabes with no skill, intelligence or ability, talking rubbish for the cameras, desperate to be famous for being famous, or just revive a flagging career. She wondered fleetingly if the newspaper printed revelations on the show's fading rock star's sexual preferences were true. They must be!

It was a bleak compensation for an empty flat and single plate of food – cheese, pickle and wafer thin bread that tasted like dust and just one glass of well deserved wine!

No-one was expecting the explosion that racked the town centre department store. No-one could have dreamed that the following events could ever have happened in the structured, health and safety conscious world in which they all now lived. No-one would ever forget the devastating loss of life on this Thursday night.

The cheap Casio hand movement now displayed the time as ten to nine. Bert looked at his watch by the light of the glowing candle then around at the grubby faces staring expectantly at him.

'Can we light a few more of those candles?' asked Brenda from her position on the floor.

'Hey, that's shop stock!' exclaimed Dave, having now regained his breath. 'You can't keep lighting them, they need paying for!'

This was the wrong thing to say as the murderous looks spoke volumes on the surrounding faces.

'…but still,' he hastened on, 'I suppose this time, its ok.'

'Could you get them?' asked Bert pointedly, a limp smile of complacency on his damaged face as though talking to a small child. Bert didn't tolerate fools gladly, and though of depressive character, he felt he had the knack to handle difficult situations.

'Yes… yes, of course,' stammered the security guard, and he shuffled off.

Bert and Brenda looked at each other. He felt sorry for the largish lady on the floor. She obviously had a great deal of common sense, and it was a shame that she had hurt herself on the steel and glass rubble in her previous blind panic to escape the building. He saw the disconsolate but friendly face of a woman used to being let down by events around her.

She in turn saw the strong jawed determination of a man used to sorting problems. Regardless of the occasional vibration in his voice, he had already got rid of that annoying guard who had kicked a tin can of baked beans into her upper thigh and assessed their situation for potential immediate risks. She trusted him.

As did Sian. Sian came from behind the cashiers' desk, and walked towards the group of people. The glowing candle was crackling nicely now, though gusts of wind through the broken window above whipped the flame about, despite its seclusion amongst the trapped and frightened people.

She was the store representative. She's seen Dave about over the previous two months since they'd begun working on the same floor, and hadn't been impressed with either his professionalism or intelligence. She needed to calm and help these people. Sian, fortunately, was first aid qualified following a recruitment campaign when Lexington's first advertised for potential employees at the new location. Her common sense desire to have an extra qualification helped to make her more employable than the thousands of other unemployed school leavers.

'My name is Sian,' she introduced herself; 'I work here. If you give me a moment, I'll see if the store phones are working and I'll try to find out what happened!' She receded cautiously back down another aisle towards a column that she knew held the in-store telephone.

A signatory beep from Andy on the floor further down the aisle indicated that he'd removed his mobile phone from his breast pocket and turned it on. 'I'm phoning for help!' he spoke up. 'This is ridiculous!' One hand cradled his wife's head, while the other pressed the keys on his latest WAP phone, the keys singing different notes as they were pushed.

Bert nodded to himself. He himself had never been able to afford a mobile phone, let alone had the desire or potential phonebook to require its use. Sandra had never expressed a desire for him to own one, and certainly never let him look at, or use hers. Indeed, there were several evenings a week that he barely saw her. Instead, she kicked her heels lying on her belly on the bed, phone pressed to her ear, giggling like a teenager to another one of her countless, nameless friends. Tyrone sat with him rather than Sandra, and *his* one sided conversation with the panting and occasionally drooling dog never once included the phrase, 'ooh yes, I know!' or 'you are bad, you are'.

Bert had long since decided that leaving his wife alone whilst she was deep in a prolonged phone conversation was the better option after once receiving a curt 'what do you want?' for his efforts to join in her pastime not long after he had bought her the phone. Subsequently, he had never had the metaphorical leash attached to him whilst out and about, and could never understand the attraction for pedestrians he passed in the street to pace about shouting into the confounded instruments while gesticulating wildly.

Brenda would have agreed whole-heartedly with him if she knew his thoughts. She too owned one as a necessary evil, but a quickly discharging battery meant that at that moment in time, it was sat on its own personal throne at home attached to the house electricity supply through another of those small black cuboid transformers that seemed to come with every new purchase.

Sydney, getting weaker by the minute from the effort of looking after his stricken better half, had never owned such a device, and never would. Their son; a transport firm's boss, had tried to persuade them for many years to invest in one, but fading eyesight and clumsy aging fingers meant that ownership was never a viable prospect. Doreen herself got into enough of a muddle with the house landline. She had never figured out how to use the in-built answer phone, and pressing the required keys following guidance through automated menus to any overseas call centre was never easy.

All three stopped to hear Andy's side of the conversation...

'Yes, yes... the Lexington's Superstore,' he was sighing emphatically. 'No, I don't know what happened... some sort of explosion. We are ALL trapped!'

He paused, clearly listening to the response from the call centre response evaluator, nodding his head imperceptibly as instructions were relayed.

'OK. We'll wait! Cheers!' he snapped the hood back down over the designer communicator and looked up at the worried faces, in time to see Dave arrive back with his hands full of large candles. 'No idea what has happened!' he reported. 'The storm has caused problems all over. They said it was giving off electrical discharges interfering with radio reception. We have to wait where we are for help!'

'Brillian'' said a jaunty voice sarcastically, 'so what nah? Jus' sit 'ere an' wait for the storm ter rip the roof off an' blow us about?'

Eddie Simpson was a half Asian, half white entrepreneur. At least, that was what he called himself. He had been in the store looking for additions to a private un-purchased collection of goods that would have provided a little income later in the evening from the lads at the 'Bear and Bush' on the main Dudley road. 'Steady' Eddie had been in many scrapes in his life, countless times requiring a quick exit or fast thinking, but this was the first time in his life that he was part of an incident that he hadn't caused or been privy to. The last thing that Eddie wanted to do was to sit with this bunch of middle class losers while waiting for the coppers to show and wonder what he was doing out after seven pm without his court-ordered ankle bracelet.

He privately cursed his career choice, but stealing to order was the only thing now that Eddie Simpson was capable of doing, following his downright pathetic performance in his school exams two years previously. It was his elder brothers' fault. It always was his fault. He had dragged him from his books for numerous illegal escapades that usually ended in Eddie's over-night incarceration or suspension from school. Eddie was used to blaming his brother for his own poor judgement. He never knew his father, but his poor white working class mother had despaired and eventually washed her hands of him; kicking him out of her house. This meant that the only life Eddie was now capable of was one of ducking and diving through innumerable private deals in order to eat, stay clothed and remain warm at night. Eddie held at least three mobile phones within the recesses of his 'poaching coat'. However, he had no idea what the passwords were in order to relinquish control to him, and they remained where they were until he could get to speak to 'Uncle Bill', his less than friendly fence who paid him below market value.

By now, the fifth floor was looking quite pleasant in the cheerful glow of the dozens of candles surrounding the group. Dave had done an admirable job of lighting them without tripping over anyone else, which Brenda, for one, was grateful.

'Let's see if we can shift some of this rubble!' said Dave enthusiastically.

Bert had a cautious prod at one of the steel beams. It held steady, but was rewarded with a trickle of water from above. Scowling with annoyance, he tried again – this time helped by Dave who strained to lift the girder. It didn't even rock in its contorted position.

Above them, a crack of lightning again lit up the room and the rumble of thunder silenced the space from conversation. Just then, Sian returned from attempting contact with store management.

'Phones are dead,' she said, 'oh that's better,' noticing the candles, 'I've a first aid box behind the desk. Shall we look at the injured?'

'Good idea,' said Bert. 'Come on, give us a hand!' He looked directly at Eddie who shrugged when he realised that no one else in the immediate area was capable, and followed his lead to help Brenda to her feet!

One on each side of her, it became apparent that a leg was broken judging by its awkward angle and oddly unnatural independent movement. Brenda, however, smiled and bore the pain with good grace, apologising for their inconvenience and trying to do as much as possible to assist in her own rise from the floor. Her now tatty flowery dress hanging from her like a rag, she limped down the aisle, hanging from the two men's shoulders, towards the counter. They helped her up and lay her down, leaving her in Sian's capable hands while they went to look for others in need of assistance.

Camaraderie was developing amongst the remaining fit and generally healthy ex-shoppers. Taking Bert and Eddie's lead, the fallen fleeing girls were picked up and helped towards the improvised hospital area, low sobbing emitting from their frightened lips as they responded to the suggested plan, hugging each other regardless of the fact that they hadn't know each other prior to the incident, but feeling better by the solidarity.

Two brooms were collected from a stand by the now useful Dave, who then snapped the brushes from the bottom, and helped Sian bind the stays either side of Brenda's leg with a roll of sticky tape. Brenda smiled gratefully, and then rested while others were assisted.

Sydney was helped from the ground and the prostrate form of his wife lifted and carried to another counter, Sydney's appreciative, but extremely worried smile their only reward.

Andy had helped his wife up. Locating with a glance around the dimly lit sales area, an exhibit of fancy cardboard boxes that contained polystyrene wrapped microwaves and, even though she had twisted her ankle, helped her hobble towards them. Helen sank a little as the boxes sagged under her weight, but she was thankful to ease the pressure on her legs.

'Yes dear,' she replied to his diatribe and dark threats of retribution for the instigators of the atrocity and lack of proper assistance from the authorities. 'But I'm sure that they are doing their best!'

'But they can't keep us waiting like this! I've paid enough in my taxes. Why aren't the fire brigade here by now?' He huffed annoyingly and fingered his expensive Siemens phone, upset that it hadn't provided an immediate solution to their current predicament.

Helen smiled her usual false smile and nodded obligingly, while actually worrying about her wayward daughter at home, and wondering what time they could expect to get back to her.

'Can I borrow that?' she asked, holding her hand out for the handset, retrieving it from her reluctant husband. Quickly dialling the home number; a smile of relief when it was answered, she dissolved into emotional tears relating the story to the child. Andy left her to it and wandered back to the main group. Unprepared to help in case he got blood on his designer coat, he still wanted to know what the consensus of opinion was. He rested, arms folded, against shelving.

From his vantage point close to the floor mounted candles, he could see the group tending to the injured; new dusters and jay cloths used as improvised bandages. Sniffing, he noticed that the smoke from the candles was getting worse. The wind had subsided a little through the broken window, though the teaming rain still noisily obvious.

Looking around at his surroundings, he noticed a heavy   plume was rising steadily towards the ceiling and…

Grabbing his umbrella he popped it open and lifted it above his head, a smile the only thing on his lips. He was just in time. The smoke had reached the sensor on the ceiling. A red warning light was flashing furiously as it decided whether or not to take counter measures, and then… the sprinklers turned on. Swishing back and forth like a garden watering system, they gave a low 'phutt phutt' sound as they drenched the entire floor.

Screams and cries of anger from the vexed shoppers didn't save them from the downpour. Hands above their heads they tried to duck the persistent fluid. Bert just stood there disbelieving. Looking up at the ceiling, he ran his hands over his face. Andy watched in amused dryness; his sardonic superior smile even wider. In the moment before the flames from the many candles were extinguished, he noticed the dirty, smeared face of his momentarily forgotten wife scowling at him.

His smile faded.

The room was now pitch-black. However the general mood within the group was still good, and after the initial shock of the downpour, almost manic laughter began. Brenda laughed, as did others one by one as amusement for the incredible situation increased.

Within moments the sprinklers ceased through lack of supply and pressure and left the dripping people wondering what else could possibly happen.

Andy turned back towards where he knew his wife was, and crept cautiously towards her.

'Get away from me!' Her words of warning were heavy with disgust and annoyance for his selfishness with the umbrella. Andy blinked in the obscurity of the dark room, and lowered his umbrella, feeling for the catch in order to close it and feeling more than a little embarrassed.

Dave was dispatched to find one new candle, and when he returned with it lit, the unspoken viewpoint was that just one would be enough.

Eddie decided that he had to find out what was happening outside. Creeping carefully across the slimy wet grubby floor, he made for the windows.

The windows were designed purely to allow light in, not for use by the public to see out of. They were positioned to make it impossible as an access route either in or out. Fire safety regulations had allowed the designers of the Lexington's Superstore to centralise the main access, deciding that it had been wide enough to negate the necessity of further entrance. How wrong they'd been? However, Eddie thought he might be able to climb the steel pipes up to the sill and see out. Years of gaining access to other people's houses had provided enough expertise and the upper body strength to allow him to clamber up like a cat burglar, and pause at the broken window.

Bert, Brenda and a couple of the others watched him with eager fascination as his figure was outlined against the residue of the huge double glazed window units, cautiously avoiding any shards of glass. He peered out at the town, the immediate area lit by countless lights of fire engines, police cars and ambulances. A thousand other passers-by were braving the weather to watch the unfolding sequence of events. Street lights far below were still glowing brightly and the railway station nearby still sported trails of illumination for nearing and receding travellers.

'What was that?'

He could see a dark shape far below straddling the street. He twisted to gain a better vantage point in order to see what was happening five floors lower. It looked like... well like a colossal snake parked on the pavement belching fire. Sticking his head almost completely out of the window he could see hooded figures in luminescent yellow bibs running back and forth around the snake. Headlights were almost obliterated by the force of the rain, and the back of Eddie's head began to get extremely wet as he craned to see what was happening. He could barely make out the fact that there were shouts and commands from the emergency services far below, but not what they were saying. Further out, he could see collections of cars around the traffic light controlled island waiting their turn to complete their circuit and disappear safely away from this tragedy, a few horns blaring unnecessarily with the driver impatience in the tumultuous and hectic weather conditions. In the distance he could make out the booming discord of another fire engine as it joined the swarm of cars on the traffic island, though displaying none of the regard for the colour of the signals as it weaved through the waiting vehicles to join its brothers.

He looked again at the snakelike shape. He wished he could make it out. If only there was a little more light by which he could see?

'Come on, for Chris' sake!' he muttered under his breath.

Just as he completed his words of desire, he got his wish. A near crack of forked lightning gave instant illumination to the scene below. The surprise and realisation of what had transpired below hit Eddie with shock like an unexpected slap in the face. From where he was, the 'snake' looked like a train protruding from the front of the building. What on earth was that doing there? Oh my god!

He fell backwards with the revelation. He lost his footing, grabbed out for a hand hold on the warped aluminium window frame hanging from the brick face, and missed. His body fell backwards, and a long wail of impending doom howled from his lips as his body arched downwards, called by the force of gravity.

He landed on a display of mirrors, previously disarranged by the explosion from off the walls. A particularly large, sharp, gilded, gold effect frame from one damaged extravagant potential purchase entered the small of Eddie's back and pierced through his stomach, re-emerging at the other side just below his rib cage as his weight sank it through. Blood bubbled from his mouth as he coughed, his head lolling in a pool of broken glass, his arms and legs limp at his sides. Bert was already there at his side, but unable to help.

The pain outstripped anything Eddie had ever known. The day he had his appendix out when he was practically conscious though incoherent following a slip up by the anaesthetist; the time he lost the

77

tip of his thumb in an unfortunately quick closing, heavy, metal studded security door... even the deep down and constantly self denied sorrow he felt for his mother's anguish when he was first arrested at thirteen for a fool hardy and ultimately pointless foray into a elderly neighbours house as initiation into his brothers group of thugs.

More screams from the remaining shoppers as they realised what had happened. Brenda shook her head in disbelief. Helen forgot the anger at her husband. Andy forgot about reclaiming his phone. Sian left another wounded girl and stepped away in shock, her hand instinctively clamped across her mouth in personal denial.

The elegant twenty-something girl began to blubber with emotion. Whether it was sorrow for the unknown bloke who had fallen, or personal feelings of insecurity and fear for her current predicament was unclear. But then Lara Lowingstein was quite a selfless person. She had just completed a year in the peace corp. helping in Africa and the middle-east whilst taking a break from her education. She had seen bodies of young children dying from malnutrition and diseases caused by pestilence, a result of famine and war caused by a poor third world government and lack of the intervention by the West... the cause of her joining the educational system within her own country of origin upon her return. But she had never heard or seen anyone die in this particular fashion before.

She was reminded of her relief worker friend once again. If only he had been here now, everything would have been all right. She needed to hold someone. .. she was scared!

The throbbing subsided a little and Eddie started to feel a little on the cold side. This was due to the blood leaving his body through the gaping hole in his stomach, spreading around him to join the already present pool of rainwater. His last vision was the grey shape of Bert's worried head looking over at him. Desperate to speak, he tried to report on his sighting.

The only sound was his dying breath

CHAPTER 7

Earlier that day, Alison had sat fuming in the steadily humming bus. Another look at the liquid crystal display on her mobile phone confirmed the time at a quarter past eleven. She wished she could use it to phone her friend, Sian, but credit had lapsed and it remained temporarily in her handbag as an over priced clock.

The traffic showed no signs of moving. Ahead she heard the distant sirens of a responding police car, but the sound came no closer having also been stuck in the back log of irate sales representatives and homeward bound house wives who were all sat between it and the incident.

The trundle of the heavy diesel engine in the bus slowed and eventually rumbled to a halt as the driver, a bearded Sikh, decided to turn them off. Nothing was moving. He had already picked up a walkie-talkie and reported into the depot that he had been stuck in the rapidly expanding traffic jam.

Noisy lads in the seats at the back of the bus became even noisier as they decided that their predicament was funny and decided to start playing a thumping game which resulted in annoyance from six of the other elderly passengers, heavy sighs and the irate scratching of heads, whilst mild yelps of pain culminated with two of the youths jostling for the upper hand on the linoleum covered floor in front of one quite frightened old lady.

She gripped her walking stick tightly and pulled her little white handbag close in, while her spectacled head shook slightly in fury and she muttered under her breath that she 'didn't know what the world was coming to!'

To the lads it was harmless fun, to the busload of prisoners it was another annoyance.

Ahead of them other drivers had now alighted from their vehicles and walked to the front of the queue in order to offer their viewpoint on the situation. The tram driver was deep in conversation with someone, his hand clamping his phone to his ear as he struggled to hear whilst being aggravated by the inconvenienced drivers. His other hand showed his palm as he tried to distance himself from the threat of physical violence.

The phone away now, he looked up at the wires above the tram. It had been running fine all morning. Why now?

The Wolverhampton and Birmingham tramway system is a marked improvement on those from a previous era. The previous tram system had last run in 1939.

Transport was important in the Black Country, as this area is known, and new forms of transport were continually being found. The Black Country has never completely discarded the past, preferring to adapt to fit present needs. Thus, canals have adjusted to new uses, and instead of canal boats of the nineteenth century, you are more likely to see cabin cruisers or converted barges moving along, making for the winding stretches of countryside and trams are making a come back in an attempt to alleviate the continuing build up of commuter traffic, with routes to out-of-town car parks encouraging 'park and ride'.

All trams are now computer controlled with the driver having to do very little for his money other than push a lever to go forward, and drag it backwards to come to a halt. The two inch diameter metal cable that looped from overhanging post to overhanging post the entire length of the track provides the power to the electric motors that turns the wheels. A sprung mechanism on the roof of the tram, keeps the grab beam in constant contact. It is a foolproof system, and one that has been around for many years.

Unfortunately, if no power was forthcoming to the cable, or if there was no contact, then there could be no forward movement of the tram. It was even more fateful that the tram had chosen that particular moment to lose its power and cease all movement resulting in the mayhem. Cars couldn't get past at this juncture of the road.

Behind them, several impatient drivers had tried to conduct three point turns across the carriageway. This manoeuvre for most had been distinctly unsuccessful, resulting in, amongst other things, a minor collision for one young sales rep, and the beaching of a Ford Mondeo across the raised central reservation by one harassed middle aged lady with three appointments she was now late for.

The weather didn't look like helping either. The storm clouds were right overhead, and the first smattering of rain was obliterating the view through the windows. Many of the cars in the complete gridlock had cut their engines, though others kept them going in an effort to stay warm by the heaters. Some lucky few turned the warm air conditioning up a little and snuggled down into their seats while they waited for resolution.

Alison was neither warm nor snug. She wanted out of the bus, though the driver wanted none of it, asking her to sit down and wait.

'Let me out!' she screamed at him, resulting in jeers from the lads on the seats. She swung her handbag threateningly before the Sikh backed down and released the door catch. The moment it had and the door swung backwards with a pneumatic hiss, she stepped out onto the pavement. She swung her handbag over her shoulder, and began the next mile of journey on foot, heels clip clopping on the concrete.

She passed the tram, the shouting voices of the driver, passengers and other citizens just one mad commotion of noise.

She wobbled slightly on the uneven pavement. Why did all the public footpaths look like patchwork quilts of white concrete and black tarmac additions? It annoyed even the disorganised nature of Alison that utility companies never felt the need to liaise with one another before carrying out seemingly endless urgent remedial works just after the council had resurfaced the necessary stretch. The upshot of this lack of communication always being that numerous red and white plastic cones were constantly kicked around the streets, and the once perfect billiard table surface descended into street level in a hotchpotch of cheap hole filling... and more importantly to Alison, she would always end up losing a heel stud.

A gust of wind whipped up her hair as she started through the short tunnel past the stricken tram. Momentarily covered from above by the ancient brick of the railway bridge, she was also out of the rain.

Desperate to get to work, she stepped out quickly, there now being no alternative to the wet windy hike to work. She had spent the last few coins she owned on the bus journey and now had no option for any other form of transport.

The wind blew about her hair and loosened the elastic band. She felt cold, wet, hungry, tired and lonely. It was only a mile to work and the dry confines of the brand new Lexington's Superstore, which she could see clearly from here, beckoned invitingly.

Looking up, she admired the structure that towered into the sky. Like a large phallic lighthouse, it dwarfed all around it. The sixth floor was made almost entirely out of glass, and the large dome that stuck up from the middle a strange concoction from this distance. Her unemployed sister was jealous because she hadn't managed to find a job there, and certain acquaintances were suitably jealous of her position as stock room deputy manager on the seventh floor. ('For how much longer?' she thought.)

She had never thought about a job as a manager whilst she was growing up. The goal each day had been to reach seven o'clock, when she could pull her skimpy teenage clothes on and then kick around the streets with her friends. The last thing on her mind at the time had been to concentrate in class, complete homework or produce reasonable exam results. Alison hadn't been alone in her attitude to her education. Pretty much most of her circle of friends, including her sister, shared her apathy whilst living their school days, determined to have as much fun as possible, to the detriment of any sound financial future.

The turning point for Alison had been a couple of days following her eighteenth birthday. Two years of living with her argumentative parents had driven her crazy. Neither of them worked. Her father had been laid off from his job at a local tyre production centre and had never found further work. Her mother was a large woman who preferred to sit smoking in front of day time television than find work, or even keep the home in an acceptable condition. The few pounds that did constitute household income were spent quickly on the vices of alcohol and nicotine. Alison, and her sister Samantha, were chips off the old block.

As she side-stepped a rapidly forming puddle of rainwater, Alison recalled the day she got her first job. She had been spending a lot of time with a particularly charming young gentleman who drove a company BMW whom she had met one evening whilst very drunk. He had been taken with her, as she remembered, and would have loved to have created a more permanent attachment to her.

However, she had a different agenda. He had aspirations of married life, children, the works, while she had a desire for quick and similar pleasure before moving on to sample the delights of others. He had been appalled at the state of her parents' home and the lack of any motivation to better their standard of living, though initially disguising it quite well. After two glorious weeks of evening drives to romantic countryside locations for amorous coupling, quiet drinks in quaint cottage-style pubs and more than a couple of missed films sat on the back row, he had decided to recommend her for a job interview at one of the stores he was Area Manager to.

To her surprise she got the position. He had pulled more than a couple of strings. She decided to do her best, never having had the remotest opportunity of work before. She hated the uniform that they gave her but decided, prudently, not to make a fuss. She surprised herself. She hadn't realised that she had the determination to pursue a normal career path.

Soon after getting the job, she had ditched him. He had become too clingy and needy. She was used to a free loving approach to life, and he had been brought up with a different take on life. She told him that she needed a little space to think. Occasionally she felt bad about it. She had seen him a few times when he turned up to monitor the progress of the new Wolverhampton store. On those days she flashed a smile and put on a well practised demure expression in order to tease him a little. Her boss knew something had gone on between the two based on the glances and aloof silences when they were both in the same room, though he never said anything to either of them.

That wouldn't stop him from sacking her now. She already had verbal and written warnings on her record. She needed the job. It had provided much-needed independence.

Her sister, Samantha, was racked with jealousy. She had also been at the pub that night that Tom Robinson met Alison. In fact, Tom had approached her first, and she blew him off because he seemed very shy, taking a great deal of delight in his embarrassment and upset. Alison only went with him because she was inebriated (again) and just wanted some fun before going home to their grotty, unkempt little house. And now Alison had a job and she didn't. It was the cause of more than one bitter argument. The household was used to arguments. The neighbours were used to their arguments. The whole street was used to the rotting, rusting beige Ford Cortina in the front garden, windows smashed with usually three cats in residence, an overgrown garden crawling through broken flag stones, and peeling off-white wooden window frames like tearful eyes out onto the street.

Alison tried not to go back to her parents much these days.

'You wanna lift love?'

A voice broke through her reverie. An aging grey Ford Fiesta sat idling at the curb, the nearside front tyre squashed into a particularly low slung metal drain amongst a multitude of cigarette butts and fading crisp packets. A blonde haired lad was leaning out of the passenger window, a smile across his stubbly face and a look of desire in his eyes. He looked in his mid twenties.

Just as Alison was about to tell him where to go, she glanced at her watch. It was well past eleven. She had no money. She was probably fired by now! She didn't want to be on this road any more!

Having noticed the blocked road ahead, a grubby lorry started to complete an illegal u-turn before her. The vast hulk of metal crunched through a puddle at the entrance to a side road before a blast of black exhaust smoke mingled with the rain and made her head swim with nausea. In the barely covered back, Alison could see a heap of ground excavation. The lorries were once used to carry coal back and forth down this road, but now were restricted to ironstone, fireclay, sand, limestone and dolerite excavated in vast quantities mainly used for the road surfacing industry.

The lorry's exhaust pipe spewed out a cloud of foul smelling diesel fumes which blanketed the road and pavement. Alison choked on the stench and was momentarily glad that she didn't have a breakfast to bring back up. Looking up, she saw a cloth-capped occupant leering through the window at her, hands obviously busy wrestling the wheel and gear shift; something she could hear clunking as though stripping cogs.

'Go on! Buy you a drink!'

'Yes!' She spoke instinctively and stepped towards the car. It wasn't the first time she got into a strange car. She needed a drink.

The lad swung the door open, flicked the seat forward, and stood out to one side to allow Alison to climb in to the rear of the vehicle. Once in, the seat was back and he was in.

The driver was a very black young man, quite a contrast to his passenger and obviously only a couple of years older. As he turned to regard her, his piercing brown eyes bored into her, a faint smile playing on his lips. His broad shoulders gave Alison a slight shudder of yearning and his obviously muscled left arm flexed as he reached for the gear stick. He looked at his friend, and they smiled at each other, sharing a private unspoken thought, before he engaged gear and lurched forward onto the, now, very quiet road.

CHAPTER 8

The firemen knew something big had happened to the Lexington's building as the fire service made their way down the Birmingham Road as quickly as it was possible to go in the crackling storm. Visibility was extremely limited. The night sky seemed even blacker than usual. No moon tonight. The Superstore was usually visible from quite a way out of town due to the large neon lights that proclaimed the owner's name from between the fourth and fifth floors.

They weren't in evidence tonight.

Smith eased the large red fire fighting unit through the gaps created by the late evening commuters as they realized its direction; their cars were desperate to move from his path, and away from the noise of the sirens. Monk hit the button to cease the noise as they rounded the final bend, past the newly built court buildings and Smith jammed the brakes on and brought the unit to a halt in front of an obstruction, the blue light still flashing quietly on the roof.

Their progress was impeded. Across the road before them sat the aftermath of what could only be described as: hell on earth. Imbedded in the building were the remnants of three cars; ghosts of their former selves.

'Bloody 'ell!' breathed Monk, aghast at the scene of destruction and demolition. 'What time do they close...? Ten, is it? There'll be some people in there then!'

The reason that the cars were sat steaming in the ground floor of the Lexington's building was a sixty foot blue and yellow tram. It had obviously jumped the track at speed and ploughed across the road, picking up and flinging the comparatively lightweight cars before it. The group on the tender could only guess at the speed that it must have been going before colliding with the waiting queue of cars. Could there have been any survivors? There certainly wouldn't be any on the ground floor.

Ten minutes earlier, twisted and crushed metal sheets – body work from the tram – had been flung around, and for the present time, was the least of anyone's worry. Petrol dripping from the cars tanks, ignited by the electricity from the dragged and broken tram cables had created an explosion that had lit up the entire ground floor, exploding with the ferocity of a war-time shell attack. Masonry, steel, glass and assorted debris now covered the total area. The steel and glass front to the building had totally collapsed over the transportation means. Broken windows both sides of the tram had helped vent a fire which had engulfed the entire interior and still continued to burn with some ferocity. The helpless fleeing occupants had obviously attempted escape, only to be caught and left blackening on the sills... dead within seconds.

The oppressive heat was obvious from their vantage point beside the tender, an inferno burning on the ground floor visible through the rubble. The rest of the store above was in complete darkness.

Breathing apparatus was going to be essential tonight.

Ignoring the rain, Tannen looked up at the building to ascertain the extent of the job. 'Is that someone looking out?' he said to Monk, craning to see as high as possible, patting his shoulder and pointing upwards.

An extremely close crack of lightning surprised them both and they ducked instinctively, faces cascading with streaming rain water.

'Where?'

They both again stared up at the disaster zone assessing the damage and planning an attack on the most imminent problems presented to them.

The face wasn't there any more.

Out of the tender now, they were unable to find any on-site official – his incident commander was due but obviously hadn't arrived yet. Two police cars were parked on the other side of the tram and another fire engine was unloading its hoses. Seeing no immediate person, Monk assumed command and started to make immediate plans for entry.

'Come on!' he shouted to his assembled team (despite the torrential rain) putting into action the normal sequence for this situation. 'Unload!'

The well-oiled and, by now, completely soaked squad, off loaded their own hoses. Connections made, the fire fight began on the flames engulfing the pedestrian tram. Aware of potential back-draft, the rear windows of the vehicle were smashed out and a slow entry made; years of daily training providing intuitive response to the problems.

No one could get in through the front of the building at the moment due to the fire and rubble. The beams from their high powered torches barely penetrated the dense smoke and fog within but Monk made plans to send someone scrambling through the wreckage as soon as feasibly possible in order to understand more fully the extent of the problem within, though the drooping lintels betrayed massive structural tribulations.

Obviously, with no hope of anyone surviving the blast in the tram and the torrential rain was only modestly limiting the flames so the group attacked them vigorously... eventually turning the hoses into the front of the building to douse that inferno too before the fire had chance to work its way through and attack the upper floors. Other attending units joined the fight from the other side, and together, the teams made headway.

The initial blast had incinerated the ground floor, before thrusting up the stair well, pushing anything and everything ahead of it. The people on the ground floor hadn't stood a chance. If they hadn't been crushed by the impact of the cars, tram or steel beams; if they hadn't been electrocuted by the cable thrashing about; if they hadn't been slashed to shreds by the flying glass, they were burnt to a crisp by the resulting fire.

As the explosion ripped up through the building it had begun to slow, the pressure of the air slashing the designer central top dome to shreds, the momentary vacuum destroying the top floor's integrity and dumping several tonnes of rubble down the centre of the building and corner fire escape shaft. It destroyed the atrium in seconds but prevented the fire from rising for the moment beyond the ground floor. The staircase had collapsed under the crush of brick and steel. The luckiest people were the ones who had died instantly rather than those who grimly hung on to life with reducing oxygen availability.

There were some people alive, just, on the third floor, and groups of generally healthy, but confined citizens on the fourth, fifth and sixth floors.

The air smelt of smouldering flesh, dust and petrol.

The public outside had barely been spared. The hammering rain the least of their worries as they sobbed sitting on the pavement, some screaming in disbelief at the occurrence before them, some loved ones obviously inside. The police and other rescuers were attempting to comfort and console these, survival blankets wrapped as many as possible, the wind causing even more of a problem for the valiant helpers. Ambulances were arriving in convoy from the hospitals close by, the medical staff running back and forth in high-visibility jackets attempting to help as many as possible back to the comfort and safety of their vans.

A perimeter of 'POLICE – DO NOT CROSS' tape, was set up by the occupants of another arriving police vehicle loaded to the gunnels with police support staff, and only just in time. Local television had heard on the police scanner of the incident and was arriving en mass to record the events for the evening news. Keeping them back to allow the services to do their job was the priority task.

Respectful requests did the job. No one wanted to cause problems at this moment; the horror of the scene speaking volumes. Comments on the cause and results of the unpleasant incident weren't forthcoming from anyone. The fire and ambulance service were well into their stride, the police helping where possible.

News teams had begun to arrive like locusts to a new field of crops. Compassion was not a prerogative with a story like this.

A well dressed reporter was preening herself whilst she sat in the passenger seat of the company emblazoned Rover Freelander, the vanity mirror less than three inches from her face, dabbing her immaculate features with the merest hint of blusher with one hand, her phone clamped to her ear with the other as she got the last few instructions and information from the studio. A producer and a cameraman were outside the car, braving the wind under an over large umbrella waiting for her, desperately trying to keep the electrical equipment and sound boom dry and scouting the vicinity for witnesses.

As she kicked open the door, the canopy was pushed over her to keep her dry for the walk to the nearby porch doorway of the court building. Microphone in her hand, she turned to face the camera, her back to the efforts of the valiant services. Tossing her head to show her hair to its best, she gripped the microphone as the cameraman took his stance. He switched the back light on, and motioned that she was now on air.

'This is Colleen McLaughlin with a live report from Wolverhampton town centre. Twenty minutes ago an explosion occurred here at the brand new Lexington's Super store. As yet we have no reports as to exactly what happened, but in the wake of the recent terrorist bombings around the country, a similar activity here has not been ruled out. However, this reporter can see what looks like one of the town trams protruding from the main entrance.'

The camera panned up and above her shoulder, showing a close up of the frantic service staff and mourning escapees. Reporters at the home studio in central Birmingham went crazy as they searched for any previously recorded footage of the area, building or trams.

'As you can see, things are well in hand. Until a few moments ago the tram was engulfed in flame. The weather has helped the local fire service to extinguish these…' she paused while the cameraman momentarily wiped the lens of his camera with his handkerchief; the rain so intense… 'flames!'

The producer turned to one side, now talking ten to the dozen into his phone. He desperately wanted the footage of the inaugural day for the town's tram system five years earlier to add to his live broadcast. Somebody stood watching caught his attention, and he waved them over.

'Did you see what happened?' he spoke urgently, discarding the phone momentarily.

'Err, yeah!' replied the young man.

'Come on then!' He pushed the dripping wet teenager in front of him towards Colleen.

The lad's trainers squelched with the wet, his trendily ripped jeans now letting in more water than was comfortable, his thin hooded jacket less use than paper. Colleen saw him out of the corner of her eye, and with the professionalism of two years of live television, brought him into the conversation.

'Now we have here a witness to the incident. Could I have your name please?' She thrust the microphone into his nervous face. The camera refocused towards the lad; his face was acne ridden and scabby. Scared!

'Err... Jason. Jason Cummings!' he stuttered.

'I understand you saw what happened. Could you describe it for us?' The microphone flicked back and forth between them, the ambulance and fevered activity a perfect back drop to the picture.

'I was in... I was inside. We was jus' looking, like. We decided to go, so we come out, like. Moment after, that tram... well, we heard this noise... very noisy, like a roar. Then that... tram come in... come in real fast, like.'

Colleen flicked the microphone back to her mouth.

'So are you saying, Jason, that as you left the store, an approaching tram didn't stop and hit the building behind you?'

'Yeah! Yeah that's it. My mates... they ran off like, but me mum works there an' I'm worried 'bout 'er!'

She touched her ear as a message came in via her ear piece. The camera worked its way across the scene behind Jason whilst Colleen regained her composure, picking out images of Monk, Smith, Tannen and the rest of the squad damping down the last of the flames, the police stood stubbornly in their orange jackets defending the area, and an incident commander arriving in a bright red Ford Mondeo, a black and white chequered band down either side of its length, closely followed by a large but understated red box truck with COMMAND written down its side in black print.

'We haven't been able to confirm it yet, but it looks like it was tram number 46.'

Jason ignored now, wandered back from the point of safety and dryness by the court building towards the tram.

Colleen flicked back her immaculate brunette hair, the sheen obvious in the limited hand held light, her perfect two piece suit perfectly crease free, and the pristine white lace-topped blouse showing a neat line across the top of her chest. She hadn't seen anything like this before, but she wasn't going to show any nervousness. She had her heart set on the anchor job at Central TV. If she could start getting the good stories, that position would be hers when that ancient old crone, the one with the crows' feet around her eyes, left. She deserved that anchor. She had worked hard for it.

She had given up a bloody good relationship to sleep with that idiot of a producer. Had to make a start on the ladder some how. Three weeks on her hands and knees with just a stupid promise as motivation. Still, she had managed to get the roving reporter position under her belt.

She was fed up of covering the heart-warming stories about the pet which had come home after three years, or the old age couple who renewed their wedding vows fifty years after some war had ended. She needed this story to show her true repertoire. She had to make a break into the big time some how. This might be the one.

Behind her Monk and his team were attempting to make an entry into the building under one of the beams. Decked out in the breathing apparatus, gloves and as much protection as they could, they were feeding a rope between them.

The other side of the, now silent tram, another team were attempting to lift the ladders to the second or third floor. Steam was rising from the wet pavements due to the intensity of the fire, the conditions were extremely uncomfortable. No one was thinking about themselves. There were people in that building. They had to get them out.

Colleen had managed to grab a member of the medical staff who was resting momentarily. The fraught bespectacled man had just seen his evening meal again despite having above three years medical experience and was quite clearly disturbed by what he'd seen. He had just tended to a woman who had had her entire left leg crushed. Her screams of agony would stay with him and wake him up in the middle of the night for many years to come

Colleen asked him to relate what he had seen to camera.

'It's horrible. The worst I have ever seen. There must have been above thirty people stood in the doorway and around here on the street!' He swallowed and blinked back the pain of the injuries that he had seen. 'No one stood a chance with the speed of it all!'

Sensing him faltering, Colleen took the opportunity to speak again. 'What sort of injuries have you had to deal with today?' She whipped her head again in the wind to keep her glorious locks of hair from her face.

'I really don't want to talk about it yet, best wait for an official release. I ought to be getting back…'

'Has anyone told you what they saw?' Colleen was unwilling to let him go, desperate for an in-depth interview, but wishing she had been able to collar someone more important.

The young medic knew enough to limit his words.

'They were running, trying to keep out of the rain after leaving cars at the curb. The tram was coming too fast. Hit some of the cars on the road. It didn't stop! No one stood a chance!'

Luckily for the medic, he was waved at by another, and, nodding briefly to Colleen, he turned unhindered to help with another discovered body.

'There you have it confirmed.' Colleen turned squarely to face the camera, her most serious face angled determinedly at the lens. 'An eye witness saw a town tram jump the track and cause devastation. There are upwards of thirty casualties!'

Colleen would have carried on quite happily trying to earn an 'Oscar' for her live reporting, but the controller at Central TV decided to cut back to the studio. The smug voice of Irene Carlson, the current anchor, came condescendingly through her ear piece.

'Thank you Colleen. We will rejoin you in a little while for an update when you have more information about the tragic events this evening!'

Colleen put on a brave, but hopefully rueful smile to terminate the broadcast in an attempt to appear both caring and sympathetic before the red light extinguished on the front of the hand held camera and the cameraman motioned that they were off air. It changed to a look of disgust. She ripped the earpiece from her ear and strode back to the warmth of their abandoned Freelander, taking the umbrella with her, heels clip clopping in the river of water running down the gutters.

The producer and cameraman glanced at each other before quickly following her, shielding the equipment from the elements as best they could, hunched over and soaking wet.

Above them, a lightning strike crackled down followed almost immediately by the heavy crash of thunder. The centre of the storm was almost overhead.

Behind them, a second fire crew was desperately trying to climb into the second floor window. The blustery wind was swaying the ladders but the fearless troop was not giving up. They already had a window open but had not yet made entry. Instead they were valiantly trying to improvise a rope lashing to hold the ensemble steady. Other members of the five-strong second squad were trying to erect giant spot-lamps in an effort to illuminate the ladder man's troubles. They were not having much luck... yet.

It was as though mother earth, four thousand, four hundred million years old, was angry, and her vengeance was tonight.

A dark coloured high-top Mercedes van cruised unnoticed around the traffic island for the third time. The volume of passing commuter traffic was normally heavy at this time on a Thursday evening, and hadn't yet abated tonight with the extra vehicles ferrying people home because of the appalling weather, plus the extra rubber necked spectators who had come out specially to gain a better view of the fascinating local incident being heavily reported on television. The van was just one more piece of annoying road clog that was now touring the roadways, braking quickly at the red lights and desperately trying to follow the meandering white road markings in the deluge of water that now covered everything.

The occupants strained to catch sight of the efforts that the emergency services were making, though not in a gawking sightseeing manner. They wanted to know for a far more sinister purpose. They needed to know how much success was being had. The rest of their plans for tonight rested upon that knowledge.

The van circled once more at a leisurely pace, before indicating left and taking the turnoff before the police cordon. A route into the town centre had already been planned.

Everything was running on time; it would soon be time for the second phase of the operation.

CHAPTER 9

'Do you want a drink?'

'Again?'

'No. Do you want a drink?'

'Yes please love!'

The girl swivelled her long legs from the bed and rested briefly, stretching. She stood and padded across the laminated wooden floor to the chair. Grabbing a light blue linen shirt discarded on the back, she pushed an arm into it and flipped it across her slender shoulder blades. She pushed her other arm in and straightened the collar. Leaving it hanging unbuttoned, she looked back at the man lying on the bed, her long legs obvious as she struck a pose for his benefit, her blonde hair tumbling around and framing her face. Her beautiful blue eyes searched his face and saw a lust returned in his.

'Beautiful!' he exclaimed.

'I know!' she replied softly and turned on her heels to exit the room.

Terry Thomas lay back in the bed, a satisfied smile now fixed on his face. His spiky black hair still retained its original style from an hour before; his designer stubble matching perfectly due to the time he spent on it that morning. It was warm in the bedroom. He pushed the thin cotton sheet down his body with a powerful hand to reveal thick black hair upon a perfectly honed thirty nine year old chest. The scrawny youth of his past just a distant memory, he now spent much of his life creating the person he had always wanted to be.

One thing a woman liked in the bedroom was heat. He wouldn't compromise on the basic necessity despite having the flat that no woman wanted to walk away from.

He had a living space that was the envy of everyone. His perfectly flat walls were painted white with a hint of mint to give them an aesthetically appealing quality. The beautifully laid floor was trimmed with natural light cedar skirting which gave a Scandinavian look to the room. Four, perfectly placed wooden framed pictures of iconic scenes gave the briefest insight to their owner.

A small, expensive wide screen television took pride of place against the wall. Large enough to speak volumes about Terry's tastes, it still didn't dominate the room. And the bed on which he lay. A beautiful ornate metal framed bed with the most luxurious mattress and the softest linen his personal shopper had ever found. The original sash windows had been beautifully restored and framed with curtains of the softest brown which matched the brown of the Mongolian hair throw cushions and bed runner.

A satisfied sigh ended his thoughts as the girl returned to the doorway. She carried two fine cut glasses containing their drinks.

'I've missed you!' he said, his white teeth flashing an alluring smile.

'I've missed you too!' she returned.

She passed him his glass but remained standing before him, shirt parted, giving him an obscured view of the pleasures within. He loved the little tattoo of an angel on her inner thigh. It was cute and appealing.

Swirling his glass, a couple of ice cubes clinking, he sipped the twelve year old bourbon and smacked his lips with pleasure. She knew how to prepare his drink. The girl sipped her own vodka and slim-line tonic and stared at him over the rim of the glass, her eyelashes almost magnified over her wide eyes; the glass pressed seductively to her lips.

The soft, hypnotic tones of 'Barry White' suddenly ceased as the CD came to an end from the silver top-of-the-range DVD beneath the television.

Terry regarded the equipment without surprise then looked back at the vision of beauty before him.

She lowered her glass, stepped forward and placed it carefully on a coaster upon the natural wood, bedside table. She padded across to the DVD player and bent over to look for the drawer release button.

Terry watched with desire for a second before calling her back to bed. Placing his glass alongside hers on the table, he lifted the covers and gratefully felt her hands on his chest as she pressed up close to his hips.

Within moments they were lost in each other again, oblivious to the increasing rain fall outside, audible now without the tunes of soul music filling the air.

Lying in each others' arms, they stared happily up at the ceiling, spot lit with two of the wall mounted stainless steel lights lost in personal thoughts. Outside, a crack of lightning broke the silence and the wind lashed rain against the windows behind the curtains.

Terry pulled his girl's head towards his face and softly kissed her hair. Her head rested on his chest and she sighed happily, flexing her hand and gripping one of his pecks. It was a perfect end to a perfect day. She had spent the day with him in his little powerful silver Porsche Boxster car. They had travelled to a little inn amongst the Derbyshire Dales for lunch and had a hand-in-hand stroll along an idyllic natural stream, stopping frequently for prolonged kisses and declarations of lust.

If only this could happen every day. But, she didn't see him that often. He worked hard for his money. He was some sort of financial market trader apparently. He had to disappear for days at a time. Always in London, or New York or Hong Kong… or so he said. But they always made up for lost time when he came back. She didn't mind. Their catching up was always wonderful.

'Some storm outside, San'!' he mused.

'Will you protect me?' she murmured into his chest hair.

'Of course I will!' He stroked down her back and patted the soft globes of her back side. A glorious shudder of pleasure sparkled down her body following his trailing fingers.

She was happy again. She didn't want it to end even though she knew it would.

'How long you got left?' His question returned her to the real world.

Glancing up towards the side table, she could see the red glow of the crystalline figures on the fancy clock. 8:29. 'Just over an hour yet!'

Terry cuddled her close. He'd be free by ten o'clock. He'd have a wash and brush up after she left. That still left time to wander down to that new fancy club on West Street. There was always a good crowd in there of an evening… always something going on.

A close and loud clap of thunder creating an explosive booming sound surprised both of them. The two lovers looked at each other. Taking it as a sign, Sandra rose again from the bed and disappeared into the bathroom.

Terry's searching hand found the remotes for the television and then flicked the Sky box through the channels, seeking out a soothing station to help pass the time.

In the fantastic wet room which had cost an absolute fortune to build, Sandra stood before the mirror and looked at her face. All around, the pearlescent liquid blue tiles shone brightly. The wall mounted toilet and stainless steel fittings an interior designers dream.

She wasn't bad looking for thirty-five. She had retained reasonable elasticity to the facial skin; high cheek bones had prevented double chins from forming and the skin around her neck was still very tight. Wrinkling her nose back and forth, she checked for creases in her forehead.

Sandra gently prodded the line beneath an eye with an extended finger and wiped away the merest blob of mascara before blinking her lashes.

Baring her teeth, she checked for anything that was out of place. Finding nothing, she licked across her teeth and grabbed the purple plastic hair brush from her hand bag. She started to slowly brush through her 'now tangled' locks staring at her reflection almost proudly.

Through the closed door she could hear the sound of the music channel being turned up over the sound of rolling thunder.

Pulling a cleansing wipe from a box in her bag, she proceeded to clean her face and then laid out her make-up kit across the top of the sink.

Without any reason, she suddenly looked up at the obscured bathroom window. She couldn't see anything. That was odd.

Terry's had bought his expensive flat earlier in the year. A reclaimed 'brown' site in Wolverhampton town centre, developers had decided to change the miserable and generally rotten factory into the latest habitats.

Last Christmas, the place had been home to rats, spiders, damp, two or three teenage drug addicts and a squatter living on a smelly disgusting mattress that had been dumped in the grounds and from food he found at the bottom of bins behind the local takeaways. It had had the peeling brown paint of years of neglect. Smashed, dirty and boarded up windows had given an abandoned and neglected look to the forgotten historical landmark. Dangerous rusted steel stairways had given way under the tidal wave of despair, and the musty mouldy internal plaster walls had long since fallen down. Dog walkers had never been able to cross the grounds for fear of broken glass and discarded syringes abandoned where they fell. People crossed the street to avoid the barest minimum of scaffolding that had been erected by the council in order to prevent one of the walls from collapsing under the weight of a displaced steel girder. The roof had lost its slates many years previously, and the remaining skeletal beams had since barely stayed up under the force of the Midlands weather and a small fire during the summer of 2003.

Now it was home to the up and coming go-getters of the area. Developers had been fighting for years to own the land for the bare minimum of financial outlay. Similar developments in the trendiest areas of Birmingham and London had proved instant hits, and they had wanted to emulate the success with this unit. Within weeks a new façade had been constructed to clad and enhance the early nineteen hundreds structure, extra hidden internal steelwork to support the building that had survived two world wars and three businesses.

New windows and roof had been a major improvement as far as the passing pedestrians and shoppers had been concerned. It no longer had a hideous edifice; the new lick of paint had transformed the whole corner building to one of almost beauty. New fencing, landscaping and car parking completed the external facelift.

Hungry eyes *now* from the passing drivers on the town's ring roads as they viewed the potential housing with envious desire!

Placards placed along the overlap fence proclaimed it as being the latest development from the Bleath Brothers. The astute high flying upper echelon management knew exactly the sort of quality that that meant. A waiting list had been quickly filled with names. Terry had jumped to the top of the list because of a connection he realized he had with the sales team on the day he had visited the show apartment on the ground floor.

Sandra had walked and driven past the forlorn warehouse many times without so much as a glance past the intermittent rusty iron fencing. She had never expected to be inside and the object of envy whenever she walked up to its security controlled front door.

A chance meeting with Terry had changed all that a year ago whilst stocking the freezers at Sommersby's. Tipping over the lip of the compartment with a heavy box of frozen chips had resulted in his strong masculine hands clenching around her waist and rescuing her from the ravages of the cold; a stilted conversation and an offer of something to warm her up later.

Sandra smiled as she recalled how he had made her feel twenty years younger even during the first conversation... the playful toying with her hair as she twisted nervously on the spot while the sharp, booted and suited man made her feel like the most glamorous woman on earth, despite the ill-fitting all-in-one overall she was made to wear and the frankly quite insultingly cheap name plaque that adorned her chest.

It hadn't taken much to smile as she met him that night as she crossed the car park to the car, and even less to condescend to an evening drink at a secluded pub where no one would recognize her.

The rest, as they say, was history.

She looked up at the window again. Many nights she had gone through this routine of replacing her make-up ready for the journey home, but this time it was different.

Standing on tip-toes, and despite the glare of the bathroom spot light, she stared through the opening at the top. Normally she could see lights from here. The lights of that new Lexington Superstore! That's right. Massive neon lights that gave her the feeling that she was now part of an expanding metropolis of life and colour in this god-forsaken town. Large glowing lights that distanced her from the quiet suburban lifestyle that she now felt trapped in, and made her feel alive. Lights that had encouraged her to continue with the current choices she was making for herself and gave her the motivation to change her dreary existence for that of a socialite.

The lights from that new store! The store where she had sent Bert! That was odd. They were usually open all evening... this probably meant that he had had to turn round and go back home.

'That's all I need!' she exclaimed to herself. 'Another argument when I get back about where I've been! Typical!'

Vehemently!

She applied the foundation more angrily now, sweating slightly from the half thought that her husband would have returned from the closed store early and wonder where she was... again!

110

'Look at this!' An anxious shout from the bedroom.

Sandra quickly closed her compact and returned the kit to her handbag. Flicking the light off, she left the room and passed the cramped kitchen and down the beige carpeted corridor to the bedroom.

Terry was lying on the bed propping his head on his hand, mouth slightly open in awe at the events unfolding on the television.

'What is it?' she queried dropping her bag at the door.

'Lexington's!' he breathed, 'it's gone up in smoke!'

The two watched the outside broadcast from a windswept girl stood before a burning building. They could distinguish the fluorescent yellow jackets of the emergency services rushing back and forth behind her, and a fire crew battling to put out the flames on a... on a tram?

The camera panned to a dishevelled, extremely damp lad who looked like he was crying and a practically incoherent conversation with him.

'Was that the noise we heard?' asked Sandra of her incredulous man as understanding pervaded her mind.

'Could have been!'

Terry had a thought. He jumped out of bed, and ran quickly to the floor-to-ceiling patio doors. He pulled back the curtains, unlocked the door, and hauled them open inwards. Sandra grabbed his dressing gown, and joined him on the tiny balcony wrapping it around her shoulders. Together they looked apprehensively towards the town centre.

The rain teemed down around them, and another bolt of lightning forked across the sky. They weren't taking any notice of the weather though; they were looking at the Lexington's building that was now in darkness.

'Bert!' exclaimed Sandra in a small voice, sudden worry in her mind; a small knot of concern balling deep in her belly.

'What?'

'He was going there tonight. I sent him for some things for me... to get him out of the house more than anything! He would be there just about now! Shit! Why didn't he get himself a phone? Shit!'

On the television a paramedic was being interviewed. They caught the number of injured. Thirty!

Sandra was really worrying about her husband now. Despite the lengthy affairs she had conducted over the last couple of years, there was still a certain amount of closeness and some love left for him.

Terry was worrying about her husband too. The husband was the only thing stopping this woman from attaching herself to him permanently. Terry didn't want an enduring addition to his life. It would restrict his life choices dramatically. She was all right for days out. She was extremely attractive. She was great in bed. But she had a lot of baggage; she was a shelf stacker. Terry wasn't ready to settle down yet, especially with a shelf stacker.

Returning into the bedroom and closing the door, he sat down on the bed and turned the volume up a little higher on the television. Sandra sank into the chair and together they watched for any more information.

Irene Carlson was on screen. She came across to the viewing public as a motherly type and attractive in a warm, friendly sense. Someone you would trust to tell the truth. She had a remorseful expression on her normally quite jovial face. She wore a sombre but attractive grey suit.

'Just to recap,' she was saying, 'at 8:30 this evening, the number 46, Birmingham to Wolverhampton tram jumped the tracks whilst travelling at an undisclosed speed and has ploughed into the front of Wolverhampton's Lexington's store. It took with it several cars.' Previous footage of the events was being looped behind her on the screen. 'Casualties so far are too many to ascertain. There are people trapped on different floors, and the services are battling to enter the building.

We go now to John Marshall with some background.'

The camera cut to a grey haired, clean cut, suited man who began to explain the history of both Lexington's and the tram system. Previously recorded footage had been found and was now being wheeled out onto primetime national television.

Stock footage showed the old multi-storey car park that had been ripped down to clear the ground. Various shots of the building construction from many different angles included an aerial shot of the final roof dome, obviously taken from a helicopter. Interviews with designers, construction engineers and Mr. Lexington himself, a London born 'gutter boy done good', added to the bulk of the story, the lingering shots of the glorious, innovative square based tower with the completely glass sixth floor topped with the ribbon cutting ceremony by the mayor and a brass marching band accompaniment.

Interviews then with a small queue of excited people hoping for employment in the new building and various V.I.Ps including some member of parliament of the time whom was now just a distant memory and bad taste in the mouth for most.

John Marshall smoothly linked the footage to the next section of his report with a serious narration.

'The building of Lexington's was a great day for Wolverhampton. Over one thousand people were employed for its construction and just under… one hundred jobs were created to run the state of the art department store.'

A video recording was played showing the scene as a camera wandered through the store, picking out the design features of the glorious staircase, escalators, service areas and superb changing room facilities on the clothing floors. Luxurious seating areas with a selection of in house entertainment conveniences for bored partners and offspring were mentioned by the young, eager company Public Relations representative and the tape demonstrated the sumptuous carpet and snack machines that had tried to revolutionize the shopping experience for the new millennium. Comprehensive Closed Circuit Television kept track of all floors, and whilst extra, more detailed scenes were relayed to the high tech security office on the sixth floor, the broader views were relayed to the screens above the padded armchairs and settees for viewing by the waiting or anxious users.

The viewer was given limited views of the high security offices at the centre of the sixth floor. Peak capped security guards were sat in the computer laden room pressing buttons, and filling forms. One middle aged, straight backed, ex-soldier with short cropped hair and a wiry moustache explained to the camera that they could monitor every section of the shop floor, the entrance hall and roads surrounding the store. He patiently explained that they now possessed facial recognition software that could distinguish the undesired elements from the visiting populace and that police could be called to attend within six minutes any incident.

'This was the store of the future!' explained John Marshall. 'Coupled with the reintroduction of a cheap and cheerful transport alternative from the early nineteen hundreds, Wolverhampton was looking to be a completely regenerated zone.'

The screen went on to show the first journey of the trams along the main road in the late nineties and the main stop in front of Lexington's Super store at Wolverhampton under a beautiful steel and plastic canopy. Views of pleased looking little old white haired ladies and gentlemen as they alighted into glorious sun shine had all been propaganda at the time in order to encourage use of the park and ride system. There were pictures now showing Mr. Lexington and an official looking council representative wearing a purple and blue sash shaking hands and beaming at anyone who would look.

Terry and Sandra sat, now holding hands, aghast and shocked at the events that had been relayed and amazed that Wolverhampton was having so much air time on national television.

The screen flicked back to showing John Marshall sitting on a stool in front of a giant green screen now bearing the slogan 'Terror Tram'. Facing the camera, he now recapped eloquently, shuffling unread paper for effect before him...

'Millions of pounds have been ploughed back into Wolverhampton in an effort to regenerate the blighted area. New buildings are currently under construction in order to alleviate the old look. The events tonight are certain to be a major set-back to the project... Losses still have not been recouped, and insurance is going to be hard hit... Irene!'

Positive her husband was still in the building, Sandra was up and already pulling her clothes on. Terry's shirt was off and flung across the chair. Blouse, skirt and shoes took seconds, her face a picture of worry. Terry watched unspeaking. He didn't try to stop her. He didn't try to comfort her.

'Do you need a lift?' he asked helpfully.

'No.' She was white and tight-lipped with concern. 'I'm going straight over there. I need to find out if he's there or not! Can I borrow a brolly?' A red, moistening eye betrayed her worries.

'Of course!' Terry left the room, still naked, in order to locate a corporate logo emblazoned golf umbrella from various cleaning equipment within the hall cupboard. No little tattoos on his body.

She pecked him on the lips as he handed it to her, all desire and thoughts of love, all memories of their day completely gone in the worry she now felt for her husband. Terry understood gladly. He let her go without question, listening for her footsteps descending down

116

the stair case, the cheery 'good night Miss' from the stationed security guard and the click of the entrance door at it closed behind her. He closed his front door and returned slowly to the bedroom.

The glamorous Colleen McLaughlin was back on screen, flicking her hair about seductively against the wind, her cherry red lips pouting in the cold wind. 'LIVE FROM WOLVERHAMPTON' emblazoned in blood red letters on a bright yellow banner across the bottom of the screen and scenes now of the fire service getting ready to remove the tram from the entrance…

'Of course, we don't yet know what structural damage it has done to the building. We can't afford for the second floor to collapse in. We've had to contact the original designer for blueprints of the building, though he has been located in Dorset and efforts have already been made to transmit details to us here. The weather is hampering our job quite considerably!' A bulky looking fire fighter was being interviewed, a gruff voice betraying some annoyance at being distracted from his duties. Monk was stressed, physically tired and determined to do his job and save as many lives as he could. Temporarily removing his helmet, he rubbed a worried hand over his head, leaving a dirty streak in its path.

'We don't expect many survivors on the ground floor which took the brunt of the accident, but we expect minimal casualties on the other floors. Though there is no power in the building, we have had contact with mobile phone from other members of the shopping public within the store…I've really got to go…' Monk turned from the camera and Colleen watched his disappearing back for a moment before turning back to the camera, desperately hiding her excitement at speaking to someone so important to the incident.

Terry shook his duvet cover, replaced his fancy brown runner across the bottom of the bed and disappeared to the bathroom for a shower.

Sandra was running barefoot through the town streets towards Lexington's, hands gripping the umbrella and little handbag, her heeled sandals swinging from the handle, unconcerned about the litter and garbage strewn down the main streets that she unsuccessfully tried to avoid. The sharp corner of a crumbling pot hole caught her toe and made her wince.

Grease now from spilt fuel. Yuk!

She felt a sudden concern for her husband that she could not understand and that she had not felt for so long now. He had never let her down… *ever*! If he said he was going to do something, then he always did. He was going to that store tonight because she had asked him to. She had cheated him into doing it so as she could self-indulge. Never mind the long day at work; he would have followed through on his promise. He was still there! She knew it… felt it!

Why? Why was she positive?

Guilt?

CHAPTER 10 *Coordination*

After being picked up, Alison had then expected to enjoy her afternoon. The two lads were her kind of people – up for a laugh – the type to take her mind of her problems. Deciding that she must have lost her job by now and wanting a couple more hours to come up with a feasible story to get it back, she agreed to going for a drink.

Sitting on the back seat of the Fiesta, the exhaust rumbling away beneath her, she looked around the vehicle and made a judgment about her saviours.

The layer of cigarette ash in the car made Alison cough. The floor held a thick covering of old butts mixed with sweet wrappers and a greasy lump of paper that looked and smelt suspiciously like old chips. The windscreen had a crack that started smack in the centre with a massive hole and meandered out to the top right of the screen causing the driver to duck his head in order to see the road ahead clearly. The central rear view mirror was a distant memory for the car, as was road tax if the peeling plastic holder displaying a 2000 date was anything to go by. No gauges moved on the dashboard, and the driver judged his speed cautiously in order not to attract attention. The passenger window didn't fit the hole properly, causing a whooshing sound when the car climbed above thirty miles per hour, and a smattering of rain to flick across Alison's face occasionally.

These weren't law abiding citizens. These were her kind of people; 'grifters' and grafters.

Her previous casual desire for a cigarette suddenly magnified. She shifted across the back seat away from the water ingress.

'Can I 'ave a ciggie?' she asked cheekily, smiling seductively and knowing exactly how to get what she wanted.

The white lad smiled and felt in his coat pocket for a gold packet bearing the customary health warning. Tapping one out, he offered the open mouth of the carton to her. 'Karl!' he said as way of introduction.

'Alison!' she returned, taking the offered cigarette and checking her pockets for a lighter. No surnames. She was still evaluating them.

'Adam!' continued the lad, gesturing to his driving friend, who nodded briefly in recognition of his name. 'Fancy a drink?' His piercing green eyes never left her face.

'Sure!' she answered, blowing a flume of smoke through pursed lips and resting back on the least uncomfortable part of the rear seat, her back scratching back and forth as she avoided the rigidity of a recalcitrant spring.

The lad's eyes flowed down her body, taking in the wet uniform, to her legs. They lifted and he turned to face forward. 'Where d'you work then?' he asked, looking out the window at a cheap furniture store they were passing, blue tarpaulin covering a selection of miserable offerings on the pavement.

'Lexington's,' replied Alison, 'but I think I'm sacked! I should've bin there for 11 today! On a warnin'.'

'Bastards sacked you?' Adam's voice was deep and low. His hands clenched fleetingly on the steering wheel, his knuckles showing almost pink for the moment.

'Yup!' Alison didn't want to talk about it. She wanted a drink. She wanted another fag. She wanted to forget the store. She was looking at the driver's broad shoulders. Another tiny shiver ran down her spine. From this angle he looked extremely fit.

The car bounced through yet another water filled pothole, shaking the occupants as they tried to ignore the jolting journey; the tyres had seen better days and the suspension was totally shot.

Adam twisted the wheel and they bounced up a patchwork curb; up a small incline and lurched into a space on a glass strewn car park. In the corner, under a moulting beech tree, the remains of a blackened family estate car, the surface below it was testament to its location when it had been fire bombed. The boot lid was in the air, two doors open and glass non-existent in the apertures. It must have been gutted before being torched. No seats, dashboard or any controls. Their Fiesta was the only working vehicle in the vicinity. Alison noticed a battered sign languishing in the weed ridden shrubs surrounding the car park. 'Stag and Horseshoe'.

'Here we are!' said Karl, amusement playing at the corners of his lips. He held out the catch and leaned heavily against the door. It banged open and creaked to maximum limit. Jumping out, he pulled the seat catch and once again pulled it forward to allow Alison to get out.

As she climbed past him, she noticed that he was only a little taller than her own five foot seven inch frame. Roughly the same weight though; a hundred and seventy pounds. He didn't step far enough back for her and she had to rub against him to make her exit, her hand bracing herself against his elbow. To be honest, now that they were in such close proximity, she felt her skin crawl a little. It was a familiar feeling at the pub on occasion, though not one that bothered her that much. Alison knew how to take care of herself... had done many times before now. But she was penniless today and in desperate need for a drink. She ignored the feelings and looked again at his better looking companion through desirous eyes.

Adam was already out the driver's door. They both slammed their doors shut without any attempt to lock them, and then started towards the white rear door of the pub backing on to the car park. Alison followed. She had nothing to lose.

The pub was one of the worst places Alison had ever stepped into. Normally she didn't care about where her drink came from, but this was something else. An uneven floor in the hallway almost tripped her twice; a mysterious dark brown stain on the walls prevented her from steadying herself, relying instead on the following Karl for a hand of support.

She gingerly followed between the two lads through a decaying archway into the lounge, a spider's web annoying her hair as she entered. The threadbare and dirty green carpet was wall to wall, but the selection of stains didn't help the poor impression it made. An ancient jukebox sitting in the corner clicked irritatingly and a fruit machine whistled various disconcerting notes quite piercingly alongside the bar. A short Asian man, in the process of thumping the big yellow buttons with stubby hands, looked up at her as she entered before returning to his random prodding.

Upon the pale brown, mouldy bar featuring uncountable sticky water rings, grubby yellow splash trays were leaking their contents. The barman, if he knew, didn't care. Engrossed in a secretive whispered conversation with a youth standing at the bar, a nod of welcome was the only thing offered Adam.

'Vodka and lime!' said Alison looking at Karl before she could be asked. Karl nodded. She went to find the cleanest seat she could under the dirty brown windows that faced the noisy street outside. Karl joined Adam at the bar. One foot each propped on the rusting silver metal rail that ran down its length, they continued a whispered conversation whilst waiting for the barman to join them. A couple of glances back at Alison confirmed that they were talking about her.

'Yes mate?' asked the unkempt proprietor eventually looking up properly, his scruffy white shirt bearing the stains of more than a couple of previous meals. He moved down the bar to the lads, his breathing racked with obvious problems as he flicked the stub of a cigarette expertly into an over flowing ashtray and wiped his hand down the front of his trousers.

They ordered the drinks and joined Alison on stools at the circular table before her. Smiling her thanks, Alison sipped satisfyingly from the thumbprint stained glass. The lads took long drinks from their 'Guiness' and 'lager' with discrete burps of appreciation. They looked at each other in a seemingly unspoken conversation before regarding their guest with eager looks.

'Do you two work?' asked Alison in order to break the silence; her watched hand brushing a collected dust ball from her skirt as she sucked her belly in slightly and imperceptibly thrust out her chest for effect. It didn't go unnoticed.

'We do this an' that!' smiled Adam mysteriously. 'We sort problems! Put things right!' He tapped the side of his nose in the time honoured 'mind your own business' fashion.

'Make good on people's promises!' added Karl, his eyes making Alison feel a little uncomfortable. She preferred Adam's warm brown eyes. He looked a little sad… like a puppy dog. She wanted to hold him and make him feel better.

'Can we help you out with your problem with Lexington's?' asked Karl. 'We could arrange some method of payment!'

'Yeah! We'll find some way to sort them out!' added Adam, shifting his bulk uncomfortably on the stool. 'We've got a job on today anyway. Might be something we could do to kill two birds with one stone, so to speak.'

Karl snorted with laughter into his glass.

'In fact, there's something you can do for us!' remarked Adam, his pupils dilating now as he became more and more aware of Alison's interest in him. 'We could really do with your help this afternoon. And then… we'll sort out your problem in any way you want us to!'

'That would be good!' smiled Alison, taking another sip, 'but it's just my supervisor who's a pain! He thinks he's so much better than everyone else.'

'Want us to break his legs?'

'No!' she sighed in exasperation.

She had many mixed feelings right now... upset at being robbed last night; wet and cold from her walk; miserable at possibly losing her job. She didn't want anything worse to happen. Maybe just a warning to the little man to get off her case would be enough. He always seemed to be telling her off for something. Why did little fat men think they have so much power? His steel rimmed glasses, faded brown tie and grey cardigan better suited to someone ten years older than he actually was. He always carried a blue biro pen which he jabbed at his A4 pad of paper whenever he saw her. She never knew what he was writing, but the look of distaste on his face as though smelling a large rotting fish, spoke volumes. Alison tried to avoid him, but he was a weasel, always popping out from behind pallets of stock that had ridden the fast, non-stop service elevator to the top floor from the delivery wagons parked in the bay behind the store, or watching as she tried to have a crafty fag sitting near a rubbish cage then preaching about health and safety or some such garbage.

As sneakily annoying and creepy as he was, he didn't deserve loss of limbs. A quiet word from this couple about respecting people's personal space might be just enough to sort all her problems.

Just as she was about to convey these thoughts, Karl rose to find the damp, dark, filthy and exceedingly smelly Men's room, leaving her alone with the current object of her affections. With Karl barely through the door, her foot was already stroking Adam's calf, and she was staring deeply into his eyes to hold his undivided attention.

Adam drained his glass and looked the girl up and down appreciatively. A large hand gripped her foot and mutual desire was born. Logically he knew he couldn't pursue this today, but it was nice to have the attention.

Karl, coming from the toilet saw it all and realized that he couldn't compete. Lifting his eyes resolutely to heaven, he plucked the remainder of his pint from the table, grinned weakly at Adam, and disappeared to stand out on the street front under the stone slab canopy.

A young girl was walking past the pub door dressed in school uniform. She looked at him with complete disinterest. Glancing at his watch, he wondered fleetingly what she was doing out of school. He lit another cigarette.

The girl's name was Claire Yates. A modern fourteen year old teenager, she hated school; hated her parents; hated her life. Thick black mascara and black lipstick plastered her face. Her teacher had told her to go to the toilet in order to remove it. She had taken the opportunity to walk through the open block door and out of the unlocked school gates. She couldn't care less about the pouring rain, which had, in the distance she had walked, created rivers of black down her cheeks and dripped onto her top. These had left everyone who saw her with the impression that spiders had created webs across her face.

Even her dress sense had caused offence. Thick black stockings climbed to a grey school skirt that was at least three inches shorter than was acceptable at Clemsall High School, a striped red and yellow tie was knotted to hang further down than was tidy, and her white blouse was playing, un-tucked around the body; an unbuttoned coat allowing the chilly wind beneath. Her attitude said that she couldn't care less. The rain streaming through the mounds of her deliberately messed up, dreadlocked hair just made her feel an individual; a rebel; a radical. Dragging her bag behind by one broken strap, it banged and scraped through the puddles. Damage to the school's books was the least of her worries. She hated school.

After one last glance at the wild looking white lad in rock tour t-shirt and jeans who was still staring after her, she turned the corner from the grubby main thorough-fare onto her much nicer home housing estate – another attempt by town planners for area regeneration. Her paces reduced to the smallest possible despite the steadily increasing rainfall. Her mom might be home – the shift patterns at the insurance agency never made any sense to her, and the last thing she wanted, was to explain why she was missing school again.

Peering around a large green bush on the final corner, she ascertained that her mother was out and increased her speed towards the idyllic little suburban semi-detached home. A low, white, wooden, picket fence bordered the little green patch of lawn and strip of planting. The neatly laid flagstones went directly from the pavement to front door, an area of temporarily unused, shared tarmac, provided off-road parking for their house and the one next door. A green front door neatly matched the garage door as well as the new plastic guttering that edged the top and side of the house. 'So conformist,' Claire had often said to her grungy friends.

Lifting the house key from a chain around her neck, she opened the front door and dragged her bag inside to the immediate lounge. Slamming the door behind her, she left the bag where it lay on the patch of grubby carpet and slouched towards the kitchen for a glass of cola drink and a packet of crisps. Catching sight of her image in the mirror above the mantelpiece, she momentarily admired her gothic make-up, quickly making a skull and crossbones on her cheek from the dribble of black mascara and with an out-stretched hand, caught the familiar ON button to the stereo system before continuing her quest for refreshment.

After a brief second to load a CD into the player, the system began the auto-play. The thumping beat of teenage music from her step-father's new speakers filled the room, the house and, unfortunately, the house next door.

Claire nodded in time with the tune whilst staring down their perfectly manicured back garden at next door's ginger cat preening itself on the recently blue painted shed, and wished that she was as carefree and un-tethered. Finishing the packet of flavoured potato snacks, she sighed, slugged back a drink from the cola bottle and wished her boyfriend was here.

His name was Johnny. He understood her because he was a rebel too. He loved the same music and never passed judgment on her. He always knew what she was thinking and never disagreed with her. Unfortunately her mother had come into her bedroom last night at ten o'clock without knocking and found his hand inside her blouse. She then threw him out and grounded her for a month. It was so unfair. She wouldn't have gone any further with him... she wasn't stupid... and what... her mother had never done that sort of thing before..? Even with that idiot that she had now taken up with... the idiot who wanted her to call him 'dad'?

Her mother was always crying. Claire pretended that she didn't notice, but her poster covered bedroom wall shared that of the toilet, and it was extremely thin. It upset her. Despite the constant arguments with her mother, she loved her deeply, and wanted no more than for her to be happy. The thought that she herself was not helping matters with her truculent behaviour, never crossed her mind.

She dropped the crisp packet on the back marble effect work top, swilled her hands under the hot tap, replaced the top on the bottle, burped, and then went upstairs to read her glossy over priced magazines. She left the music pumping away downstairs, upsetting the elderly couple next door, who even though were quite deaf, could still hear the sounds of the reggae music through the cheap construction of the houses.

Kicking her shoes off at the bedroom door, she collapsed on to her cluttered bed and plucked a periodical bearing a sample pack of the latest skin cream and detailing an article about 'how to get the boy that you want' from the floor. Around her, the faces of a hundred stuffed teddy bears looked blankly at her for the remainder of the afternoon... oblivious now to the fact that the administrative staff at her school was wondering where she was.

Her mother arrived home late. She never realized that her daughter had been home all afternoon, and after switching off the wailing sounds of the latest boy band, she disappeared though the little hall into the kitchen in order to start tea for her unappreciative family.

She had had a bad day again – always some problems at work with irate customers, fraudulent claims and money motivated management. But she balled her feelings up into a little knot in her stomach and left them there.

No one would ask about her day. No one would care.

'Leave work at work,' her one close friend had once advised her over a rare coffee morning.

Helen was barely coping, but she had been brought up to do the right thing by everyone, and would never be seen to be unable to deal with any problems presented. Andy would be home soon. They had to go out later for a new toaster... and he wanted to change their TV... again!

CHAPTER 11 *Consideration*

On the fifth floor now, Helen was now close to screaming. It was the final straw. Watching a man die in front of her was not something that she had ever wanted to see. She felt pity and worry when she saw pictures of the latest middle-east war. She sent money to the phone-in appeals. She never expected to actually watch a man fall to his death.

Bert's resolve was rather more stoic. Resting Eddie's head gently to the ground, he removed his coat and delicately covered the body.

As upset as he was, he was also curious as to what Eddie had seen. Plus, it was getting very warm on the floor. He was concerned as to whether there was a fire burning below (or above) them. He sat back on his heels and looked around the dark floor at the frightened faces.

Sian was looking to him for support. He decided that someone had to take charge. Evaluating the faces around him, he negated the possibility of Brenda who was hurt, Dave, useless, Andy, a prat, Helen, too upset. Sydney and Doreen weren't with them mentally, if only just physically. The young girls were far too emotional. Sian was looking at him. Bert stood up.

'Err... folks!' he started. The muttering of conversation ceased around him. 'Err... people!' he said again. 'I think we ought to come together. We need a plan of action and we need to stick together!'

Another clap of thunder punctuated his words.

'Can we all come over here towards my voice?' he carried on, 'please!' He was rewarded with the shuffling of the few remaining shoppers on the floor doing as he had asked and joining the few injured people around the improvised hospital area. In the light of the candle, Eddie's dead form could be seen prostrate near by.

'Don't look!' said Bert to Lara, as her trembling lower lip let her down. He raised a friendly hand to offer to hold her. She collapsed with some sense of relief against his chest and sobbed silently down his shirt. Embarrassed and feeling a touch awkward, he patted her shoulder affectionately.

'Right,' he continued, 'a man has just died because he left the group. We can't see too well in this light. We daren't have too many candles 'cos they'll set off the sprinklers again, and this place is a death trap now that everything has moved about. I suggest we sit here and work out a plan together...'

Silence!

'Does anyone disagree?'

Andy sniffed as a prelude to speaking. Realizing this, Helen laid a warning hand on his arm and looked directly at him with an un-smiling face. Andy got the message, and he expelled the air, any words he was contemplating left unspoken.

'I agree,' interjected Sian, 'that gentleman didn't need to do what he did. It was stupid.'

Another muffled wail from Lara, still clinging to Bert's rapidly dampening shirt. Sian half smiled ruefully, wishing that at that moment, she also had someone to hold her. Instead, she was in charge of first aid. The thought returned her focus.

'Dave!' spoke Bert.

'Yes!' His head snapped up at the sound of his name.

'Tell us about this floor. Any entrances, exits, rooms... anything!'

Dave swallowed. All these people were looking at him for his response. He'd never had this number people expecting words from him since his slurred wedding day speech, when his inebriation had spared any embarrassment about public speaking. His new bride had pulled him back into his seat after two minutes of disgracefully poor mumblings about it being the best day of his life.

'Well... well there's the middle stair case, and... well you know that... an escalator in the middle. In one corner there's two lifts...' Dave got into his stride and everyone listened.

He explained that the store had three lifts in the corner. The main one didn't stop at this floor, but merely carried stock from ground floor to the stock room on seventh. A service elevator carried required stock up and down the building, and the customer lift was used for disabled access only. Toilets in the other corner were self contained for both staff and customer use.

'No other method of travelling between floors?' asked Bert. 'We know the police know we're here, but we ought to have an alternative option!'

'There's the dumb waiter!' interjected Sian.

'What's that?'

'It's what the cashiers call the money chute!' continued Dave. When there's too much money in the tills, security come round to empty them, put it all in strong boxes and send it up a small lift to the cash office on the top floor.

'I think we need to explore the possibilities of using one of them for escape.' Bert was a little worried. He felt like he'd been there for hours. He was now cold without his coat. He was damp following the drenching from the sprinkler system; he was distressed at holding a dying man; the only feeling that he wasn't objecting to, was the warm body of the young lady currently holding him.

'Get a grip!' he told himself, 'you're married!' He eased her up, checked she wasn't crying and untangled himself from her form.

'I'll check these possible exits over,' he said to the assembled group. 'Dave, can you show me?' Dave jumped to his feet, eager to help. 'I think the rest of you should stay here together!'

Andy caught his arm as he made a move to follow Dave, the look of distaste and superiority evident even in the dim light of the candles. Helen and a couple of the others looked up in surprise and interest. The pressure of his grip on Bert's elbow told him that this man was not happy and more likely than not – a trouble maker. As Andy leaned in, a strong smell of Kouros aftershave mingled with unpleasant breath assailed Bert's nose. It wasn't enjoyable but Bert smiled weakly.

'So, who put you in charge?' Obstinately! Provocatively! Andy asked almost spitting venomously with his own frustration. He blocked his wife's face from his field of vision, determined to add his opinion, confident that he didn't like this scruffy little man.

'If you have a better plan, let's hear it!' returned Bert almost good naturedly, his own voice calm and even, despite the aggravation and weariness that he was actually feeling. All he wanted to do was collapse where he stood, but concern about their present predicament demonstrated a need for imperative action. The weather was obviously hampering rescue efforts and his own limited knowledge about building design based on his occupational experience told him that he wanted to be somewhere else if this particular building decided to collapse.

'We should all just sit here and wait for rescue. Lexington's has a corporate responsibility to make sure that we are safe. If they don't, my God, there's going to be trouble. I don't want to be here. They'll come for us in a few minutes!'

'What if they don't?' The question was simple, spoken just above a whisper, and conveyed all of Bert's anxiety. However, it was Helen who had spoken, joining them quietly.

'They've got to!'

'Look, you're worrying these people,' said Bert calmly. 'If they come, they come. If they can't, then I'm gonna know I didn't just sit here!' He looked between Helen's concerned face, and Andy's belligerent one. 'I'm bored anyway,' he lied and finished with a weak grin. He didn't want trouble with Andy. Enough had happened tonight without fisticuffs in the half light. He shrugged Andy's hand off; his immaculate attire and presentation irked him a little as he stood there in his tatty t-shirt.

As a knowingly scruffier individual, Bert was always a little overwhelmed when talking with the better dressed, as though in the presence of a superior, moneyed high flier who would look down on him for his manual labour look and deride him for it, if not to his face, then behind his back.

A nonsensical illusion; a barrier in his sub-conscious; an evil inner voice – one that he never dared to share with his always immaculate partner for fear of immediate ridicule – one that contributed to his depressive demeanour. He had tried to smarten up many times, but something always seemed to happen when there was no possibility to change or prepare – always when he was in his best clothes and it would be... 'Bert'll fix that... Bert'll crawl under that... Bert'll carry that!' and in the end the over consuming regression occurred almost instantly. The trouble was that he'd created a monster... a monster of himself... a man that everyone had accepted a long time ago as the one for the job and as he stereotyped others, he himself was also stereotyped and given little opportunity to alter. Who was it that had covered Eddie's dead body?

Andy looked at the tall scruffy man. He hated not being on the front line; he wanted a hand in his own destiny. There was no way he would just sit back and watch another find a way to save the group.

'Well, all right then!' he growled begrudgingly, his taut lean face almost white with latent abhorrence. If, as this man thought, the emergency services couldn't reach them, then he supposed it was a good idea to try to find a way out. He turned abruptly and meandered away.

Lighting another candle, with one last look at an apologetic Helen, Bert and Dave cautiously made their way to the corner of the sales floor to check the unobtrusive lifts for a means of escape.

In the steel framed security room on the seventh floor, Philip Warden was regaining consciousness. He found himself lying in the tangled mess that was once the hub of the building. He felt cold and damp. It was dark. It took him a few moments to realize and remember where he was after initially thinking he was at home in bed.

'What the...?' he muttered to himself under his breath as he comprehended the seriousness of his situation. Gripping the console above, he levered himself upwards, feeling for his plush and extremely comfortable swivel chair, he sat down and rested, evaluating his predicament.

He remembered watching some youths on one of the floors upsetting other shoppers. His security partner had disappeared for a crafty fag break. He remembered radioing for an active patrol to watch for them as they descended the floors. He recalled being half way through a bacon sandwich from the canteen... the entrance hall exploding. That was it! He had seen something very large coming in through the ground floor entrance hall before everything went black.

'Why am I all wet?' He felt the damp around him and wondered why he could feel the wind, and why could he hear the storm so loudly?

Straightening to his feet, hands tentatively feeling for holds in the dark, he moved to where the key-coded door usually was. An empty gap surprised him, and he gripped the doorframe.

It was lucky he had. Feeling feet discovered that the floor was non-existent the other side of the door way. Philip found himself staring out at the rolling black clouds above Wolverhampton. Where there was normally a large, comprehensive stock room, it was now open to the elements. The wind, howling at this altitude, almost knocked Philip from his feet as he appeared in the doorway. As he steadied himself, he found he had a panoramic view of the entire north of the town. Where there used to be the rails and balcony surrounding the ornate central dome of the atrium was now nothing. He peered down into the hole before him positive he could see a mound of rubble.

Heart sinking with the feeling of loneliness and abandonment, he backed up to the relative safety of the strong room, glad it hadn't disappeared along with the rest of the floor. Instinctively grabbing for the tools of his trade, he quickly found that the phones didn't work. Patting his jacket pocket, he found his own mobile phone.

Dead!

Drat it! He was positive he had charged it last night. He shook it thinking that maybe his fall had damaged it in some way.

Further inspection was pointless in the dim light. Where was his partner? He was never around! Damn him!

He sank back into his swivel chair in an effort to calm himself. A crack of lightening illuminated his controls around him and confirmed that every single one was dead and covered with a layer of dirt. Resting his head in a hand propped on the desk, he wondered about his options... he couldn't reach anyone... he couldn't see where he was going... there was no way off this top floor. He was stuck.

A loud clang shook him from his contemplations. The bell above his desk was clanging. A moment of consideration brought back the purpose of the bell. It was the mechanical indication that there was a bullet to arrive.

A bullet was the informal term used for a cash pod from a sales floor. A security guard on the appropriate floor loaded the pod with cash; vouchers, credit card slips or whatever else was required, put the pod in the dumb waiter then pressed the bell for immediate delivery to the security office. The system had a mechanical back-up in case of power failure. The bell was operated by a mechanical linkage not dissimilar to that on a bicycle – the dumb waiter itself had a mechanical winding handle for emergency operation, though it had never been used by hand before. The motor which controlled its operation was normally very efficient and very fast, thus earning the nickname... 'The gun', and therefore... 'The bullet' for the cargo which rode the system.

Philip looked at the bell clanging before him. It was no good pushing the button to operate the motor as there was no power. There couldn't possibly be anyone sending money up with the condition of the building as it was… the only thing it could be was someone on the sales floor trying to contact him. He looked as closely as he could at the bells. He thought it was the fifth floor calling. It meant that there were people still alive below him. There must be someone who had called for help.

Heartened slightly by his thought processes and eager to let others know that he was here, Philip started the manual wind to bring up the tray from the fifth floor, hoping the noise and immediate reaction to the bell ringing would let those below know that there was life above. It was very hard work. It had never had to be wound manually since the store had been built. The wind mechanism was already quite rusty.

Two floors below, Dave was showing Bert how the bell system worked.

'…and we'd push this to let those in the security office know that there was money coming!' He pushed the recessed red button high up on the wall.

'How big is the shaft?' asked Bert contemplating the thought of people using it to climb down.

'Well… there are actually five little shafts side by side,' explained Dave knowledgeably, 'one for each sales floor. In total the shaft is about a metre wide, by that much deep.' His arms moved apart to half a metre, as though a fisherman demonstrating the size of a fish he had recently caught.

He gestured towards a drop down panel which provided access by the staff and Bert bent to look closely at the chute.

A discrete, large, metal, drop down scoop provided locked access to the shaft. Tapping the lock with his finger, Dave delved into his jacket pocket for a set of keys. Fumbling the candle slightly, he found the appropriate one and unlocked the access.

Bert pulled the flap down and peered in... a complaining twinge of pain coursed through his lower back. The result of many years of completing others' bidding, the slight curvature of the spine aggravated a previously bruised vertebra, caused as Bert recalled, in his youth when on a particularly hot summer's day afternoon with an exorbitant amount of adolescent exuberance, he had spent a few hours shipping bricks in a rickety old wheelbarrow for a neighbour. An impending rear house extension necessitated that a delivered pile on her front lawn was transferred to the back garden. A couple of quick and healthy trips had given him false confidence in his physical abilities, and the allure of promised financial remuneration became a craven desire; further journeys each held progressively more weight. The result was an evening groaning in a Radox fuelled bath which had done little to dispose of the pain. Although by the following week it had receded, the damage had been done; his back would never be as strong as it could have been.

He could see nothing in the shaft and relieved Dave of the candle. The flickering flame illuminated the sheet metal shaft once through the aperture. A draft was evident as it tossed the flame randomly, and as Bert got his face through the entry, could feel it on his cheeks. Peering down, he could see nothing but blackness. A strange creaking sound was emanating from above; Bert listened in a futile attempt to identify the noise but dismissed it quickly.

'Does this go right to ground floor?' he asked. His voice was muffled but had a strange echo to it.

'Yeah!' confirmed Dave, bending to see what Bert could.

'It's not very wide… quite deep though.'

'There's one big shaft which feeds five floors. Can you see the tables?'

Almost climbing into the chute now, Bert could see, by the glowing light of the candle, a steel sheet metal platform below and to the right of him - suspended by wires.

'I can see one,' he said, 'quite a long way down.'

Dave twisted to see as well, getting his face as far in as possible. 'That's the one for the next floor down. They return the tables to their floor after they've delivered, ready for the next trip. They don't half shoot up this tube as well… well; of course, carrying money…they've got to.'

'Can we climb down this shaft?' asked Bert logically, thinking through the problem.

'Well…' replied Dave. 'It's big enough. You'd get in all right. The problem is that when you get to the bottom floor, if the hatch is locked, there is no way through.'

'We could bang. The fire brigade might hear us.'

Philip upstairs was tiring fast. He wasn't feeling well after being knocked unconscious earlier – his head was aching and he was feeling a little shaky. He had pulled the heavy bullet up by hand and there had been nothing on it. He had hoped for a message or anything to let him know that he wasn't alone in this nightmare. It had worn him out. Desolately, he released the ratchet which held the steel slab, and let it disappear downwards out of sight.

'What's that whooshing noise?' asked Bert suddenly twisting his head around to check it out. Above him he could hear the sound of whining cables and of rubber wheels rolling in the tight space. The echo of the noise gave it an eerie quality.

'Let's have a look!' said Dave.

Bert balanced the candle on the ledge and using both hands to grasp the sides, withdrew from the shaft. Within a second of his head leaving the space, and letting go of the lip, the large heavy steel platform descended at speed past the opening, smashing the candle into smithereens and plunging the two men into darkness. The chute rattled as the steel slab passed the breach and continued downwards into the darkness momentarily before coming to an immediate and sudden halt. Cables twanged and quivered to a sudden stop.

'Wow!' breathed Bert, under his breath, aware immediately that he had just got out with seconds to spare, knowing that he could have been crushed.

'Blimey!' added Dave, 'someone's upstairs then!'

'What?'

'You press the bell. The guy upstairs winches the table up with the money, takes it off, and then just lets it go. The weight brings it back down again.'

Bert was back in the shaft again. 'Hello!' he shouted upwards. 'Hello… anyone there?'

Philip's eyes snapped open. He could hear someone calling. He lifted the shaft cover and leant over the hole to shout back.

'Hello! I'm up here… hello…hello!'

Bert could hear the panic in his voice. He wanted to help but didn't know how to.

'Are you all right?' he shouted to try and calm him down.

'I'm stuck up here. You've got to help me. Are you the fire brigade?'

'No!'

Bert wished he could say yes. The pleading in the man's voice was worrying. He wanted to give him hope and help him, but he knew he couldn't. He had to be honest but a thought struck him.

'Can you climb down to us?'

Bert sent Dave for another candle. He needed some light.

Confident now that there were to be no more surprises from above, and having a decent floor to crawl out on, he climbed back through the gap, testing his weight gingerly on the diamond plate table held by the steel cables. It was a tight cramped space, making him feel more than a little claustrophobic, but looking up towards the downwards draft, the knowledge that he had to help someone eclipsed all fears. The thin sheet metal sides buckled back and forth when he touched them, giving a clanging echo which ricocheted up and down the tube. Bert was glad that his bulk could be accommodated within the narrow space and even happier when Dave returned and handed him a lighted candle.

'I can see you... just...' shouted Philip from above.

'Is there no other way down?' asked Bert, '... are you sure?' He had been hoping that this might be an exit route for the people on the fifth floor; he hadn't expected to add to their number by someone from above.

'No. Pretty much the whole floor has disappeared!'

'So who are you?'

'Philip. I'm security. We've a strong room up here which has stayed intact.'

'Can you climb down to us?' asked Bert again.

'I don't know if I should. I shouldn't ever leave my post!' Philip's voice betrayed his dilemma. He knew his job. He shouldn't leave until relieved by another. That was the point of 24 hour security, and a point drummed into him by the Lexington's area management staff. But, despite a few jokes about World War three being the only reason to desert his post, no one had ever mentioned this scenario.

Bert's concern was the stability of the building. He remembered seeing the images of the Twin Towers in New York collapsing after the planes had hit in that fateful September. The planes had hit near the top, collapsing a floor. The weight of the floors above that one had been enough to crash down into the opening and have sufficient power and speed to break down into the next... and so on... bringing them down. The last place Bert wanted to be in right now was in a tower after an explosion.

'You ought to come down. We've got to get out of here.'

There was silence for a few moments. Philip contemplated his options. If he stayed where he was, he hadn't left his post. He would have defended the store's money and done his duty. He would be an exemplary employee. He might even get a promotion. However, the rest of the seventh floor, as far as he knew, had collapsed. His mate who should be on duty with him was missing – he presumed that he had been crushed by the rubble and his room might be next to go. He knew in his heart that they didn't pay him enough to put his life on the line… he was scared. He decided to try and get out.

'I want to climb down but I can't…' he called eventually, '…there's no rope or ladder. If I had something I'm sure I could! There's nothing up here to use. I need a rope.'

'Can't you use the cables?'

'I'll rip myself to shreds on them.'

Bert thought for a moment. There had to be something around that they could use. 'Hold on Philip! I'm gonna send you up a rope if I can.'

'I can't wind the bullet up again. I jus' can't!'

Bert slid back out of the chute and righted himself in front of Dave. Swallowing nervously he said, 'Are there any washing line poles on this floor?'

'Yes, over there!' Dave gestured towards the side wall. 'What for?'

'Grab two for me,' Bert instructed, '… oh, and some washing line and masking tape.'

146

Dave did as he was asked, scrambling to be useful.

Bert turned back to the dumb waiter opening and checked over the scoop which covered the aperture. Deciding that it was purely a covering and not a security feature, he positioned himself carefully, before high kicking at the metal door. The impact hammered his toe. Nothing else happened. Taking aim again, Bert gave two kicks in rapid succession. This time the door gave a complaining creak. Encouraged by this, three more pounding thumps resulted in the cheap hinges giving way and the metal scoop falling the short distance to the floor, clanging as it hit and rolling away with another kick behind it.

Dave was at his shoulder. 'Wotcha doing?'

'Helping the guy upstairs!'

Bert unwrapped the packaging from the goods that Dave had brought. Threading the washing line through the top of one of the telescopic poles, he angled it into the hole in the wall. Pushing in the button, he extended the prop as far as it would go up the chute before letting it pop back out into the topmost hole. When it had reached its maximum height, he pushed the rest of the pole in. Reaching for the second line support, he wrapped masking tape around to hold and attach the bottom of the first pole to the top of the second. Extending the second prop, the contraption continued its journey up towards the waiting sentinel, taking with it the nylon rope.

'Can you see anything yet?' he shouted up into the tunnel. 'You should be getting a rope on the end of a pole.'

'No!' Philip was peering down into the gloom.

Bert hated it when he was looked on with envy for his height. It was almost discrimination… 'Could you reach that for me, you're tall?' or 'you've got long arms, how about..?' He never dreamt of saying to a smaller person… 'Could you pick that up off the floor, you're short?' Oh no, the other way it sounded rude. Besides, to his mind, more stuff got dropped on the floor than put on high shelves. The fact that as he put his hands above shoulder height the blinding light of excruciating pain hit him squarely between the eyes never figured with anyone, least of all Sandra, who, as the years passed, had less and less patience with any of Bert's health problems.

His height was handy now. Gritting his teeth, Bert reached into the opening and hoisted the bottom of the second pole up as far as his arm could reach. Philip at the other end, reached down. Suddenly, contact was made, and Philip withdrew the end of the washing line. He pulled the rest of it up through the chute. Doubling the rope, he knotted it around the desk leg and dropped the rest back down the hole.

A crack of thunder directly over head made him breathe a little faster as he kicked his legs over the side of the chute. It was a tight fit and he was scared. He could just imagine either sliding straight down and hitting the bottom in a crumpled mess or sticking half way down with no hope of rescue. Wisely, he decided to take his jacket off; he'd have more room without it on. He slung it over the back of his swivel chair. A gust of wind whipped moisture through the doorway and made him shiver again.

Swivelling around to face the desk leg, he pushed cautiously back into the chute, gripping the edge of the hole with grim determination, feeling the wire down the side of his face, and pushing the extended telescopic props to one side with his feet. There wasn't enough space to bend, so his body hung limply from his hands.

'Come on. You can do it,' encouraged Bert from below, the clanging of Philip's feet on the steel sides informing on his progress. 'Not much further now!'

'Yeah,' he panted back, now gripping the double rope with first one, then two hands. Grunting with effort he continued his journey. Philip's weight brought him down. Playing the washing line cable out one hand at a time kept his speed steady and his advancement sure. The sides of the chute offered no grip for his feet and the metal platform cables were greasy and rough on the occasions he swung into them. The muscles in his arms began to ache. His fingers were numb and sweating, and his grip was beginning to loosen. Sheer panic kept him holding on. A bead of sweat extended across his hairline and dripped down past his eye, causing him to blink furiously.

He was over half way down.

Bert kept peering up into the chute, but was reluctant to stay in there in case Philip made a sudden descent. The view was non-existent anyway with the lack of light and the panting, grunting noises in the tube gave no indication of his distance away. He looked around from where he stood for something to cushion the platform but saw nothing suitable.

Four metres to go.

Philip's resolve gave out. It was too much. The wire was now too slippery with his sweat, and the panic, fear and upset was too much. The muscles in his arms seized and his resulting plunge was immediate and fast. One flailing hand tried to catch something... anything. It caught one of the steel cables and barely gripped. It was enough to slow his movement, but only just, and at a price. Small shards of twisted steel from the cable ripped into the palm of his hand lacerating his fingers and causing immediate agony.

'Aaargh!' His scream of pain and worry warned the waiting two men of his imminent arrival. There was nothing they could do as he landed on the platform before them with a resounding thud. The cables rippled again in the tight enclosure and the platform vibrated. The tightness of the enclosure kept him upright, but the shock of the landing jarred his ankles, and another scream of pain ensued.

Bert and Dave hastened to get him out; he emerged sweating, his hand covered in blood. They checked he could before they stood him upright. He shielded his damaged right hand with his left and was doubled over with the pain in his feet. Greasy black streaks ran down his face and ripped clothes.

He looked all right. He was alive. He was relieved to be with other people. The loneliness of the top floor was disappearing with the closeness of his two helpers.

At that moment a bolt of lightning hit the building.

Down below, on the street corner, Colleen McLaughlin was preparing herself for another live broadcast; touching up her make up and brushing down her suit. Monk was preparing the second ladder unit to make eventual entry to the second floor. Sandra was just turning the corner past the shuttered, scruffy and graffiti scrawled entrance to a TV repair shop. The viewers of Central TV were watching the live transmission of the panoramic scene over the shoulder of the gently talkative and reassuring Irene Carlson.

The lightning took everyone by surprise.

Any electrical current or discharge takes the path of least resistance and lightning is no exception, striking wherever the path to earth is easiest. This may be through the fabric of a building, in which case intense heating along its path can cause considerable structural damage or even fire. High buildings are generally equipped with lightning conductors from their highest point to earth – thick copper rods along which the energy travels harmlessly to the earth. Lexington's didn't have anything like that before hand, and now…

It hit the metal frame of the security office on the top floor which now had turned the building into a gigantic lightning rod. The sparks flashed for what seemed an eternity, jumping off the roof in a remarkable resemblance to a firework display and up into the sky like a roman candle; and sparking across to the large exposed pulley wheels that once controlled the lift, like the filament in a light bulb.

Outside, Colleen's hand went to her mouth as she instinctively ducked in horror. Monk, with years of training and expertise behind him, jumped clear of the ladder as did his squad, landing and rolling on the ground like soldiers. Irene went quiet as she stared at her desk mounted monitor in disbelief. Sandra staggered back in shock against the small lip of the step into a shop doorway, before losing her balance and landing on her knees amongst the cigarette ends and suspicious smells; twisting her ankle and causing a loud yelp of pain.

The chances of a person being struck by lightning are small. In a thunderstorm one of the safest places to be is in a car because any electrical charge to earth will pass through the outside of the metal body and not affect passengers. Philip realized that a metal chute would not have been the best place to be.

The lightning recoiled down the chute and sparked around the opening, sending the three men crashing to the floor in alarm, their candle skidding across the floor extinguishing as it went and causing the huddled group at the cash desks to scream in fright.

Bert noticed that Brenda and Sian had gripped each other, Sian instinctively covering the wounded woman in an effort to spare her any further possible danger. Helen cringed on her stack of stock boxes and Andy recoiled in horror. Lara fell to her knees and bowed as low as she could in an effort to ball herself into a position of safety... unnecessary now that the worst was over. Bert thought she had cried his name, but couldn't be sure.

The lightning and sparks subsided and the three men looked at each other in the dim light, their faces drained of colour with how close they had just come to death. Mercifully there were no eruptions of flames or fire on their floor.

Philip realized he had done the right thing climbing down and escaping. Though not the brightest of intellect, he knew that if he had stayed where he was, he would have been dead now on the top floor in the steel security office coffin. He would have been fried alive.

'Thanks!' he whispered and Bert just nodded.

Monk had a lot on his mind. Apart from some stupid reporter keep trying to call him over to take part in a broadcast, he had to think about making an entry into the second floor of the Lexington building, as well as plans to remove the tram from the entrance. The commanding officer had arrived not long before and relieved some of the pressure from him by taking charge of incident. He was aware that other fire crews had now been requested from neighbouring districts and that coordination between the emergency services was proceeding smoothly. He had been left to decide on an entry strategy.

The teeming rain was not making his job easy. Everyone was soaking wet. Visibility was dire and double checking everything had to be the order of the day to ensure that there were no mistakes.

"Jones!" he shouted to another of his team, "I need to know if the tram is taking any weight from the building! Crawl all over it if you have to. I need a report a.s.a.p. Johnson, check the back of the building. Is there any other route in? Where are the fire doors? Take the ram. Find out for me – I need to know. Is there any other way in at all?"

"Right you are sir!" Jones shouted back, and with an eagerness that he didn't really feel in this rain, endeavoured to do Monk's bidding.

"Yes, sir!" responded Johnson, setting off at a jog.

"Tannen... Tannen. I need the jacks." Monk directed his colleague to retrieve the pneumatic jacking system from the lockers on the sides of the fire tenders that would be needed to brace the openings. "Smith. Help him!"

"Yes sir," was the responses – discipline above all else.

Monk stood at the side of the tram gauging the risks and options. He decided he needed another crane unit as Jones was climbing down from above to make his report.

"The entrance to Lexington's has collapsed over the roof of the tram, but I can't see that the building mantle has been affected. You need the blue-prints to be sure, but I think the tram can be pulled back without upsetting anything."

"Smith. Check the ground at the rear of the tram. Jones. Check underneath. I want to know if we can shift this bastard back safely. Tannen, what's the state of the wheels and transmission? Will they turn?"

Monk left his squad to continue the necessary safety checks and went to find the other tender crew. He needed to know if they could reach the second floor. He found them battling the elements the other side of the tram near the street corner. Their tender was already positioned with the steadying rams extended. However, the wind was creating massive problems for the crew who were desperately trying to extend the ladders.

Checking that they were doing their best, and that the Incident Commander was supervising, he returned to the tram with the goal of removing the blockage from the front of the building. There must still be people alive in there, and they were counting on his speed and efficiency in affecting entry in order to save their lives.

Colleen McLaughlin watched him eagerly.

"I can see more activity here behind me. This number 46 Wolverhampton Tram is creating a blockage to the entrance of Lexington's, but it looks like the fire brigade are getting themselves ready to move it... woah!" The wind blasted past the entrance to the court buildings, whipping the sound boom around and knocking the cameraman sideways.

As he steadied himself and regained his composure, the public viewing the live programme were caught up in the activity unfolding before them, the cameraman's balance adding to the excitement that they were feeling in their cosy, warm and safe houses.

Terry Thomas glanced at the television as he lathered his face in aftershave. The blustery conditions on the show were mimicked against his windows giving a very vivid and surreal image of what was happening outside. Watching the picture veer to one side as the cameraman lost his balance, proved an entrancing one and he sat back down on the bed to continue observing the developments and started to pull his clothes on.

"The weather here is terrible!" continued Colleen. "Mike, are you OK?" Her hair was again flipped around her face as she extended a hand down off screen as a gesture of compassion to pat her cameraman's arm.

It was making excellent television. The producer was almost apoplectic with glee. He had never been to a scene of really important news, and yet this was almost tantamount to Bosnia, or the Falklands. He was hoping for more exciting work later in life. This coverage would get him that.

"The storm is whipping up gale like conditions. The lightning is refusing to abate, and the thunder is adding to the nightmare behind me. It has not stopped raining and the streets are almost rivers. The fire brigade is going to have to do something about that before they can do much else because it making any activity: treacherous."

Irene Carlson broke in. "So can you tell yet what their plan of action is? Are the services going to go in through windows or is the tram to be moved first?" She held her ear piece to catch the reply over the static created over the airwaves and gave a rueful smile to camera.

"At this time," answered Colleen nervously brushing down her jacket again, "it is unclear what the plan is. However, more fire fighting units are coming as we speak, and I believe that they are trying more than one strategy in order to save the people trapped inside..."

At this, the howl of more sirens obscured any more words, and a flashing blue hue enveloped Colleen. The camera whisked around to catch the arrival of two more tenders to the scene and followed their slowing down in front of the ambulances and cars. Their arrival had not surprised the IC who flagged them and gave them precise instructions; directing them to park behind the tram. The other was to reverse and park.

Another news crew had arrived and parked illegally at the traffic island. Ignoring shouts from the police, three people jumped from their grey Transit van and rushed with their equipment towards where Colleen stood.

Her producer saw them coming and widened his arms apart in an effort to slow them down. Colleen watched as he bent his head close to the leading man and pointed back towards the island.

They turned to watch as a police car pulled up behind their abandoned radio station emblazoned van, and two officers jumped out in an effort to find the driver and get it removed.

The first man turned extremely reluctantly and returned to his vehicle. The producer looked gleeful, and came back to his spot, leaving the other two unhappily trying to keep their equipment dry whilst looking vainly for somewhere to set up their broadcast.

"Other news agencies and spectators are trying to get here," continued Colleen professionally, "but this area behind me is already packed with many emergency workers and the injured. The police have constructed a cordon around the incident and as yet are not allowing any one to enter...

...It looks like the emergency services, right at this moment, are attempting to address the problem of the flooding roads."

"Is this a necessary precaution?" asked Irene from the comfort of her studio, "surely the flooding isn't that bad!"

The camera panned past Colleen and took in the scale of the problem around the Lexington building. The storm drains in the area had been built in the 1950's and connected to the main sewage systems to take the excess water out of town towards the pumping stations on the outskirts. They had not taken into account at the time that the excessive use of concrete and tarmac over the next fifty years would erode the surrounding fields and woodlands that had supplied a natural soak away for any rainfall. The subsequent half a century had gradually, but very surely, eaten away at this land, concrete chewing remorselessly at the green belt, spreading away from the town centre like ripples from a stone, thrown into a pond. With no natural exit for rainfall, the archaic and out-of-date town plumbing tried desperately to cope. Of course it couldn't. The fancy new roads and high concrete kerbs contained the rising water as well as a swimming pool would have done. The small selection of gutter drains were over-flowing with water, gushing up like geysers, the created basins over flowing, the camber of the road cascading the water deeply across the narrow pavements to the shop fronts.

It was hampering the efforts of the emergency rescue services. They were almost knee deep in water, the splashing back and forth taking more effort than the actual rescue work they were pursuing. The camera picked out Monk sending his men beneath the stricken tram to attach ropes to the undercarriage, breathing equipment being used as scuba diving gear as they checked for reasonable mounting points. The camera panned back to the IC who was now directing one unit to attack the rising flood around them. Pumps and hoses were being extracted from the unit at double speed by the crew.

"The depth of water is beginning to affect the operation. At this rate, we will need boats to float the survivors out of here, rather than ambulances. Yes Irene... the flooding is getting substantially worse. In fact, though we are on steps here, the water is almost at this level!"

The camera focussed at Colleen's 'Jimmy Choo' four inch spike shoes and perfectly toned calf muscles to demonstrate the height of the water as it lapped at the top step.

"I see!" said Irene, "so this is turning to be quite a race against the elements!"

"Well the time is now twenty past nine. The fire crews have been here almost thirty-five minutes, and in that time the weather has got significantly worse." Colleen checked her little Gucci watch on her wrist. Although cold, she was more excited at the prospect of reporting live on the rescue operation, and the shivers down her spine were not because of the damp. Another fleeting glance over the producer's shoulder confirmed three more unmarked police Range Rovers now adding to the melee of vehicles, the bright yellow jackets and uniforms obvious inside despite the poor visibility.

"I have seen more high ranking police officials turning up to check the progress of the fire crews... I can see that they are reluctant to move the tram from the entrance, but need to in order to make entry to the building. Ladders are proving ineffective in this blustery wind." Colleen almost had to shout this last bit at the camera, as the wind, which seemed to know it was being talked about, gusted again.

Monk's team were attaching winching gear to ropes around the trams axels. He was desperate to get it removed, though a police forensics team was now here, warning him that it was a potential crime scene and needed to be left as untouched as possible.

It was a very thin line they were all treading between doing all they could to rescue the people within the building, and leaving the crime scene unaffected for police forensics investigation. A compromise had been reached... the tram could be moved back over ten metres if otherwise left alone.

Monk was desperate to see that happen.

The plan was to move the tram back out of the shallow basin in which they were now paddling and up the slight slope towards the tram station from whence it had come. The wheels had suffered slight damage but seemed otherwise still able to cope with the journey. A crane had been requested, but so far was having problems with the journey to the town centre. Plan 'B' had to suffice for the moment. Sturdy spikes were being driven deep into the ground and all manner of pulleys were being mounted in order to get the tram rolling.

As Terry Thomas pulled his coat on, a last look at the television showed a small movement as the tram began to roll backwards away from the entrance to Lexington's.

Without much interest in the tragic scene, he punched the power button on his remote and made towards the door of his flat, the objective of taking his Porsche Boxster out towards Highley, a little village outside Wolverhampton with a warm and welcoming tavern, and a warm and welcoming barmaid was uppermost in his mind.

Sandra, unaware of this, was sitting in the doorway of 'Ranjit's TV Repairs' nursing a bruised and swelling ankle, sobbing quietly to herself. With trembling hands, she again dialled her home phone from her fancy mobile. Again, the unrelenting ring went unanswered as Bert's little terrier pricked up his ears from the easy chair where he was sleeping and observed the noisy object with an air of disgust.

A group of lads across the street who were loitering in the entrance of a clothing store noticed her distress. Nudging each other, they all turned to regard Sandra with an air of hostility, cupping their cigarettes with hands at their faces. As though in uniform, all had logo emblazoned sweatshirts with hoods, blue jeans pulled down beyond the line of decency, and the white waist bands of their underpants showing.

Sandra was intimidated. She had to keep moving. Trying not to slide on the dirty ground, she staggered to her feet, pulled her skirt back down as far as it would go, and set back off into the rain, trying not to get blown against the poorly rendered side wall of the shop which bore the residue of chewing gum and various other squashed and lingering foodstuffs.

Her ankle was sore, but she had to keep moving. The umbrella was useless in the rain as a covering to keep the rain from her, but ideal now as a make-shift walking stick. She concentrated on moving a step at a time, very careful not to drive the tip of the brolly through her foot. She rounded the last corner and entered Market Street which ran across the back of Lexington's store. It was deserted. Everyone who had been unfortunate enough to be in the vicinity of the area that evening, had graduated to the front of the building, in order to watch the rescue operation. The police had cordoned off the area between the entrance to Lexington's and the tram station opposite. No one was at the back now. Johnson had investigated the possibility of access and conceded it was impossible; heavy steel doors were the only other access point, but would withstand anything that they could throw at it. He'd used the ram several times to question the door's integrity, but to no avail. There would be no entering the building this way. All attention was focussed on the events unfolding at the front.

Market Street was dealing slightly better with the tremendous down pour, and was expelling the water down Woolpack Street towards the paved area used for the Wednesday morning farmer's market in Queen Square near Blaise Street.

The original Wolverhampton Wool Fair, founded in the reign of Edward III to be held in July each year had fallen into disrepute during the late eighteenth century after its original purpose had been virtually usurped by a pleasure fair. In the years before it had ceased, Wolverhampton was a busy mart for the sale of wool, and attracted attention from merchants and traders from all over Britain and the Continent. It had turned Wolverhampton from a sleepy farming town into a bustling market town catering for a large portion of the country's wool trade. The heritage of the town now interested no one. Only the names for the streets remained.

Sandra slowed her pace and rested against a pillar box; a canopy marking the entrance to the indoor shopping mall 'Phoenix Centre' provided a little shelter from the driving rain. Sandra was soaked through to her skin, her garments clinging; her hair a sodden dangling clump, matted against her face; her make-up almost a dim and distant memory.

She glanced at her watch. Wiping the moisture from its face, she could tell that it was almost twenty-five past nine. Breathing heavily, she swallowed, lifted her foot up to the pedestal on which the box sat, and massaged the bruised ankle for a little relief.

A dark, high top Mercedes van turned into the road ahead of her, driving very slowly. It idled up to, and past the Phoenix Centre, cutting its lights and pulling into the kerb behind the Lexington Building. Sandra watched with interest. Something about its demeanour didn't look right... almost furtive; the windscreen wipers, despite the heaving rain, were working on intermittent speed as though desperate to prevent anyone seeing through. The tyres, obviously brand new rubber, squelched slightly even at low speed and cut through the road water creating swathes of wake in their path.

Trying to shake the feeling as just ridiculous, Sandra dropped the now damaged umbrella on the floor and knelt down to her ankle, trying to ease the pain building up at the base of her calf.

The engine was cut and the van sat there quietly in the dark. The sound of the rain splattering against its roof clanged noisily in stark contrast with the waterfall effect everywhere else. Darkened windows prevented any indication of movement within; gentle hissing from the bonnet as the warmth of the engine evaporated some of the water from above; dirty rainwater dripped from the wheel arches.

Sandra decided to ask for help. She could barely walk now and needed assistance. The pain was creeping up her leg, and with the effort of moving, had begun to pull the ligaments in her other leg. Pushing the worries to the back of her mind, she straightened as much as possible, and limped to the edge of the kerb, her naked feet splashing in the puddles. Bracing herself for the depth, she stepped into the gutter, the running cold water almost soothing to the inflammation. The force of the rain took her breath slightly as she crossed the road to the side of the van.

"Hello!" she called, "hello... is any one in there?" She tapped sharply against the side of the van.

There was no answer from within. Sandra leant against the side of the van for extra support, and continued limping down the side to reach the passenger door. She reached up slightly and knocked on the window.

No answer.

Almost on tip toes now, she pressed the side of her hand against the window and shielded her eyes as she desperately tried to see in.

She couldn't even see her own reflection in the rain streaming windows. Sandra sighed with worry and pain, concluding that the person within was either too rude to help or perhaps preoccupied and probably wouldn't help her anyway. She decided to continue her journey to the front of the building.

All of a sudden, the side door to the van slid noiselessly open. A smelly dirty hand reached around and clasped her mouth, another reached around her waist, and within a moment, she had been hoisted into the vehicle, and the door slid closed behind her.

CHAPTER 13

Tim Slater was in serious trouble. This Thursday morning he owed 'Big Sam' fifty thousand pounds, and every day it wasn't paid that figure got higher. He opened his eyes and the daily realization of his predicament hit him again. Blinking and lying still, he looked up at the ceiling, his arms at his sides; his body covered with a single sheet.

Slater was twenty-two year old lad, tall with curly fair hair and of limited intelligence. According to his father at regular intervals throughout his formative years, he would never amount to anything, and unfortunately the prophecy was coming true. Despite every idea and attempt at breaking into the 'big-time', nothing was happening to help him out. His daily period of dawning comprehension reminded him of the sequence of awful occurrences…

Slater had left school at sixteen with the bare minimum of exam grades. He had never been very good, or very eager to keep up with his schooling, and continued association with the less talented of his year group kept him extremely short of achieving anything beyond complete contempt from his teachers. Further education was not an option. Understanding that his father was disappointed with his results prompted him to try a series of manual work jobs including labouring on building sites and stacking shelves on a supermarket night shift. They all ended with dismissal for either stupidity or ineptitude.

The loss of his job at a building site for new local housing estate by a national construction firm caused the greatest distress. The deal had been the best Slater could have ever hoped for: he had had a contract for forty-five hours a week; overtime as and when needed; on the job training and scope for career advancement. However, though Slater did not have a driving license, it hadn't stopped him purchasing an old battered 1988 Peugeot 205 GTi from a drinking friend and driving it to and from work without tax, insurance or MOT. A collision with the rear of an elderly gentleman's car waiting at a zebra crossing one Tuesday morning caused enough of a commotion that police were called and discovery made of his illegality to drive. The result was that Slater lost his job; the car crushed under a government initiative on untaxed vehicles, and a lasting police record including a driving ban for five years.

His father's emphatic and repetitive 'told you so!' hurt.

Slater was more upset than his parents realised. A credit card that he had been nursing from a short-sighted bank for several years had recently taken a pounding with purchases based on his recent job prospects. New tyres and alloy rims hadn't come cheap for his car; a minor Friday night drug habit to keep up with his more affluent friends had eaten up a couple of thousand pounds and splashing out on gifts to impress the girls in night clubs - thousands more. Slater could never be bothered to get a license or make his car legal.

After his foray into nightshift work ended with him being found asleep on a pallet of sugar hidden in the back stores instead of stocking over one hundred and sixty cases of goods into the tins aisle, and arrogance towards his supervisor instead of pleading for forgiveness – Slater was out of another job… his father barely acknowledged his existence.

But it was just after his twentieth birthday that his parents almost washed their hands of him.

By now, borderline offensive tattoos had appeared down his arms and an eyebrow piercing had appeared to try and formulate a more macho image in order to detract from his rather weedy appearance otherwise. Money was appearing without a recognisable source and his mother's nightly crying pushed him further away. His doting mother had continued to be a buffer for arguments between her son and her husband, and though it was a source of regret and displeasure for his parents, Slater continued to live at home rent free, preventing his father's retirement for an additional four years from work as lorry driver due to the now poorly depleted family funds.

Slater decided he would make money buying and selling drugs at the clubs on Friday nights. Contacts with several shady characters had set him up with a source of supply, and his natural 'effervescent' personality created an outlet for them (at a little sixty or seventy percent mark up) to the young clubbers waiting in line outside the latest trendy place in which to be seen.

It had worked well for a couple of months. His parents had been suspicious of the quantity of jewellery creeping around their son's neck and appearing on his fingers, though none of the loans were being repaid to the family account.

A moment of weakness and another argument brought the torrid business blatantly forth from Slater's lips... now proud of his venture and determined to aggravate his family once again.

The upshot was that Slater had had to find his own flat. Despite his dealing, the income was not steady enough to provide worry free living, but this didn't trouble him and more borrowed money found him a beautiful, if empty, flat in the latest development on a canal side property. He'd not had the intelligence to clear previous debts, and his new commitment added to his overall financial obligation. A minimum of new furniture was put on another credit card, but the wolves were already at the door.

At the time, Slater's confidence was un-shaking, positive that his life would change for the better with the next deal... always with the next deal. His friends laughed at him – behind his back. To his face they tried to be encouraging because he insisted on buying the drinks and throwing his money around. They weren't stupid!

The price of cocaine steadily rose following a local crack down on his suppliers. Customer numbers and consumption through Slater had peaked due to other small time players appearing on the scene, and retail price had to be competitive. He had to cut his prices to clinch deals and didn't have an alternative avenue for sales

Slater was in financial trouble and spent most of his time avoiding creditors or phoning the selection of money lending companies advertising on television and in the backs of newspapers. He had no luck; he wasn't a homeowner.

Slater was in a lot of financial trouble but it was in his twenty-second year he made his worst mistake…he asked 'Big Sam' for money. With little thought of the future beyond getting rid of his debts, Slater borrowed just over forty thousand pounds to clear his problems. Sam lent it without question.

For nearly a month, Slater slept well at night. He had the acumen to clear, then bin his credit cards, pay his rent up to date and had enough left over to flash a little more cash at the clubs.

The call had come at the beginning of September…

'Tim?'

'Yeah. 'oo is it?' Cocky. Self-assured!

'Sam!'

Gulping. 'Err, 'ello Sam. D'ay recognise your voice! What can I do for you?' Nervous. Panicky. Quavering!

'I'm checking to make sure you're all right. Friendly concern, like…' Sam's voice maintained a quiet but even paced menacing growl.

More swallowing and a nervous cough now from Slater's end of the line. 'Tha's good o' yer!'

'Well, there is one other thing!' Sam paused for effect, knowing full well that by now Slater had sat down where he stood, his bladder pressing for the toilet. He knew that he had that effect when he called. He had a couple of business associates that were sometimes present with the customer when he had to make the second or third call. 'You've had your first month off. I need a payment… an instalment.'

'Shit!' thought Slater. His thought processes hadn't really progressed beyond the end of clearing his debts; the unwavering belief that he would soon make the deal which would clear his troubles still paramount in his mind every day. 'Err... yeah Sam... 'caus'.'

'My boys'll be round tomorrow night at eight for two hundred quid. Make sure you're in!' He paused again. He hadn't finished the conversation and no one had ever dared to put the phone down before he did. 'Interest is adding on!'

'Wha'...?' Slater was definitely feeling very weak at the knees despite being sat down. His tattoos and piercing weren't making him feel very macho now. He desperately wanted to cry with the dawning realisation that he'd messed up somewhere along the line... and messed up big time.

'Competitive rates of interest. Remember. You now owe forty-three grand. Two hundred quid at eight tomorrow night.' With this, 'Big Sam' rang off the line.

Slater sat on the edge of his imitation white leather settee still holding the phone – the dial tone droning in his ear. His shoulders sagged; his scrawny chest caving; his knees knocking together. Suddenly the phone fell to the floor. Slater ran to the toilet, fell to his knees and retched repeatedly into the bowl. He wished he could step back in time or just disappear into thin air. He'd never appreciated the concept of a loan shark before.

Slater lay on his bed. That had all happened a month ago. Almost daily, the phone calls had come. He had managed to pay what

171

was expected at the beginning, but it was wearing him out and had totally affected his life. He had called in every debt, sold everything he could and scraped every last penny together to pay, but still the amount had crept up rather than decreased. His senses were now numb. He now owed fifty thousand. There was no way he could meet the expectations and had made an alternative plan. Yesterday he met with 'Big Sam' to voice his agenda after an altercation with one of Sam's helpers...

The wall mounted communication panel buzzed. Slater looked at it in puzzlement. It was five thirty in the morning and he had barely slept with the worry. Yesterday he had had to avoid the weekly collection by staying away from the flat and only crept in just after midnight when he was sure that the place wasn't being observed. From then on, he had watched the minute hand of his clock creep round unhurriedly while he waited for day break.

He decided to ignore it in the hope that they would go away. Unfortunately the buzzer went again and again. They must know I'm here! Still dressed in last night's rags, he ran from the room and down the hallway to fire escape. Smacking the bar down, the door popped open with a cacophony of warning beeps and Slater hit the metal escape staircase at the best speed he could, jumping and leaping down the steps two or three at a time, wincing as his hips took the brunt of the hand rail as he changed direction at each level; his face a mask of fear and dread; his breathing just tortured gasps.

Too late he saw the man waiting for him, arms folded as he leant against a Biffa flip top bin. A big, bald, ferocious looking white guy with a thick, plain black bomber jacket, jeans and the largest steel capped boots Slater had ever seen. His face was creased into a sneer because he knew that they always tried running.

Slater's momentum took him to the bottom step before he could stop. The man's hand grasped his hair and tugged him the remaining rung, slinging him to the dirty ground in front of the bins; a boot kicking him smartly on the rear to force his progress. Slater's arms flailed around in an effort to get up, but the man was already there, massive hands grasping his collar and belt as he effortlessly lifted him up. Slater watched the ground recede and then felt his innards almost explode as the man kneed him in the ribs, effectively winding him and creating a bruise the size of a small town on his thin bony body before dropping him back into the surplus rubbish.

'No... please!' Slater's thin, pitiful, pleading voice meant nothing to this man. 'No... we can work this out!'

He enjoyed his work. Sam had said to just rough him up a little – show him what forces there actually were in this universe. There was always the promise of next time! He was the 'encouragement' that people sometimes needed.

One more thrashing should do the trick. Grabbing the back of Slater's neck, his hand squeezed enough to gain purchase and lift him back to the vertical. Slater's hands were waving pathetically before him, protesting at any further attack, but could do little except hang there limply, feet trailing on the ground as the man delivered his last blow, an open hand to the side of Slater's head with enough force to leave his ears ringing, a thumping headache, but nothing broken.

'I need to see Sam!' Slater now knew what he had to do.

The man grunted and indicated his waiting car. Slater climbed to his feet and meekly followed – any desire or ability to run and keep running, totally wiped from his body. Only one course of action was left open to him because if he ran, they'd find him.

'Tim...Tim... come in!' Sam's massive hand gestured towards a chair in front of the desk and returned his frame to his huge leather office chair. His many chins rippled as he made himself comfortable, the starched white collar of his crisp silk shirt cutting in and spilling flesh towards his dark blue Armani suit. He twisted the knot of his matching dark blue tie to make sure he looked as good as his obvious bulk would allow, the gold of his many rings glistening in the daylight from the floor to ceiling windows.

'What can I do for you?' he growled, the jowls of his clean shaven face rippling. He adjusted the smart silver frames of his glasses and observed the quivering wreck before him. 'You're paying all right, except for this week. Chuck hasn't reported any problems when he's had to meet you... you've still got use of all your body parts... just!' He chuckled as though the thought was amusing to him. It sounded like the rattle of a machine gun.

'Yeah... erm...erm!' Slater's mouth was very dry. He could barely speak. He knew Chuck very well by now. He doubted that 'Chuck' was his real name, but more like his stock-in-trade. No doubt

Chuck could give him more of what he had suffered that morning. His hand touched his bruised jaw gingerly.

Chuck was a very large black man whose neck was actually wider than his skull. He was over six foot six and had arms and legs the width of tree trunks. Though always dressed immaculately in sharp suits, the shaven head and close cropped goatee beard gave him a menacing appearance, as did the way he stood as though on parade in the army, hands clasped behind his back. He rarely smiled, self-conscious of the gap between the top front two teeth, preferring to growl when he needed to talk, through sneering lips. He had been 'Big Sam's' right hand man for as long as anyone could remember, a loyal stalwart of his team – despite many offers over the years of alternative employment from possible rivals.

'You want a drink of water?' asked Sam amenably.

'Please…' Slater needed a drink. He needed the toilet again, but then again… he needed food. He hadn't been able to afford much in the way of food recently and had been surviving on scraps of generosity from his friends.

Sam graciously returned to his feet and waddled to the table of refreshments by the window. Stooping, he poured a glass of water, set the jug back down and turned to face Slater. Over his shoulder, Slater could see the view from the penthouse which doubled as both Sam's office and home. He could see most of the West Midlands conurbation, the homes and businesses stretching out below the tower block like a sprawling patchwork quilt of sights, colours and sounds.

The vertical blinds had been pulled back from across the windows to allow as much of the morning light in as possible.

'I can't pay any more!' Slater blurted it out. There was no other way. It was now or never. The repayments were killing him, and he couldn't live like this any longer. He couldn't cope with another beating.

Sam remained where he was, glass gripped in a podgy hand at waist height, his inscrutable eyes searching Slater's face for evidence of humour or fear. He saw fear. It wasn't the first time he'd had a quivering crying husk of a man before him speaking those exact same words. This wasn't a joke. He frowned and pursed his lips.

'But... but I know a way I c'n make good!'

Sam was listening. Always with the deal. They always wanted a way out of their foolishness. It wasn't Sam's fault that this snivelling worm had come to him for money... he hadn't made him... hadn't forced him. He knew the deal when he signed – well – most of the deal – he needed to honour it.

Chuck, stood behind Slater, flexed his muscles beneath his suit, the crinkling of the fabric obvious to both the other men.

'I have a friend... I 'ave inside information abou' a cash office... lots of money... I c'n get it!' Slater's voice betrayed the panic he was feeling.

Sam had heard similar speeches before, but made it his duty to listen before passing judgement. On occasion the blubbering wrecks before him had made good, and life went on, especially theirs. He crossed the Persian rug on the natural wooden floor and placed the glass on the desk in front of Slater and returned to his own seat.

'Go on!' he rumbled; the sound of a distant jet plane.

Chuck sniffed apprehensively.

'Well look,' Slater slurped his water, spilling a little down his front in his haste. Sam ignored it. 'Look... there's a buildin' in Wolverhampton, a new building with new security. I know a way in. There mus' be at leas' two hundred and fifty thousand in cash in there by Thursday night!'

'Go on!'

Slater slurped again at the water and fumbled the glass slightly, returning it to the desk. Sam's eyes narrowed at it fell noisily to the top. The glass remained intact, the fluid within sloshing back and forth for a moment before settling.

He sold the job prospect to Sam.

Lexington's was a new building on the outskirts of the Wolverhampton built opposite a tram station. The whole design of the building concentrated the façade, signage and windows at the front, leaving the other three sides generally unattended with no parking allowed. The back of the store held the main freight lift which had locked and alarmed access to a lift shaft. Slater's friend had worked on the building of the specialist design and could guarantee access to this shaft with inside knowledge of a metal service ladder flush with the back wall which ascended directly to the top floor. The cash office was situated on this floor and protected by two guards who made regular trips down to the sixth floor for the staff amenities. The safe within was operated with an electrically controlled lock with a back up circuit routed through an independent generator built into the stock room.

Slater's plan was to create a diversion at the front of the store, force access at the rear, hit the cash office whilst security were otherwise preoccupied and be out before anyone noticed.

'When?' One word question.

The store had comprehensive security. Cameras covered every inch of the sales floors and a direct line to the police station could call for assistance within moments. After closing time, the police made more regular patrols across the front of the building because of the public transport stations and the crowds of young people meandering drunkenly to their various watering holes. During opening time, they generally left the area alone because of the countless drop offs and pick ups from the shoppers.

On Friday mornings, a security firm collected the takings. Because of the exorbitant cost, Lexington's only paid for this service once a week which meant that the whole week's takings sat in the cash office safe on a Thursday evening.

Thursday evening would be the best time, just before closing. Tomorrow evening! Thursday!

'What deal are you offering?' Sam's interest was aroused. Normally the prat before him (who was usually begging for the continued use of his legs) was talking by now about robbing his parents or ripping off a girlfriend or business. This job was showing a lot more promise.

'Well... you say I owe you fifty grand now. I expec' a two fifty haul. I need a few things so... fifty,fifty?' His voice faltered with the offer of the split.

'What *things* do you need?' Practical question. Sam noticed Chuck shifting his weight from one foot to the other and flexing his muscles again. It wasn't the first time he'd heard a similar conversation. The two men shared these moments with almost a perverted relish.

'Well, the job needs a diversion at the fron'. I need transpor', and a way to cut the power, like... I need one other bod' to help with the safe.'

Sam grimaced across laced fingers at the nervous youth. He shook his head slightly with feigned displeasure. 'At this rate, we won't need you!'

'Well look,' nervous babbling again. 'I know a way in like. I 'ave the key to the freight lif' doors. I know where the safe is, but I don't... I don't know how to knock ou' electrics.' Slater could see the whole thing going sour. The money he had spent on his friend from the building firm, and all the effort he had put into priming this guy for information after the chance conversation two months ago, could all have been a waste at this rate.

Sam thought for a moment. It would be a useful job. Two-fifty wasn't a massive haul, but this toe-rag owed him fifty (which he wouldn't get otherwise), but for one night paid labour, could stand to come out with enough to make it worth while. If it didn't work out, he'd still have the pleasure of knowing that Slater had lost the use of certain limbs and still in debt until the day he died.

'Eighty,twenty!' he countered, 'in my favour!' His tone was brisk and no-nonsense. It didn't invite a rebuttal or bargaining.

Slater looked around nervously at the hulking figure of Chuck. He hadn't any options. It was either this way, or no way. He could still clear fifty grand depending what was in the safe. He was hoping that with the run up to Christmas, people were spending more and that none of the security arrangements had been changed. Still, he was all out of options. It was either this way… or Chuck!

'And the debt's off?' he asked in a timid voice.

'Of course!'

Slater gave an almost imperceptible nod and cast his eyes back down to his lap – a beaten man. He knew he wasn't going to get rich from this, but it would square him up with this shark and save his limbs from potential breakage. The new bruise beneath his thin shirt gave an involuntary throb of pain.

'Go downstairs and wait at the front door of the building. I'm sending someone to *look after* you!' The words held a menace though inflection in his voice was something Sam rarely achieved with his vocabulary.

Slater shuddered again before standing as Chuck moved to one side, glowering down at the lad as he made his way back through the door, down the corridor, and back down the stairs. His receding steps from shoes with thinning soles were heard for a few moments.

'Get Adam and Karl in here!' directed Sam, closing his eyes in contemplation and breathing softly through his mouth whilst deep in thought, unaware that he was blowing his cheeks out.

Chuck left the room and within a few minutes was back with two other men who meekly followed him in and stood, unspeaking, before the desk.

'I've got a job for you lads!' Sam spoke without opening his eyes. Adam and Karl knew enough not to speak.

He recounted the necessary facts of the operation which he wanted to happen the following night. There was no point in waiting. Slater might get cold feet. Broken legs and missing fingers didn't help Sam get his money. He told them that they needed to find a vehicle for the use of and prepare a little surprise for the front of Lexington's. 'Talk to Huggins from 'special ops'. He owes me a favour.'

Adam and Karl nodded with understanding. It wasn't the first time they had been called upon to assist with their boss's work. Despite their shabby appearance in jeans and t-shirts, they were very capable at making little jobs flow smoothly... they were men of the world and more than proficient with organising 'surprises' for people.

'The boy Slater is downstairs waiting for you – he'll tell you the rest. Make sure he takes all the risks – not you. No names and... don't get caught!' Good help was easy to find. Loyal help was a little thinner on the ground. Adam and Karl had proved themselves before at numerous functions. Sending them off with a paternal but metaphorical pat on the back was the least he could do to ensure they remained focussed on the bigger picture.

Sam looked directly at the pair. 'Take precautions!' He nodded his head towards the door, and the couple took it as their cue to leave. Karl plucked a cigarette from behind his ear as he got to the door and jabbed it into his mouth – looking up to search Adam's face in mutual anticipation of the next forty-eight hours.

'Gentlemen!' Sam shouted.

They turned from where they stood in the corridor to look back at the big man dwarfing the desk.

'Once you have the money… you won't need Slater!'

Chuck slammed the door from within, leaving Adam and Karl standing alone in the hall beside a giant green fern.

Adam's big brown eyes smiled as his lips twisted to a half grin. 'Sounds like fun!' he said. 'I have an idea!'

Slater awoke late that morning with the knowledge that today was the big day. Today he would change from petty crook and small time drug dealer into a big time burglar; today would change his life forever. He only had a couple of hours before those two picked him up.

He pushed the single sheet off his body and stared at the clock on the wall. Midday already. He'd been up most of the night plying what used to be a friend with drink. It had worked. He had got what he needed.

He choked and ran retching for the toilet.

Across town, Karl finished his cigarette and threw it to the step. His foot twisted momentarily upon it as he dispelled a last puff of smoke into the chilly air. He returned into the broken down public house to rejoin Adam and Alison – there were plans to be made and a job to be done.

As he rounded the pillar to the lounge area he could see Adam and Alison getting better acquainted on the same piece of grubby side seating. With a deep breath of suppressed jealousy, Karl took the stool at the opposite side of the peeling table, prompting the two lovebirds to separate and look towards him.

Adam looked more than satisfied, but hesitated to meet his friend's eyes. The two men had a lot of history together, and each knew of the other's problems and pleasures. He rested his broad shoulders against the threadbare seat back upholstery, the frayed hem and remaining tassels shaking against his weight as the aging stitching groaned with the strain. He twisted his head slightly instead and stared through the murky windows at the passing traffic.

Karl tried to smile. It was a false twitch of his lips that barely concealed the yellowing crooked teeth of a habitual cigarette smoker, his eyes stayed harsh and unforgiving. The afternoon's job was of paramount importance and this girl needed playing very carefully now, otherwise she would have been a complete waste of time.

He checked his watch. It was after twelve already. They had an appointment to keep with Slater, and they didn't fancy letting him off the hook for his promises to Big Sam. However, an extra... expendable person was needed, and Alison fitted the bill quite nicely.

'Wha' we're gonna do… babe… is get you another drink, an' then work out how to sort ou' your supervisor problem. Come on… drink up.' Karl watched as Alison reached for her grubby glass and smiled again as the clear liquid disappeared over her tongue and drained quickly. Abruptly he stood and sauntered quickly to the bar, ignoring Adam's arm that was reaching around the girl's shoulders. As disappointed as Karl was on the particular roles that they were playing… they still needed playing. Karl plucked the coins he needed for another Vodka and tonic from his back pocket and thumped them down on the counter with a grunt to the barman.

Adam pulled slightly from Alison's proffered lips but continued to stroke her neck slightly with one finger. It was time for tit-for-tat… one good turn for another. He had to keep his eye on the prize.

Karl rejoined them at the table and Alison took the glass enthusiastically and sipped again.

'Thing is babe,' started Karl, 'is tha' we could do you a favour… if you do us one. Your supe'visor. He needs a little chat does he?'

'Yeah,' broke in Alison. She had to put them right on that score with these two; the last thing she needed was worse problems with work. She was over an hour late and quite frankly, had no desire to go in at all the way she was feeling. Robbed last night; hunted now by her landlord; and more than a little inebriated with the 'hair of the dog'. She was subconsciously assessing the different excuses she could use for her absence today – deciding what she had used before and what she hadn't. Should she profess illness – family problems – transport failure – abduction? If she played it properly, she might be able to have a couple of days off. No money for shopping (or drinking) though – and still over a week until payday. Bloody salary. She saw enough people down the pub at a weekend being paid every Thursday. It just wasn't fair that she had to get her money monthly. The crosses she had to bear; it just wasn't fair.

'Just a chat though… show your muscles,' Alison appreciatively stroked Adam's brawn, 'but you can't mention my name. It'd make things worse!' She took another large sip. 'And no beating him up… I don't need that hassle.'

Adam and Karl shared their knowing look. They had no intention of pursuing Alison's problem. What they did need however, was Alison in a particular place at a particular time. They nodded sagely as though in complete agreement with her.

'How do we know what he looks like?' asked Adam.

'If we drive to the store… every day at three o'clock he stands out the back of the store to take stock in. We have a delivery… I could point him out!'

Things were looking up for Adam and Karl. It meant a chance to do a little extra research before the big event tonight. It had been worth picking up this girl – a stroke of genius – the store uniform had been a giveaway… and what's more… a willing participant. No need for threats or intimidation. Bonus!

Karl glanced at his watch again. They needed to pick up Slater as well in a bit. There was time for another drink though.

'And what favour could I do for you?' asked Alison, more than aware that her help had been requested. She fluttered her eyelids as seductively as she knew how and looked obviously at Adam's crotch.

'Nothing like that!' Adam growled with a smile. Flattered. His mind was on the job in hand. 'We need you to deliver a parcel for us.' He was more than aware of what he was turning down, and truth be told… she looked a little too rough for his tastes.

'OK?' Alison would have preferred other jobs, but that seemed easy enough. 'As long as you're sure there's nothing else I can do for you!' She replaced the glass on the table and licked her lips slowly, holding Adam's gaze with steadfast determination. 'When and where?'

'Oh, don' worry about that,' added Karl with a forced smile. He tried to keep a level head, but was getting a little angry inside that the girl wasn't all over him instead of Adam. Jealous. He desperately maintained his careful tone and tried to ignore the blatant flirting between these two. It was bloody hard being a third wheel. 'La'er tonight. We need you on the main tram from Birmingham to make the delivery. But there's plen'y of time yet. One more drink an' we've got to fetch someone!'

Adam nodded in agreement and Karl rose one last time to collect a round of drinks.

They collected Slater later. As they pulled up outside his canal side property, the youth was already sitting on the elegant front steps waiting for them. As the battered Fiesta drew up, Alison peered at him from the back seat, regarding the dishevelled and ill-looking boy with disgust – he appeared extremely malnourished and pale and the facial jewellery just looked out of place on a little boy trying to look big.

Slater climbed into the backseat without a word and sat nervously fidgeting and playing with the threads hanging from his jeans at the knees. Neither Adam nor Karl attempted to engage him in conversation.

Next stop was Lexington's. Alison directed them around the rear of the building and they pulled to a halt opposite the back entrance, cutting the engine of the Ford quickly so as not to draw attention to its rattle and tried to look as though they were there to collect someone from the Phoenix Centre.

The rear of Lexington's was already open. The heavy metal doors had been opened to their extreme, clipped back against the walls on either side with hook and eye metal fasteners. An internal roller shutter had been wound up, but not as far as possible. A tall thin man wearing the company colours had just clipped it with the top of his head on his way through, and was now gesticulating angrily to another shorter man to raise it further, and rubbing his sore spot briskly to alleviate the pain.

Neither of the observed two men looked happy as they watched a large box van draw up alongside them in the loading bay. Also purple, it had the name of the store emblazoned down its length. The tail lift was up for transit, but the driver was quickly onto the task of dropping it. They had a delivery window of ten minutes as agreed with local council and the driver had no desire to be there any longer than he needed to be.

Alison picked out the taller man as her supervisor and both Adam and Karl nodded understandingly. She hid her face with her hand and peeked through slatted fingers. Holding her breath momentarily as the object of their scrutiny surveyed the generally quiet street, she was positive he had seen her. Instead, he looked back down at his clipboard.

Slater harrumphed with annoyance. He had no idea why this woman was with them in the car but didn't currently have the confidence to tackle the two men in the front seats about it. He was displaying extreme nervousness and chewing the remains of his fingernails, ripping jutting nail with teeth through pursed lips and blowing the residue to his lap.

'OK!' said Adam, 'we've got him. What time does he leave tonight? Ten?'

'No,' replied Alison, sweating slightly in the crowded car, 'eight o'clock tonight. He parks on the car park nex' to the tram an' bus station! An old blue Mondeo! Yellow front bumper!'

'OK!' said Adam again, 'we'll see to him then for you. We need you to do something for us now! Important job!'

'Yeah,' added Karl. 'Dead easy... we need you to ride tram 46 to Birmingham New Street an' back. Go to the address we give you... not far... an' collect somethin' for us. Small parcel! Nah... Not drugs!' He saw the bemused expression on Alison's face. 'A mobile phone. Trouble is…' Karl wondered how much to say, 'we ain't got the time to go! Other things on… you know how it is?'

'Yeah sure… got nothing else to do today now!' Alison watched as her troublesome boss signed the offered clipboard from the driver, waved a curt goodbye and closed the two heavy rear doors to Lexington's. The driver climbed the couple of steps to his cab, started the engine, and disappeared down the street and past the little traffic island. She fancied a trip to Birmingham – check out the new Bull Ring. She kept trying to find time to go!

'Bring it back on the eight o'clock outta Birmingham tram. It gets here for eight thirty. We'll meet you… an' by then… we'll have had a chat wi' your boss and everythin's okay. Wotcha say?'

'Yeah, sure…' Alison wouldn't have cared if it had have been drugs as she hadn't been particularly averse to them in the past, and fully expected to be taking them again in the very near future. The passing hope had been that she was chatting with a cheaper supplier. If she stayed in with these two, who knows what contacts they would bring for her? 'I need cash for the fare… I ain't got a penny on me!' Why should she pay?

Slater ignored his new partners as they drove on and parked at the tram station, preferring to stare at the passing traffic kicking up puddles of rain water and the windswept passers-by hurrying past. They left him sulking in the back seat as they took her to board the vehicle, pushing a little money and the slip of paper with an address into her hand, though Slater didn't fail to notice the kiss Adam gave her before they turned back to rejoin him.

'Wha' was all tha' abou'?' he grunted as Karl returned to the front seat, car door slamming loudly and poor suspension grinding under the abrupt weight.

Adam stayed outside for a moment, his own phone glued to his ear, deep in unheard conversation whilst absent-mindedly kicking the front tyre.

'That was our diversion!' crowed Karl with pride, twisting in his seat to observe Slater now straddling the back seat.

'Wha'?'

The driver's door creaked open, and the car bore the new weight as Adam's mass tested its integrity.

'She's due back here at eight thirty tonight. She's collecting the mobile phone which we will ring when we are ready. One call and it will blow the brakes on the tram.' Adam stared at the rear of the vanishing tram with a mixture of emotions and sighed.

Karl gave him a quick sideways glance, again annoyed that Alison had been interested in only one of them, but professionally focussed on the task in hand.

'The tram won't stop. It'll crash into the barrier an' cause *so* many problems. It should give us the chance to get in through those back doors.' Karl was almost chortling with glee. Bitch. Adam always seemed to have the luck with the girls. He wouldn't be wasting much time worrying about her.

'You sure?' Slater was dubious. He had left the diversion to the two lads who had told him yesterday that they had it sorted. He hadn't expected them to drag someone else into the equation.

'Yeah! No problem. I fixed a small device... a simple bomb... on the tram this morning. Held the tram up – told 'em I could see a problem on the roof. Whilst the driver was looking, I nipped underneath and placed it next to the operator's system on the underside of the tram before running off. It works by remote. The trouble is – we don't want to be there to set it off, and the range is too small.'

'We needed someone on board to blow it for us!'

'An' tha' girl said she'd blow it... an' you trust her?' Sceptical now. Didn't she work for the store? Had the same uniform on as he he'd seen on others there.

'She doesn't know about it!' Karl sniggered. 'As long as she's on board that tram... One call to it and... boom!' Karl spread his fingers wide in enthusiastic demonstration.

'An' tha's the diversion?' Slater was very tired but now a little more inspired by the news about the diversion. He recalled one science lesson he had attended at school. He had never usually paid much attention, but the teacher had been very informative on this occasion about the explosive nature of a balloon filled with petrol placed in a microwave with a tinfoil strip. He supposed it wasn't difficult to make a bomb. It was always on the news about terrorist bombs made from fertilizers.

But for the moment, his ribs were still aching and he was more than a little hungry. The small amount of food he had begged from obliging acquaintances yesterday had come up that morning into the over priced bathroom toilet that his pride had insisted he rent.

191

Again… the feeling of sorrow tugged at his heart and the desire burned to turn the clock back in order to make better choices for his life.

'Yup!'

'Wha' makes you think she'll be there?' Antagonistic.

''cause she wants our friend here!' Karl gave Adam's bicep a friendly squeeze and shared a laugh with him.

'Huggins'll make sure she gets on the right tram!' added Adam. 'I've checked with him… everything's good his end. I've told him I put the piece of equipment on tram 46 this morning. It's still running on time… even after our little hold-up this morning. As long as she's on board… it'll go OK!'

Slater closed his eyes as they restarted the car, and wondered if they'd buy him a burger if he asked. He could do with something to fill his stomach. The lack of food was affecting his energy badly, and giving him bad breath.

Neither of the two men was aware of, or in any way interested in, his needs. The plan was going smoothly and they needed to pick up the van and get ready for later. The Fiesta pulled out past the court buildings and joined the thronging traffic to drive past the fancy international hotel and Japanese car dealers back to the Stag and Horseshoe. A police Volvo, its lights blazing and siren shrieking to an uncaring population, sped past them.

The three men sat in silence within; each of them entertaining their own thoughts and expectations of the day.

By far, Slater was the most nervous. He had the most to gain or lose today. Big Sam was not someone you messed with, and if these two psychopaths were typical employees, then he didn't stand a chance if he failed to deliver.

Neither of the other two men was particularly worried. If Huggins' electronics didn't work, then he would have incurred Sam's wrath, and Slater wouldn't get the money. If it all worked out fine, then the evening would go with a blast.

Alison had saved them a lot of trouble, but there were always people like her to help out. Willing and unquestioning! The trouble was that she had no sense of what was right and wrong... limited conscience.

Always the easiest people to manipulate!

Give them a sweet and watch them go.

CHAPTER 14

Sandra was sitting in the back of the van on a smelly, disgusting, but thankfully empty, potato sack. Her hands were fixed together behind her by what felt like a plastic cable tie that was cutting into her wrists, and her mouth was gagged with an old woollen sock that was making her dry heave as she tried to keep her tongue from touching it. Her muffled screaming had just earned her a smack against the side of the head which had brought tears streaming down her face, and she now lay resting against a tool box, a broken woman.

The rain pattering on the roof instantly reminded her of their Welsh caravan holiday in Portmadoc last year. Sat in the middle of a field full of sheep with her husband... at the time all she had wanted was a chance to see her lover. As she remembered, it had rained pretty continually for most of the week and watching Bert leave the van twice a day with the terrier for a walk had almost been a relief. She had reluctantly agreed to go purely because of the disappointed look on his face after she had initially refused and the fact that she couldn't cope with his depressed drinking every night when he thought he wasn't going to get a holiday.

She snatched her mind to the characters before her.

Three men sat looking at her. Two wore balaclavas, the other; a pale but fresh faced young youth with curly hair did not. She didn't know who had hit her, but she thought it wasn't the youth because he was rocking on the spot, gripping his knees and looking extremely worried. He was wearing a dark fleece jacket that looked extremely baggy on him, threadbare and ripped jeans, and a pair of the worst scuffed shoes she had ever seen.

Sniffing back her tears, she looked at her captors. The biggest one, built a bit like a bear, was sat on the rear interior wheel arch. He wore a thick black woollen sweater and black jeans. Black gloves and the latest style, black Rockport trainers, completed his attire. Squatting down as he was, he looked a little like an orang-utan with his arms draped in front of him, and he rested on his knuckles. Peering at his face in the dim street light filtering through the windscreen, she couldn't even make out his eyes through the holes cut in the balaclava.

The other covered man was now sat cross legged beside her. He was a lot smaller than his friend, through dressed in a very similar manner. His eyes seemed to stare unblinking at her through their slit and gave Sandra the idea he was extremely wired... obviously high on something. He smelt of tobacco. The reek in his clothes clogged the air and took her breath. She thought that maybe this was the man who had hit her. Little worm! Fear almost gave way to anger as she watched him search and then toss her little handbag to the back of the van.

Self conscious that her now very dirty and wet skirt was riding up, she shifted her weight in an effort to drop it down. Although she wasn't naked, she felt very uncomfortable and helpless. She was cold, and the wet clothing was chilling her body. The smaller man reached out and slowly trailed a fore-finger up her leg from ankle to thigh, causing a fresh burst of sobbing into her smelly sock gag; her damp hair shaking fresh droplets of rain water into her face as she quivered in revulsion. He saw her little angel tattoo and his finger stopped in admiration.

The larger man leaned forward supporting himself with one hand and grabbed the hem of her skirt from the top of her thigh. Just as Sandra was about to scream the best she could, he pulled it down to cover her legs. As he sat back on the wheel arch and the smaller man turned to look at him, Sandra resisted the temptation to cry again with self-pity and stared at him with almost silent relief.

'Come on!' grunted the smaller one, obviously unhappy with being shown up and unlikely to argue with the bigger one. 'Are you ready?' He looked directly at the miserable white lad who by now looked close to tears.

The lad grunted his affirmation, untangled his arms from his legs and started to feed himself towards the interior handle of the Mercedes Van side door. As he gripped the plastic pull, Sandra decided that he must be under duress.

'What about her?' growled the big one. Sandra decided he was possibly Afro-Caribbean based on his accent.

'She can stay in here!' The smaller one's voice was cocky but he was obviously a local. 'She won't be any trouble!'

'What you gonna do with her?'

'I'll make sure she can't get out or spoil the job!'

'Mmm.' Grumbling. 'Bloody nuisance!'

Slater pulled back the handle and hefted the door back on its slide. The rumbling of the wheels in their groove was deadened by the

196

sound of the rain. The effort took his balance, and his elbow landed on Sandra's battered and extremely sore ankle as he fell backwards into the central floor space.

As she screamed in agony, the bigger one grumbled, 'bloody idiot!' and whacked the lad's shoulder with a hand built like a frying pan. The force pushed the lad almost out of the van, the momentum enough to also help him up. He crawled out to follow him and the two figures disappeared from Sandra's view. It left just the smaller hooded man who was now staring at her again.

Nervously glancing around the inside of the van, she concluded that it must belong to a builder or construction worker of some kind. The floor was littered with off-cuts of plastic pipe, over flowing wooden boxes, rings of insulated wire and those coloured little plastic box holders that fix to a wall mounted grill in order to hold screws and such like; apart from sweet wrappings and empty crisp packets. Her leg had already grazed itself on the myriad of screws and nails that besieged the false wooden floor and dust, cut plastic cartons and packaging were spilling from a black bin liner beside her.

Suddenly he pushed his face close to hers, his eyes staring at her. She could see only the coldness of hate. The smell of his breath through the balaclava was over powering… an unmistakeable mixture of tobacco, beer and fast food. Her eyes flicked up and around in the desire to escape, and his hands clenched her shoulders to hold her still. Over his shoulder, she could see only a short ladder clipped to side mounts on the opposite wall and lengths of copper tube hanging below.

Fear rose within her like a tidal wave. He was pressing his cheek to hers now and the revulsion was getting worse. The smell was quite over powering and she thought she'd choke. Moaning into her gag, she knew he was going to hurt her. 'Bert!' she thought, 'please help me!' She was sure that this was going to be the last moment of her life.

Barely had this notion crossed her mind, then the sudden realisation of how she had treated her husband for the last goodness-knows-how-long, engulfed her in a wave of self-loathing. It wasn't Terry Thomas she was appealing to, or the previous joker who had just used her for sex, but her steady and undemanding husband. Bert was always there. Softly speaking and helpful; he was the man who always asked her how her day was and brought her tea every morning in bed. The man who tried to give her everything she needed, wanted or desired. The man she had denied and pushed repeatedly away. At that moment, she swore that if she got out of this alive, she would make it up with him. 'Please God! I promise!' She promised she would do anything for him if only this nightmare would end. She'd take him back to that caravan near Black Rock Sands and spend the week in his arms... she'd...

Her last thought before a sea of blackness engulfed her consciousness was that she did love her husband, and that she was sorry.

Karl dropped the girl down onto the potato sack and stroked her again from toe to thigh – this time uninterrupted – and back down again – feeling the taught skin on her leg; fingering her glorious little tattoo; his breathing a little more rapid than before. He lovingly replaced his object of pride, the Italian made Beretta nine millimetre hand-gun which he had retained after procuring it during a previous job, back into his trouser pocket; the grip had made an excellent wound on the side of her head. Blood was already dripping to the floor. He checked to make sure that she couldn't free herself and tied another plastic cable around her ankles to be sure. He stroked the grubby hair from her face and traced a laconic finger around her pliant lips. It had been a good idea to steal this van...blooming well equipped... everything you could possibly need for an evening out. He smirked then scowled to himself as he wondered who the girl was. Not a copper! Could be someone who worked here? Would she be missed for half an hour? A sudden nasty thought crossed his mind...

In the teeming rain at the store's back entrance, Slater had found the discrete manhole cover in the gutter that his friend had described, no more than a blemish in the smooth face of the pavement, and inserted a mini crank handle into an accommodating slot. The cast iron lid popped up, and Adam hefted it out of its fissure. Looking down, they could see the rough circular brick face describing a downward cylinder, just wide enough for a man to climb into. The rainwater running in the gutter poured down the open hole creating a sloshing sound as it went like water down a plughole.

After swallowing loudly in an unconscious display of nerves, Slater followed the waterfall into the ground, climbing down the jutting rusted footholds that stuck out from the sides at irregular intervals, searching, in the light of Adam's pointing torch, for the loose bricks that he knew would be there. Three metres down, he found them; a haphazard array of mismatching bricks that had been piled into the wall rather than cemented in. He pried the first one loose and tossed it free. Three seconds and then he heard a loud splash below him. More bricks followed until enough were missing that the hole in the side wall was big enough to get through. Panting from the exertion, he reached for his own pocket and plucked out a torch.

Suddenly there was a high pitched screech. Slater almost lost his footing and his torch, but managed to hold on to the brick face banging his bruised body again on the side wall. He could feel whiskers in his face. He was almost screeching now. The downward light of Adam's torch picked out the face of a large sewer rat showing its teeth. Slater recoiled as far as he could but the rat turned and disappeared.

Bloody Hell! The canals weren't far from here. Slater recalled a dim and distant History lesson on the local area when he was sure he'd been told about Wolverhampton's storm drains and canals being linked in places. His heart was palpitating; his face whiter than ever.

Above him, he heard Adam replacing the manhole cover, the metal on concrete noise echoing loudly in his tomb. There was no way back now. He had to move forward. Please let that rat be more afraid of me than I am of it! Any light from above was extinguished. Slater was now completely alone.

However, a little recovered and encouraged by the rat's fleeing, Slater directed his own light into the hole and saw a tunnel running towards the Lexington building. Another deep breath and he climbed in; keeping his mind on the job. Gotta do this! Gotta do this! Sam'll kill me if I don't!

He crawled the five or so metres along the mud and broken brick in the tunnel. Head height was minimal. It smelt damp and dank and peculiarly of wet hair. A steady dripping sound freaked him slightly but he knew that he had no choice. At the other end he came to a metal grill held in place with a hasp and padlock. This needed the key that his friend had given him. Fumbling slightly as he tried to direct the light held in his mouth, he eventually released the lock and the grill swung outwards. Slater stepped out in relief into a small enclosed brick room – the basement of the building – tall enough to stand up in, but completely devoid of anything other than a layer of dust and a family of rats climbing through a hole made in broken brick in the far corner. A narrow set of stone steps ran upwards. He couldn't hear anything beyond the screeching of his cellmates.

Directing his light around the room he could see the many concrete pillars holding up the concrete plate roof above him. It looked almost clinical in its construction. Slater's imagination started to play tricks on him. The shadows created from his torch light by the pillars started forming into an army of zombies and vampires, all eager to feast on his flesh. A low moan and his irregular breathing pattern descended to scarcely contained sobbing.

Quickly now, he ran up the few steps to the solid metal lid in the ceiling. Praying fervently that the information was correct, he heaved his shoulder against it. It obviously hadn't been moved too many times in the past. It resisted momentarily before creaking up and allowing Slater out into the bottom of a lift shaft. He replaced the lid and sat on it trying to draw lungs full of better quality air and steady his nerves.

There was the roller shutter and there was the main desk holding paperwork, a bunch of keys, leaflets, stock books and phones. He'd made it. Standing and taking the mini crank again, he inserted it into the manual wind mechanism and energetically turned it. The roller shutters climbed slowly upward exposing the heavy external steel doors. Three metre long, heavy box iron rods braced the door by hanging freely on hooks fixed to both the doors and the frame. The cradles effectively braced the doors into their aperture, and were the store's main line of defence against the outside world.

No one would have got through this door from outside. It had been designed to withstand the local phenomenon of ram raiding. Local gangs had recently decided that subtle illegal entry into buildings was not their style and had begun to steal suitable vehicles that could be ploughed into a business premise at high speed, taking the front windows and doors out and allowing easy entrance. They would then dash around stealing as much as they could, as quickly as they could, before running out and escaping in another waiting car. To combat this fad, unsightly waist height concrete pillars had sprouted from the pavements in front of shop windows to deter the possibility of them being next. Concrete pillars had not been an option on the delivery entrance. On this particular door there was enough steel to prevent the army, fire brigade, or any one else from getting in from outside.

Slater had inside knowledge.

He moved each bar in turn, letting it clang to the floor. Snatching the bunch of keys from the desk he tried each in turn before he found the one that opened the three locks on the steel doors. Turning them gratefully, they swung open easily to allow him to see the van still parked at the kerb.

Slater stood there panting, covered in mud and wishing that he was dead. That part of the operation had only taken a couple of minutes, but he felt like he'd just run the gauntlet.

Just as Karl was about to put his thoughts into action, Adam was back at the van's open doorway - leaning against the ceiling ridge and blocking some of the light from the street lamp. Karl immediately tried to forget his sadistic idea and covered the girl over instead with a mound of overalls; banishing the thought of that little angel from his mind.

'Come on…. What's keepin' you?' Adam snarled in his low voice. 'We're goin' in!'

Karl looked at him and then at the mound of cloth that was the girl, a pleading look in his eyes. Adam's shaking head answered his unspoken question.

'Not today pal!' said Adam softly, 'come on, stay focussed on the job. There's plenty of time for all that tomorrow. We'll go up the old hospital road... and have fun!'

Karl nodded reluctantly knowing full well he was right.

'Is everything ready in here?'

They looked around the van. Since they had picked it up last night from outside a house in Perton, they had worn gloves. A stupid sticker on the back commenting on the fact that it didn't hold tools overnight had been pointless. Adam and Karl were far too astute to be taken in by that. Many years boosting numerous and varied types of vehicles had come in handy – the theft swift and unnoticed for well over an hour, and until they'd picked up Slater that afternoon, they'd kept it in a large but discrete lock-up at the back of a miserable pub on the Birmingham Road. In fact, the only person not to have worn gloves whilst in it... was Slater. Idiot!

The body of the girl lying in the van wouldn't affect Adam or Karl later, but Slater's character would hopefully be tarnished forever. Indeed, it had been Slater who had dragged her into the van in the first place... on their command of course.

Taking the advice, Karl was soon out of the van into the rain. He slid the door closed and they joined Slater at the open freight entrance. They barely acknowledged his achievement in getting them into the building, and Slater didn't dare ask for praise.

Torches were pulled out and turned on. The waving beams picked out the bare breezeblock walls and hundreds of black - iron and steel tubes which dribbled down the walls around them usually carrying power and water. Adam pulled the heavy steel doors closed to avoid prying eyes and indicated that Slater should lower the main roller shutters. The last thing they needed was someone else finding the way in.

As Slater sweated again, they directed the beams up, and could just about see the bottom of the lift suspended above them, caught halfway between floors when the power had cut out. Running up the side of the shaft was the recessed ladder that Slater had talked of. The information had been correct.

They started to climb up. Karl went first, Slater followed, and Adam brought up the rear. A rhythm was soon achieved and the climb went steadily. Through the walls they could hear the shouts of the rescue services almost into the ground floor by now. Adam was sure that he had seen the tram removed and cutting equipment being brought in from the fire units to deal with the first two cars as they completed a slow drive past the police cordon when they arrived.

A high pitched screeching metallic whine confirmed his thoughts, as Monk's team, inside the shop, were attacking the car doors in an effort to find any survivors. He glanced at his illuminated watch face: 21:40. The team had planned to be at the top floor a little before 22:00. This would mean that the tills would have been emptied and maximum amount deposited upstairs.

The ladder had been designed to be for instances of service only. It was set only a couple of centimetres (an inch) from the wall by regular mounting points. Every time Slater grasped for the next rung up, his knuckles scraped on the wall and caused a fresh gasp of pain. His shoes had very little grip, and having to climb using practically only his toes was getting tedious and slippery. Karl didn't look back down he was focussed on getting to the lift. His gloves and new boots were perfect for this... he was a monkey scampering up. Adam, at the bottom of the group, was strong enough to force Slater's pace and keep him from slipping off.

The bottom of the lift was getting closer and closer with each step up They passed the ground floor lift access. The doors had buckled in and still held a lot of heat. They kept climbing. The whining of the cutting equipment was soon no longer audible, and the walls had long insulated them from the sound of the rain. No one spoke. Maximum effort was made to make the climb as quickly as possible. Only Slater kept looking down.

The lift was reached. They had to get through it and out of the top in order to continue the climb. They couldn't squeeze past it any other way. Slater's friend had talked of trap doors top and bottom to allow entry. They hoped he wasn't wrong.

Torches were now directed to the metal frame at the base of the lift. A crisscrossing cats-cradle of box steel braces secured the floor. It had been designed to take the load of two pallets of stock with each trip. There had been no room for poor manufacture. Each pallet could weigh anything up to a quarter of a tonne. The last thing

Lexington's could afford was stock tipped down seven floors. The health and safety implications of getting it wrong had been enormous. Lives could be lost if crushed by falling stock. There to one side was the trap door, two metres by two metres, resting on box steel. The panel was flush with the rest of the floor, but held no locking mechanism.

Karl, gripping the ladder with one gloved hand, swung out, reached up and pushed gently at the panel with the other.

It didn't move. Annoyed, he looked back down at the anxious upturned face of Slater. There shouldn't be stock in the lift at this time of the evening. Seeing no comprehension of any problem, he tried again. Still no movement was forth-coming from the obstinate section of steel. Brilliant! The last thing they needed was a pallet of stock sat in the middle of the lift floor blocking the access.

Despite his fear at this height and the fact he had wrapped as much of his body as possible around the thin metal ladder, Slater could see that Karl was having problems. 'There's no lock,' he babbled quickly. 'They don't lock 'em. 'ealth 'n' safety see. Push it harder!'

Grunting behind his balaclava, Karl forced himself to belt the underside of the steel panel as hard as he could with the flat of his hand. It bounced, and he heard the unmistakeable grunt of someone above, followed by a little shriek. He belted it again, and this time the panel flew up into the air before crashing down inside the lift space with a resounding clatter. Simultaneously, a woman shrieked again, a man's face appeared at the opening, and Karl instinctively aimed a sharp up-cut which caught the man square on the bridge of the nose, sending him careering backwards.

Karl pulled himself quickly in through the bottom of the lift, and by the light of his torch, he could see a largish woman sitting in the corner holding a purple uniform in her naked lap. An almost entirely naked man was lying flat on his back across the floor, unconscious, with an obviously broken nose; pouring blood dribbling down his left cheek and forming a rapidly widening pool below him. Strewn across the floor were the man's jacket and trousers plus two pairs of abandoned shoes… the man's shoes looking very shiny by the light of his torch. He must have been a security guard judging by the cheap standard issue protection tat attached to a belt that had been cast aside in the rush for personal pleasures.

'What the..?' muttered Karl incredulously. 'Who on earth are you?' He finished drawing his legs through the hole and flashed his light around the boxy space to check for any other people. Behind him, Slater started his entry… The force of Adam's hand proved a power without argument. He bashed his bruised hips again on the lip causing an outbreak of mumbled swearing.

'Please… please don't hurt me!' The girl had caught a glimpse of his covered face in the flashing and darting light and realised immediately that these men weren't there to rescue her. 'I'm Sally!'

'Of course you are, love!' laughed Karl softly, offering a hand to Adam who had now appeared at the gap. 'Wotcha' doin' in here?'

'We got caught in the lift when the power went off!' whimpered Sally apologetically into the hem of her blouse, her big eyes trying to catch a glimpse of the strange men in the weak light.

'Who's he?' growled Adam taking in the spectacle without any outward display of surprise and getting to his feet.

'James. We were trying to keep warm!' All four people looked at the decreasing drip of blood from his face and the large pool in which his head now languished.

'I'm sure you were, love,' Karl sniggered callously. He hadn't the time or the inclination to be nice to her. They were here on a job. OK, it wasn't a massive job. It had been planned over an afternoon fry-up at a Greek owned café near the Phoenix Centre, followed by making private arrangements for Slater to take the fall in a way that neither they, nor Big Sam took any blame. But Big Sam was counting on them to nurse-maid the imbecile with an eyebrow piercing in order to get to the goods. Most importantly of all, they had to get the hell out of there before anyone realised what had happened. They'd executed worse and more hastily planned operations than this in their time working for Sam.

'Well, we couldn't get out... and we couldn't see anything... and...' Sally descended back into floods of tears, her thin blouse now pressed to her face trying to block the awful episode from her vision and therefore render it not happening.

Sally had had an on-going liaison with James for a couple of months now despite her recent engagement and approaching wedding. They both enjoyed the regular evening trips between the floors with the usual private subsequent joke about the earth moving. Neither expected or wanted anything further than instant pleasure from the affair. James had been married to a lovely girl for more than two years now, and was best friends with Sally's fiancé. It was just that James on occasion liked something more to hold on to; his wife was a stick-thin fitness freak and Sally fitted his desires and secret fantasies quite ably. Truth be told, Sally was jealous of his wife though she never let on and just enjoyed the nightly attention before returning home to plan her perfect marriage. Dieting was too much effort despite a yearly promise to herself. Besides, she wasn't doing too badly for sex and complacency was easier to adjust to than exercise. With James, it was lust, nothing more, but the fright of discovery was more powerful than any emotion she had ever experienced before. She had prayed for and expected the power to come back on and for them to complete the ride to either the top or bottom (she couldn't remember which way it had been going now when the power cut out) without anyone being any the wiser as to their shenanigans, and certainly not for her prospective husband to have any inkling.

'With this…' Adam dubiously poked the prostrate body of James with his foot and watched his head flap from side to side causing a renewed stream of blood.

James was naked except for a pair of patterned brown boxer shorts, a cheap Timex watch and one black sock. The tool of his desires had shrivelled beneath the fabric and looked almost pitiful in its present predicament. His reasonably fit form hadn't stood a chance against Karl's surprise attack. Privately, Karl was more than pleased with the outcome. Darting the torch beam across the floor and up the walls, Adam soon found the other, quite holey, sock hanging on the lift control panel with a lacy bra; a pair of white lace knickers balled beneath; no handbag evident.

Sally quivered into floods of tears again, the plump mounds of flesh around her waist undulating with the force of her distress, her streaked blonde and brown hair spilling down over her face along with the paths of tears. She had no idea who these three people were beyond the fact that they were obviously up to no good. Two of them were totally covered from head to foot; and the scrawny looking lad looked more petrified that she was.

'Bloody 'ell,' breathed Slater. 'Not another one! Wha' we gonna do wi' 'er?' He sank into the opposite corner and held his face. Everything was going wrong. Earlier today they'd been messing with some girl from the store – fussing over her like she was royalty... then some stupid cow came knocking on the side of the van and they couldn't take the risk that she wouldn't mention the van to the police, and now these two clowns had smacked a bloke up and got a fat naked chick wailing. He was sure he'd have to leave the country after this. His face would be public knowledge within 24 hours on every news show.

'Shall I kill her?' Karl retrieved the small gun from his pocket and hefted it in his hand. 'She's in the way. Do you think anyone'll hear?' His voice held the latent horror of enjoying the prospect.

Sally decided he was the one to watch out for before suffering another outbreak of howling tears, her head now almost totally covered by the thin purple cotton cloth, in total and utter fear, her little fat toes clenched in panic and legs rubbing together causing swells of fat to jiggle in a mesmerising manner.

'Shut up you!' Adam snapped at the girl. 'Leave her. Let's keep going. We can get her later!' to Karl, and 'you shut up an' all!' to Slater. Adam took charge of the group, ignored the girl who had stopped crying immediately, and directed his light to the ceiling. 'Where's the access panel?'

Slater recovered and returned quickly to his feet, staring up to look for the irregularity in the ceiling metal pattern. Within a second he had seen it. 'There it is!' He pointed to a section above the floor access with the cross hatching pattern going a different way to the rest of the ceiling.

'Come on then!' Adam laced his hands together to make a foot hold and wearily bent down to encourage Karl to step up.

Reluctantly, Karl moved away from the girl and placed his right foot in the hold; a hand on Adam's shoulder. The girl peeked out from under her clothing, intrigued as to what these three were doing. Careful not to step on the open hole, Adam hoisted Karl with practiced ease. As he ascended, he punched the panel with his palm, popping the loose panel up into the empty space above. Karl finished his graceful move by grabbing the lip of the new hole. Swinging momentarily, Adam altered his grip and pushed him up. Within seconds Karl was sitting on the roof, peering down into the lift space.

'Now you!' No choice in the matter. Adam indicated that Slater should follow the same manoeuvre. In due course, after banging his elbow again on the metal lift frame and scrapping a layer of skin from his shin, he too was sitting on the roof and out of Adam's sight.

Adam swiftly kicked the guard's belt through the trap door and listened to it plop softly at the foot of the well far below him. Strewn clothes followed. Satisfied that she would stay still now, and with agility far beyond his size, Adam jumped for the ceiling and swung for a few seconds before using Karl's assistance to wiggle through the space.

After waiting a minute, her silent crying almost finished, Sally thought they had gone and started to slowly get to her feet; the remaining store blouse clenched determinedly to her bosom despite the fact the room had returned to pitch black. Suddenly a light was directed into her face, and her free hand had to lift immediately across her face. She blinked, almost blinded.

'Stay where you are or I'll shoot you!' The instruction came simply from a deadly calm voice with a significant underlining click as Karl's gun was cocked for firing.

Sally's regaining confidence collapsed completely as did her legs. She fell to the floor, her buttocks slapping the ground like a water balloon, and shuffled back into the corner sobbing hysterically, curled up in the foetal position. She thought she had been about to die. She wanted her mom.

The light disappeared. She couldn't hear them. She was left with the sound of James' shallow and irregular breathing through a broken nose.

The three men continued their steady progress up the shaft. They had to get there quickly. They were doing all right for time until they reached the fifth floor.

CHAPTER 15 *Perseverance*

Second unit fire officer Hughes made a successful entry into the second floor window of Lexington's Super store. It was duly noted by his watching supervisor in the log book as Hughes eventually ducked his head through the broken window frame, denying all attempts by the howling wind to throw him to the ground. He climbed down a second jerry-rigged ladder to the floor inside. The exertion was still less than he used during his training exercises at a tower situated at the rear of his fire station. His powerful flashlight picked out the frightened faces of the few shoppers, now hovering in his vicinity as he descended the last few rungs to the men's clothing department.

Celebration was the last thing on their minds right now though. Flicking his light from one to another, he noticed that all their expressions were apprehensive. He instantly understood why, the moment his flashlight picked out the mound of rubble that had balled out of the central staircase when the roof collapsed. Amongst the concrete, steel, glass and goods lay the scattered appendages of other people. They were sticking out at awkward angles some still with torsos attached, some clothed, some bare, and some squashed grotesquely. The heat on the floor was almost unbearable and a fog of smoke covered the ceiling. The fire on the lower floor had caused the temperature here to rise. Hughes swallowed. Training never completely readied you for this sort of sight.

'Any still alive?' His open question was obviously one that the small group of couples had asked of themselves before. There were signs of some rubble clearance attempted by the men of the group, their hands still bearing the dirt and scars of their endeavours.

'We got two out... but one... but one died!' A nervous young Chinese man spoke for the rest of the group, his diminutive and attractive girlfriend gripping his hand passionately, her own face showing the effects of many tears and pity.

'Show me!'

The group reacted as one and directed him towards the fitting room area. As they were on the second floor, they had the benefit of the glow from the street lighting, which helped to a great extent. Hughes found a body covered over with an anorak lying on the carpet, and a coughing ailing man sat in one of the armchairs under a huddle of fleece coats. He lifted the top of the anorak and briefly noted the lacerated body and gaping head wound of the middle aged man beneath.

'We got him out, but couldn't do anything for him,' said one worried older man, fiddling with the buttons on his dusty torn jacket.

'I phoned 999, but they said they'd do what they could,' said a woman who looked very tired and depressed.

'You did your best!' said Hughes simply. 'Any one else?' He looked at the suffering man in the chair, who had been punctuating their conversation with a racking cough. Hughes had only basic medical training, but recognised the sound of a collapsing lung.

The man's eyes searched Hughes' face pleadingly. He knew he wasn't well but trying to maintain a certain dignity.

'No one else,' said the Chinese lad, 'we heard a couple of shouts for a while, but we couldn't move the rubble. Honestly we tried... we really did... they stopped after a while.' His face creased into lines of distress, though kept from crying out loud.

'You did well guys!' Hughes could see that this group needed a bit of encouragement. They had evidently tried to do what they could, then sat here for half an hour worrying about the ones they couldn't help.

He plucked his radio from the sling around his neck, pressed the button and called in what he'd found. 'Blue 2 Hughes! I'm in!'

Static briefly before Monk's voice came back.

'What's the state in there?'

Hughes recounted the numbers of people safe, injured and dead. Turning from the group for a moment of privacy, he related the horrors he'd seen on the stairwell.

A particularly blustery squall shook the remaining windows around the top of the sales floor. They all ducked instinctively. Their nerves were getting more and more tattered after their traumas this evening. It was an evening none of them would forget for the rest of their lives.

The Chinese couple had had a sheltered upbringing. From affluent families in their homeland, they had come to Britain for an extended education. An upbeat outlook on life filled with the trappings of materialistic ownership and the added benefit of a credit card without upper limit, meant that they worked hard, but loved to shop. The beseeching, pleading look on one dying woman's face as a particularly sturdy girder had slowly crushed her spine would forever give them disturbed night time horrors and eventually lead to considerable counselling. Futile pulling and fevered activity whilst she was tangled inextricably amongst the escalator wreckage had not helped her and the bubbling blood from the petrified woman's mouth whilst she had tried desperately to scream, was up until now something only seen in a predominantly gory horror film. That sight alone had changed their youthful exuberant attitude to life - to one of dark dread.

The girlfriend had made herself into the tiniest ball she could be, and took refuge under the coat rails, howling with fear, whilst her man had continued with the unsuccessful and vain attempt to help others who were also trapped.

His darting eyes and broken glasses were testament to his altered perspective on life, a previous almost permanent smile completely wiped from his face.

As Hughes looked around the group, the image was reflected in the others who had all, to some degree, attempted to be heroic. Hughes knew that he himself was heroic. He was paid to be. He was trained to be. It was the life of a fire-fighter… whether rescuing a cat from a tree, or a screaming home owner from the upstairs window during a house fire, he was usually the first one who made entry and assessed the situation for the others. He was first-up. He *was* a hero.

These people here should never have seen what they had... but fair play... they had stepped up to the mark and done their best.

The coughing man needed emergency medical attention.

'Is everyone all right to walk?' Practicalities now. They had to get out. It would mean another floor cleared and a little more of the job completed.

'He can't!' An elderly gentleman indicated the coughing man. 'Crushed foot!' he added in way of explanation. 'I couldn't make it either... I have health problems!' he was almost whispering at the end.

'Any one else can't?' The fireman gazed around at the group before him. A couple more tentatively raised their hands; elderly people.

The face of another fire man appeared at the window and Hughes assembled the able bodied deciding to look at the more problematic people afterwards. They had to get out as many as they could, as soon as they could. Standard practice now. They had to be ferried down the ladders one at a time. He pushed the Chinese girl forward first. Her face showed the anxiety she was feeling as she gazed back at her boyfriend. He in turn nodded encouragingly in order to give her a little more confidence.

A harness on a nylon rope was thrown down to them. Looking up, the incoming rain stung their cheeks; Hughes caught the harness and swiftly buckled the frightened girl into it.

Mouth wide in a silent scream, she was helped up the ladder towards the waiting crew member then down the other side, a pulley wheel fixed to the remains of the double glazing frame spinning freely as the rope passed it, but enough to check her progress in case of a fall. One down, many... many more to go.

Colleen McLaughlin was almost beside herself with excitement at the spectacle. She had the camera zoom in on an emerging figure over the lip of the broken window, showing a fireman assisting her all the way down the ladder to be practically mobbed by waiting medics and half carried, half dragged to waiting vehicles parked near by. Across the region, the live images were beamed into the homes of hundreds of thousands of viewers.

On the opposite side of town, Claire was watching the events unfold with firsthand concern. Her mother was trapped in the building. She had considered getting a taxi there, but during their brief telephone call, her mother had forbidden her to do anything other than follow the events of television, with instructions to phone back if anything to explain why they were stuck there. For the last twenty minutes, Claire had been attempting to phone back, but Helen's mobile phone was unable to receive the incoming signal for some unapparent reason. Claire was frustrated and had no idea what to do in order to help the situation.

She was quite still as she watched Irene Carlson's lucid report on the situation, tears now beginning to stream down her face as she hugged her legs. She began to rock back and forth in fearful aggravation, scared for her mother.

The flooding had begun to retreat from the steps where Colleen stood. Privately she was extremely pleased, though tried to maintain a professional deportment throughout the worrying few moments as it climbed to where she was. She hadn't wanted to get her expensive shoes wet, but had come to the conclusion that the trade-off – shoes for the story – would have been worth it to stay still. She flashed a grateful look towards the third fire unit who had been busy on the pumps and continued her coverage of the first escapee – relatively dry.

Irene Carlson smiled knowingly as she watched her rival's frantic attempts at staying level headed and coherent with her report. She herself had had to do enough live reports in her youth, and spoiled more than one pair of shoes facing inclement weather. It was her turn now to sit back in the warm studio and watch the younger puppy panting furiously, desperate for the bone.

Monk was happy with how the operation was proceeding. Giving his commanding officer a report, he commented on everything they had managed to achieve…

'Third unit is manning the pumps. Looks like the storm 'ay over yet and there's a lot of water comin' down. First unit has shifted that tram. It's only been pushed back a little – black in there – crime investigation is on that – find out why it went off the tracks. We've cut out two of the cars from inside – no survivors on the ground floor yet and we're just getting to the main staircase which is blocked up solid. Fire escape is a no-go! Second unit has got into the second floor

– found survivors on that floor – though having problems gettin' them out.'

'How safe is the building?' The commander knew he was going to have to make a press appearance and decided to confirm all the facts first. Looking around, he could see that the events of the evening had attracted a lot of curious spectators despite the atrocious weather. Around the police cordon, people were lined up, the space above their heads bristling with umbrellas. A very determined news crew had almost set up a full camp on the steps of the court building opposite and desperately trying to catch his eye as he monitored the situation.

'Cursory inspection only so far... we're still waitin' for the main architect and plans. We're pretty certain that it ain't gonna move in anyway. All the pillars on the ground floor seem undamaged except one. Hughes is on second. Same story up there it seems. Top floor caved in... right down the centre of the store. Story is... lot of dead... main access I think... caught a lot of people.'

'How about the higher floors?'

'No hope of gettin' in them yet! Wind is against us with the ladders but we've sent for another crane. There's no power and we can't fix it yet 'cause everything is controlled from the top floor... we don't know how much of it is left!' Monk had a never-say-die attitude despite the very slow progress his team was making. The plan of attack was changing almost every ten minutes. The building design and weather was competing against them... and winning at the moment. He looked at his watch. Quarter to ten. They needed the plans of the building. He couldn't believe that when they had built the store, they hadn't deemed it necessary to build secondary access. Okay, the main staircase was one of the widest in any store in the country, but still... Johnson had told him that the back elevator shafts were impassable through the heavy steel security doors. He wondered if they could access the lift shafts through the back of the ground floor of the store! Maybe they could once they'd cleared the wreckage inside. The trouble was the explosion had fused a car to the racking systems and plastered it across the back of the store. Insurmountable masonry from above had made a huge pile in front of this mess and smouldering stock and fittings were still causing poisonous fumes and problems for them. As far as they could ascertain from vantage points around the area, isolated fires had broken out across the building on different floors and would need to be tackled when they could get there.

'Any way in through the back?'

'Well, we know there's a damaged pillar which could have caused massive instability. There must have been a fault in the building, otherwise the top floor wouldna' gone. We thought about forcing a hole through, but that could have a devastating effect on the back wall, and the last thing we need is for that to go – they'd be no chance of gettin' any out. The back doors are at least two inches thick!' Monk stopped to wipe sweat from his head again. His skin was almost black now with the soot and grime but after years in this job, he was used to problems it brought. 'No - this is gonna take a lot of manual shifting... brick by brick! We're on it. Another twenty minutes or so and we should find the lift shaft!'

An assortment of ideas were beginning to form in Monk's mind. Another way into the building had to be possible. They couldn't climb in from the bottom, they couldn't climb up the side, but maybe they could come in from another direction. His mind ticked over as he debated the quantity of equipment that they had on site. Surely they could find a way to utilize it.

'Keep at it, Bill! There are more troops on the way. We should have a total of at least seventy-five here within the hour.' The commander heaved a sigh. With bad weather like this, there was always a massive drain on resources. So far tonight, there had been yet another warehouse fire near the wharf... thick black smoke pouring into the sky despite the torrential rain... a pile-up between three cars on the expressway requiring cutting gear and the coroner, and appalling flooding across some low lying land beneath a residential tower block in Brierley Hill. 'It never rains, but it pours,' he thought ironically. He resolutely made his way through the rain towards the court buildings thinking that he might as well make a public report. This was the bit he never looked forward to. In the heat of the moment he knew that he was as eloquent and calming as he could be – the viewing public had to be appeased – screaming and crying people pawing at him through a police cordon didn't help him do his job. Tomorrow he'd watch himself and hate what he saw – hate what he sounded like. Still... there were people in there and everyone would want to know what was being done. A lot of dead people as well.... when they could reach the bodies.

Behind him, another youth was being rescued from the second floor window. Ahead of him, Colleen McLaughlin was almost jumping on the spot as she saw him approach.

Monk disappeared back to the tenders, positive that they could use the inflatable slide to get those people out of the second floor window. All they needed was a second vantage point. He watched gratefully as he saw the crane unit turn off the main road and pass through the police cordon before coming to a halt with a hiss from the air brakes. Shouting orders to the crew, he ran to the unit and climbed the rungs to the cabin. It was time to try a new strategy.

CHAPTER 16 *Illuminating*

Slater was getting very tired. Every muscle in his body was screaming at him to rest. His knuckles were scraped raw, the bruises on his torso were throbbing and something in his head was beginning to bang like a drum. Each breath he drew took a Herculean effort and he felt deprived of every other sense. He couldn't see anything; he couldn't smell anything; his mouth was dry and the only thing he could hear besides his own attempts at maintaining life, was the carefully measured in takes of oxygen by his two 'companions' as they climbed with efficiency.

Karl was way ahead of them. Scampering up like a monkey, he had turned his torch off a long time ago in a bid to save its battery power. Karl didn't mind the dark. It reminded him of his early childhood when his mother abandoned him every night to look for work. Lights were never put on before she went out, and if she came back early, as she frequently did, he was always under strict instructions to go straight to the airing cupboard - at the sound of a key in the door - and lock himself in until he was told he could come out. Strange noises from the bedroom lasted an hour... the welcome click of the front door latch as someone left, and then floods of light as he was allowed back out. He had been ten years old before he found out that that was not the usual childhood and that most people had proper meals every day.

A woman with sweaty underarms had come for him one day. He remembered his mother's refusal to look at him as he was collected and taken through the front door for the last time. Never knowing a father, he had been taken to a care home on the outskirts of Birmingham where he met other children of his age.

His teenage years had been a blast. He'd been given permanent homes many times, but he had always refused to cooperate with his new parents. What was the point? They meant nothing to him! They couldn't teach him really cool stuff, like which wires you needed to strip in order to hotwire a car, or how to bend a pin to jiggle a lock. Only the other kids in the care home could teach him that! If he was badly behaved enough, he could be back with them each time in a matter of weeks learning the next new thing.

Adam was climbing steadily below him. He was a quiet man. Adam had had a slightly better childhood than his friend. His tale of woe was one of dyslexia and an inability to keep up with his peer group because of his failure to understand despite an initial desire to do so. A likeable youth, one day he had just given up trying to continue the normal lines of education and started to fend for himself – wheeling and dealing and retrieving debts. He'd met Karl, one morning, trying to 'boost' his car. Instead of the expected beating, words were spoken, an easy alliance was formed and this soon became close friendship; a mutual respect.

'C'n I rest?' Slater was desperate to slow the pace a moment. He had no idea what a heart attack felt like, but he was getting a constricting pain in his chest and his breathing was becoming extremely erratic.

'No!' Adam's closed fist found Slater's rump on an upward swing causing a squeal of pain as another part of his body began to hurt. Adam was not in the mood for Slater's wimp like behaviour.

'Please!' Slater stopped moving. He had to have a rest. He hung there hugging the ladder, his tortured breathing shaking; pain coursing up and down his left side. He felt light headed and dizzy. The loss of blood at his hands was making him feel queasy.

Adam had to come to a rest below him. There was no where to go until he moved. Above them, Karl was aware that there was something wrong. He stopped, flicked his torch on and peered down.

'Wha's goin' on?' he called down in a half whisper, annoyed at the delay. If this joker had half the fitness that he himself had, they'd have been up to the cash office by now.

'This prat wants a rest!' Adam's voice dripped with contempt.

Karl pushed the button to illuminate the face on his cheap wrist watch and peered closely at it. 'We've only got ten minutes. We can't stop now. Give him a thump! Get him moving!'

'No… please no!' Slater shuddered. All he wanted was a couple of moments for a break. He stared down at the ominous dark shape of Adam below him, the free hand swinging freely, visible in the poor light of Karl's torch.

'Move!' Adam's threatening tone terrified him, and that hand reached up towards him. 'Move, or you'll be goin' down there!' The meaning was obvious – and it was a long way down.

Petrified, Slater tried to do what he was told but his arms could not take the punishment anymore. He grip slipped on the next rung, as did his feet a split second later. Hanging by one hand, he banged against the ladder causing a jolt of pain in his ribcage and he screamed in pain. It was just too much for him. His sweaty, grimy and bloody fingers couldn't maintain their hold and his hand lost its grip on the rung. He fell.

Adam realised what had happened with Slater's accompanying scream ringing in his ears. He instinctively grabbed out and caught Slater's arm as he fell past him, having the unfortunate effect of breaking it cleanly as his fall was arrested and the unlucky youth was slammed yet again into the side wall. Adam grunted with the effort. After another scream, Slater passed out. Adam privately debated the point of holding onto him.

Karl descended the rungs as quickly as he could; Adam grimly clung to his, the weight of the scrawny youth more of an inconvenient shopping bag than a broken man.

Philip had been escorted to the make-shift hospital area of the floor and was now being assisted by Dave. The two of them were recounting the events leading to his escape from the top floor and his narrow avoidance of electrocution. They had noticed each other around the building over the last few weeks but never had much more to say to each other before than the customary 'all right?' greeting that men do. Conversation flowed freely and Dave was looking more cheerful than he had all night. No one from the store had even acknowledged his presence as an employee before, let alone wanted to chat with him.

Philip's story about the missing top floor had wowed all listeners. He repeated it several times, getting braver and braver each time, embellishing the tale until it almost sounded as though he was a television action hero – as though he alone had kept the small room bolted on in the high winds.

Bert had been mobbed again by the young blonde girl who had called him a hero. She had clung yet again to his increasingly tatty shirt, and though pleased beyond measure of her appreciation, he knew he was a married man and eased her off gently – professing pain.

Finding her inner strength and resourcefulness, she quickly found a half-depleted bottle of natural spring water and a handkerchief to tenderly pat his cuts and bruises. Lara's tender hands proved adept at the nurturing while Sian watched with a half smile. Bert appreciated her efforts and for a few minutes, relaxed with less care about their situation. He tried to recall the last time Sandra had ever looked after him with as much concern... and couldn't. He relaxed.

Helen still seemed to be ignoring her husband, who was wandering aimlessly around the remaining stock fixtures under the pretence of looking for useful items. Helen still had the phone and showing displeasure at its inability to work; probably the storm affecting the signal. The old couple were asleep now, propped against the desk, holding each other. Sian had managed to ease Doreen's discomfort and they rested appreciatively.

Quarter to ten. Still no one had come for them. The stormy rain outside had not calmed, though they hadn't seen lightning for a while. The draft from the window was cooling. Bert decided to continue his search for an exit route and got up for a wander - when Andy caught up with him.

'What now?' Andy's cantankerous approach to liaison was never going to help any situation though this time he kept his hands to himself. Despite the fact that his tone still held antagonism, his body language suggested that he was more receptive now to the idea of trying to make his own fortune. He walked half a step behind, following the taller man towards the back of the store.

'I don't know! No way down that hatch. I'm gonna try the lifts now.' Bert was wishing he could close his eyes, click his heels together, and be whisked magically back to his beloved Tyrone. He wondered fleetingly if Sandra was home yet. She said she'd let Tyrone out for a toilet break when she got back.

'Look!' Andy searched for appropriate words. 'Well...erm...well done with... you know...' It had never been easy for Andy to praise any one, as well his wife and her daughter knew.

'Thanks!' Bert cut him off. Though he appreciated Andy's efforts at apology, in his heart he really couldn't be bothered with the man. He had other things on his mind. They still had to look at the lift shafts. Maybe they could get down them in some way. The logic in his mind told him that if they had been passable, the rescue services would have used them by now – but he wanted to see for himself.

A faint, distant, muffled but echoing scream surprised both the men. They looked around at the rest of the fifth floor group. No one there had heard it. It had come from ahead of them.

'Lift shaft!' said Andy.

They hurried to the metal doors in the corner of the room and after a tenuous prod, decided they needed something to pry them open with. Glancing around, his candle held aloft, Bert saw a long heavy metal knife sharpener with a black plastic handle hanging in its packaging from a hook. Snatching it down quickly - the candle on the floor - he ripped the cardboard from it and inserted it into the small gap between the frame and door causing a long scratch and a metal on metal scraping sound which put their teeth on edge.

Bert heaved on the handle, the frame providing a fulcrum, and the solid kitchen utensil urged the doors to move. Some success; the doors rattled a little. He pushed it in a little further then heaved against it again. Andy was at his shoulder, trying to get his fingers into the expanding gap. One more heave, and the door half opened with a shudder.

The sharpener discarded, both men forced the door back into the frame and looked into the new darkness beyond. Andy stooped and plucked the candle from where it lay and offered it into the space.

What they saw surprised them both. A pair of thin legs and feet was hanging just a little way in at head height. Baffled. They looked at each other. Bert took the candle with one hand, gripped the door frame with the other and peered in as far as he could. There was a body hanging just above him… and… was that someone else above him?

Bert struggled with the concept in his head. Could this be rescue services coming up, or people from above coming down?

'What the…?' Andy's head had joined him in the space to look up. Neither man could comprehend what they saw.

Adam made an instant decision and spoke.

'A little help please!' Without waiting for an answer, he swung Slater towards the two faces below him. Andy reached in to grab the youth, and after depositing the candle once again on the ground, was assisted by Bert in manhandling him onto the shop floor as Adam let go.

Slater slumped onto the ground with a crunch like a sack of potatoes. Though not heavy, his dead weight was enough to make both men pant from the effort. In the dim light they could see his arm twisted grotesquely at an odd angle, his clothes covered in drying mud, the smell of the body almost possibly a decaying corpse.

'Who is he?' voiced Andy.

'Is he dead?' added Bert.

'None of your business!' A tough new voice had joined them from behind – youthful but intimidating and ominous.

Swinging round, the two men were surprised to see two figures dressed totally in black joining them from the lift access. A big one and a smaller one. The smaller of the two was carrying a gun. It was pointed directly at them.

'Hay… hold on!' spoke Andy incredulously. 'What you doin' with that?'

'Just shut up!' Karl advanced on the group and both Bert and Andy took involuntary steps backwards, their hands rising in time honoured fashion. Behind them a commotion of sound started as the other fifth floorers realised that something was wrong and began to stand up. Andy started to sweat with worry in his designer clothes; the draft between the open doors of the lift to the broken windows was giving Bert a chill.

Karl waved the gun at the two men. 'Grab him and get over there!'

They did as they were told, half carrying, half dragging the unconscious youth towards the rest of the group – Karl and Adam followed slightly behind. Brenda held her hand to her mouth to prevent herself from screaming. Some of the younger girls clung together for mutual support. Dave and Philip slunk back, completely out of their depth. Karl was enjoying the effect he was having on these people. Adam was thinking about cutting his losses and getting back out. He caught Karl's arm and held him back.

'This isn't a good idea!' he whispered harshly behind his mask. 'Too many people. What we going to do with all of them?' His thumb jabbed towards the group who were now giving an involuntary able impression of a surprised hen house.

Karl thought for a moment whilst staring at the cowering group of shoppers before him; Slater lying prostrate and lifeless on the ground. He was enjoying the evening. It was barely ten o'clock. The

234

emergency services hadn't yet interrupted their progress and they were only minutes behind their own set schedule. However, with this number of people caught up in their scheme, the chances of a clean getaway were looking more remote... or...

'It's all right,' he whispered back, 'we've just got a few hostages now! Easy street, man. Let's grab the money.'

The hostages were now whispering with each other and drawing back into a group. Andy had the presence of mind to hold Helen's hand. She accepted his support gratefully, their previous differences forgotten in light of the current events.

'Quiet, you lot, or you'll get it!' Karl cocked the hand gun again to make his point, his finger stroking the trigger lovingly. As before in the lift, silence fell almost immediately. Karl loved the power he had when holding this weapon. More powerful than at any other time or moment in his life. Years of teenage oppression galloped to the front of his mind – middle aged white do-gooders – all trying to teach him, correct him, change him. And when he hadn't changed – getting rid of him – losing him – snubbing him. He'd love to vent his frustrations on some of these – several reminded him of previous prospective foster parents. 'An' stay still you!' Condescending assholes they had been.

'We're not armed robbers and hostage takers,' whispered back an annoyed Adam, dragging Karl's mind back to the reality of the situation, 'we're debt collectors. This is too much trouble – for not enough money!'

Karl knew he had a point. It wasn't the ideal situation, but then, he was proud of the fact that he could always roll with the punches – adapt to the situation and improvise and overcome. All he needed was complete discipline from these people and everything would be fine; Adam would come around to his point of view and finish the night's work.

'Slater says that the back up genny running the 'lectrics on the safe is in the corner of the stock room. Can't be hard to find, nor the safe in the security room. It's only just up there. I was almost there when this happened…' he motioned the unmoving body of Slater. 'How abou' it? I'll stay here an' keep this lot in check – you nip up an' see what you can see.' Karl got into his stride now. 'You'll be five minutes max! If it's no go, then we're out of here. What we lost?'

Adam debated the plan in his mind. A lot of effort had gone into getting all this ready and it would be a pity not to see it through. The trouble with the tram this morning… it was a shame about that nice girl… but besides Slater, no one still left alive had seen their faces. And like Karl said… five more minutes and they might come out on top.

'Yeah… OK!' Adam accepted his friend's plan, 'with one exception. I'm gonna need someone else to help up there with the safe!'

Slater had told them that the main store safe was the size of a large fridge, constructed as part of the steel frame of the security office and main frame of the entire top floor. Built as one, it negated any possibility of being moved. The heavy door was built to provide

236

main access to the front but with a smaller integral area accessible only with two keys through a separate door. The on-duty security guard carried one key, the current cash room supervisor carried the other. The main door was electronically controlled through the latest Japanese technology. But, as with most things, it was only as good as the people who fitted them. The London based company that had fitted this particular model tried desperately to only employ the most reputable and honest of people. Unfortunately, the internet is home to all the information anyone could want on any subject, from a school based report on King Henry the eighth – to – well to the latest Japanese technology. And all sold on by anyone wanting to make a little money on the side.

Despite being almost a complete idiot, Slater had done his homework well enough. Sheer terror at having to face Big Sam had been enough to focus his mind and find all the angles on every aspect of this job.

The safe took its power from the main local power supplier. If this failed for any reason, a back-up generator kicked in instantaneously to keep the flow constant. The moment the safe lost that power for any reason, a back up locking circuit engaged, using enough retained battery power, forcing backup bars to automatically brace the doors, which would render the unit inoperable for a time delay of seven days. However, for a split second, as the unit registered the loss of power and begun countermeasures to ensure its safety, it was powerless to prevent entry. It was like opening a fridge door – a fault undetected by its manufacturers, but found accidentally by its installers. It had to be a simultaneous act, shutting down the circuit and turning the main handle, otherwise it would be a massive, useless lump.

Slater groaned on the floor; his eyelids fluttered. 'Who do you wanna take? Slater's out of it! I've gotta stay here 'cos of this lot!'

Lara clung to Bert's shirt again, petrified. She had seen the violence and intimidation of gun crime whilst abroad with the peace corp, but somehow, back in Britain, in her local store, she never expected to see it. It seemed out of place and more frightening in some way.

Bert had sunk to the floor and pulled her with him. This was getting silly – what else could go wrong? Still – the pressure of Lara's warm body, rubbing against his own much colder one was quite welcome in the most fundamental way. Regardless of the situation, the fleeting thought that maybe Lara liked him crossed his mind again. Come on Bert! Stop it! I'm too old for her and I'm married! He shook his head, glanced across at his coat covering the deceased Eddie and wished that he hadn't been so dramatic with his earlier actions. The coat was more than a little threadbare but would have been very warm and appreciated at this moment in time... and who were this pair?

Behind them, Sian was still tending to the injured, determined that she wasn't going to let these two men in black distract her from her duty. Brenda's wound was weeping again. It needed changing.

Karl looked at her again as once more she moved to redress the wounds. 'I told you to stay still!' He spoke with a pause between each word. It sounded intimidating.

Sian regarded him defiantly for a second before ignoring him to continue her ministrations. She wouldn't be intimidated. Karl and Adam shared a look of disappointment before Karl fluidly raised the gun again.

The explosion of bullet from the barrel shocked everyone. The loud bang filled the small silent space, sparks, and Sian disappeared behind the cash desk almost instantly. Horrified gasps of anguish, and Bert tried to jump to her aid, while everyone else cowered again.

'Hey hero,' taunted Karl, 'sit back down or your girlfriend gets the next one!' He aimed the firearm directly at Lara's head and held it steady, the muzzle almost in her face, the barrel an ominous silver missile in the poor light, the open end huge from her perspective.

Lara whimpered and Bert quickly sank back to the ground an arm around her shoulders to quieten her. He didn't want to get anyone else killed. Just do was they wanted... for the moment.

'I'll take this one!' said Adam, indicating the seating Bert, quietly impressed by what he had seen of him for the last few minutes – he looked strong and able. 'You – come with me!'

'If he causes any problems, I'll pop her!' Karl was happy with the plan. Things were looking up already. Ten o'clock though. They'd better get a move on. 'You, hero, you're needed, get up!'

Bert took slowly to his feet, wishing to god that he could smack the smaller man right between the eyes. He assessed the possibility of success and decided against it. He looked handy with that gun – and proved it was real. Lara's trailing hand ran down his leg as he stood, and he grasped it momentarily, giving it a squeeze of confidence before making his full height.

'You ARE gonna help him! If you don't – I shoot her,' Karl indicated the trembling girl at his feet. 'Any funny business – I shoot her!' Getting into his stride, 'cause any problems – guess what – I shoot her!' Malicious now. Evil. Sneering.

'What about that poor girl you shot?' Bert found his voice and a little confidence egged him on. 'Is she dead? Do you care?'

'What's it to you?'

'Can't we check?' Bert's courage was momentary. 'I'm not going any where until she's helped!'

Adam grunted and showed Karl his wrist, conscious of the time.

'You go!' Karl indicated that Andy should be the one to check.

Andy gulped. His legs felt like jelly as he released his wife's hand. All eyes watched him as he left Helen's side, picked a lit candle from the floor and walked around the back of the till island where he stooped and lowered the light to the fallen girls face. There in the exact centre of her forehead was a neat round black hole; her eyes were closed and she was slumped unnaturally. A surprisingly minimal

240

amount of blood was seeping from the wound. He recoiled at the sight and gasped for breath, holding back a vomit.

'Well?' Adam was anxious to get going.

Andy shook his head. 'Dead!' he took a long slow breath. 'You bastard!' False confidence coursed through his veins. He steadied himself before his legs gave way beneath him.

Karl chuckled and bent down to Slater's body in order to remove the torch from his pocket. Popping it from its confines, he stood tall again and bragged... 'excellent shot, me! Here...' he tossed the light to Bert, who caught it unenthusiastically as Slater moaned again.

He prodded Slater's unresisting body with his foot and assessed his necessity now to the operation. The last thing Karl wanted now was someone there who knew who he was – waking up and blabbing it to all around. He loved the anonymity of the balaclava. Glancing up to check with Adam in the dark, a silent decision was made. Re-cocking the gun, he directed it at Slater's forehead. Slater moaned as consciousness slowly regained and his eyes flicked open. Karl fingered the trigger again.

'NO!' shouted Bert, but too late. For the second time the muzzle flashed and the room filled with sound. Slater's head lolled with the force, and he too was gone, spared at last the pain of living in a world where he had never quite fitted in. His body jerked and the head wound was obvious, even in the meagre light.

Brenda vomited, Lara screamed once, Sydney clutched Doreen to his chest and Helen fainted flat on the ground.

Karl was on a roll now. He'd only ever killed one other person before tonight, and truth be told, that was more by accident than design. Putting the frighteners on one young man for unpaid debts, he and Adam were 'chatting' with him on the top floor of the Phoenix Centre car park across town. The resulting unfortunate plunge backwards and crushing collision with the pavement below had not been part of the idea but the result of nerves and general clumsiness. Big Sam hadn't been happy that night... the guy still had a few payments to make, but after a night's sleep, relented with his displeasure. It was a result of that incident that they had been moved up to 'special operations' as Sam called them having shown a sadistic streak. Sian's murder was due to intense frustration, and now Karl decided that one more made no difference.

He ignored Andy's quick dash to his wife's side, but watched curiously as he knelt lovingly, covering her tenderly with as much of his body as he could. 'Well – get going – with him... or else!' he waved the gun at Lara again, illustrating his point quite effectively.

Bert sighed, knowing he had no choice in the matter, but promising himself the chance later. He walked towards Adam, whereupon Adam turned and strode quickly back towards the lift entry. Bert followed at a minimal distance, unsure of what was going to be expected of him. Behind him he heard a slight wail from Lara and a quick glance showed she was left on her knees, the man in black stood above her playing dangerously with the gun.

'What am I doin'?' he asked the larger man. He wanted to know what was expected of him. No doubt the purpose was not good.

For a start he was wearing a mask – that wasn't an indication that they were on an innocent mission. 'I want to know what's going on!'

'Climb!' One word and a very clear instruction – not a man to be messed with! Adam stood to one side and indicated that Bert should go first. As Bert passed into the lift opening, he weighed himself up against the hooded man. Roughly the same height, but this bloke was almost twice the width. His biceps were bulging under his black top, and he had an air of intimidation, if not any sign yet of a gun.

Grabbing the frame once again, Bert swung himself out to the ladder, stepped across onto a rung, and began to climb. Adam followed a few seconds later.

CHAPTER 17

Bert made good progress up the ladder. Adam was happier now that he wasn't nurse-maiding a weak fool from behind. Although he didn't have gloves, Bert skilfully avoided skinning his knuckles, and for the first time didn't miss his coat – the effort he put in warmed him; sweat dribbled slightly down the small of his back. He held the torch clenched in his teeth, so that the light danced slightly on the breezeblock walls as he ascended, scaring a couple of small spiders and showing up the soft but steady fall of dust from above. He tried not to cough; his mouth fixed open with the plastic handle of the torch, but considered his position in the situation.

He couldn't believe what he had just witnessed on the fifth floor. The other bloke must have been a nutcase – still – his friend here hadn't tried to stop him. Bert weighed his options. The guy below him hadn't yet shown a gun, but that didn't mean he didn't have one. The guy was obviously a good four stone heavier than he was, and most of that looked like muscle. He wouldn't stand a chance with hand-to-hand combat. He could try to kick him down the shaft from above, but it looked like he didn't have a problem with climbing, plus he was just a little too far out of reach... and if he failed, he could imagine his own destiny!

But then, Bert had a conscience that over rode everything. He could never dream of killing someone else, no matter what the provocation. An eye for an eye and all that. No way. He hadn't the nerve to do that. It was one thing protecting what was dear to him; it was another premeditating a guy's murder. He couldn't do it. Hit him, arrest him, tie him up – yes – n o problem – but not kill!

The thought of Lara's pleading face and soft downy lips came to mind. If that other bastard touched her, he would... he would... I would what? He wondered what it was exactly he could do. It was a powerless, depressing thought. The man killed a young woman because she wouldn't stand still. What hope would he have trying to assail him? No good! Whatever it was he was going to do, it would have to be planned and thought through first. He could just imagine being arrested and being sent to jail for hurting that bloke, whilst he was released and given compensation for his troubles.

The world today was all cock-eyed. You couldn't defend yourself any more. The law was an ass – it favoured all the wrong people. Shit! What am I gonna do? He'd better not hurt Lara.

Am I falling for Lara? Jesus no! I'm married.

Bert reached the top of the shaft. His head bumped the concrete top, and directing his little light around, could see where the strong metal cables disappeared through to the pulleys and mechanism above.

Adam came to a halt just below.

'What now?' asked Bert trying not to show how frightened he was, but instead display as much indifference as possible.

Adam didn't reply. He picked out the closed doorway that was the access to the seventh floor. A tiny lip was enough to rest one large foot on, the other remained on the rung of the ladder, and he spread-eagled himself across the void.

Bert looked down with interest, waiting for his moment.

A long metal 'jimmy' appeared from the confines of Adam's top; a quick, deft movement, and the doors slid noiselessly backwards. A rush of wind howled into the space like the scream of the devil, battering the two men mercilessly. Bert felt the chill as the rain assaulted Adam standing in the doorway.

Adam completed his step onto the seventh floor. 'Come on!' he said without passion, turning to face the oncoming hostage and ignoring the weather conditions.

Bert climbed back down the last few rungs and jumped into the open doorway. Adam's large arm grabbed him as it looked momentarily like he was going to fall backwards, and hauled him to safety. Bert rested his hands on his knees and breathed deeply, half pleased for the man's assistance, half annoyed that he had needed it. The force of the blowing gale battered him again, and he staggered slightly to get his back against something solid.

Adam removed a thin nylon line from another of his pockets and looped it around Bert's waist; tying it securely with a large knot. He neither offered explanation nor made apology as he tied the other end to himself.

Is this for safety, or is he worried about me running away? Bert accepted it without complaint. He could just imagine being blown from this place, and they were a long way up. He didn't mind being tied to this big bruiser.

They looked around them. By the lights of their torches, they looked upon a scene of complete devastation. Over five metres to their left they could see the security room, still intact. 'Everywhere' else was missing. There was no roof. The floor looked like it had caved in from the middle, taking everything else with it – like water in a sink down the plughole. Boxes of stock had been crushed; pallets ripped apart and lifted floorboards like jagged rocks against the night sky.

Bert longed for his coat again. The rain slowed slightly.

The beam of his light had less effect now, but directing it downwards, he could see the treachery of the conditions. He had to be careful where he stood... was that the next floor down through the steel girders? Bert crouched down and confirmed his suspicions. Wow! The steel frame of the building had remained intact, but the partition walls, floor and ceiling constructions had just dropped off, like a shirt from a clothes hanger. A builder, architect or someone was going to be in deep shit for this one. There was no way they had used approved fixings and materials. Why is everything done 'on the cheap' these days? Bloody cowboy builders!

Adam was beckoning him to follow.

They crept steadily along the broad girders, careful of the fact that they were glistening wet and very slippery. The wind buffeted them occasionally, and twice Bert almost slipped from the perch, before Adam's surprising grace saved him from falling with a powerful hand in the right place.

The lights picked out a bloody arm, extended from the debris below like King Arthur's sword from the lake. The wrist was limp;

fingernails had been torn from the flesh. It looked like they had died trying to scrabble from the rubble. Bert shuddered again, almost in tears.

Adam's torch showed the face of a girl caught amongst some bricks; her body no where to be seen. She looked almost peaceful. Serene. Tranquil! Calm after the chilling events of the evening. Her eyes were thankfully closed, her face showing no other sign of distress.

Dead! Of course!

Adam was as eager as Bert to check out their location. No words were spoken as the chilling horror of the scene was a surprise to both of the men... a peculiar fascination for them both – almost possibly the aftermath of a nuclear detonation.

A fluttering or wings near their heads surprised Bert. Whirling his arms like a windmill, he managed to stay upright then lashed out into the empty space, confused as to what had upset him. Flashing his torch around, Adam soon spotted the gulls that had found the scene of devastation and started sorting amongst the wreckage for anything edible. They seemed to have found a section of interest and were almost fighting each other for access to it. Both men hoped that it was someone's discarded meal or the site of a canteen area that they had found and that they weren't turning on anyone's dead body. The two men regarded the birds with distaste and calmed themselves.

Picking their way across the girders, the rain had very nearly ceased, even though the wind hadn't. Above them, huge black clouds hurtled across the sky as though late for an appointment. The moon almost peaked out, but then disappeared completely.

'Over there!' Adam was pointing to the space behind the security room, where a constant humming sound was omitting. He changed course and a gentle tug on the line encouraged Bert to do the same.

As they got closer, Bert could see that it was a generator like the one he had at work. A handy, compact device, it could run almost forever on a thimble full of fuel, providing a constant direct current supply. He used his for a little portable black-and-white television in his shed in the gardens at the rear of the community centre. After lunch everyday, he'd switch it on and watch the midday news and a stupid quiz show before returning to the endless chores expected of him. Useful devices. They wouldn't cope with anything too big though.

Luckily bolted to the frame, it had avoided joining the drain of concrete, steel and stock down the central staircase. The warmth was obvious with a tiny spiral of steam climbing from it into the cold air. This was obviously what the bigger man wanted to find, judging by the sudden interest he took in it. Bert went to kneel down and was knocked back with a quick swat.

'What?' he blurted out belligerently.

'Leave it!' replied Adam without embellishing on the reason. He himself was getting a touch nervous now. Despite the cold night air, he was sweating underneath his head covering and wanted to breathe deeply without the constant tickling of clinging hairs on the balaclava in his nose.

The rain stopped. The sudden change was enough that both men noticed. A steady dripping of water from the lift pulley wheel and motor onto the broad widths of the girders beneath were suddenly audible. Without having to squint now, Bert surveyed the landscape around them, instinctively looking for well known landmarks and features, the main roads drawn in street lighting.

He could hear the distant shouts and yells of people on the road below them. Sirens were obvious now, as was the flashing of warning lights. They obviously had spot lamps below – they roamed the side of the building and peaked at the top – searching for survivors and people at the windows. The whine of an extending crane arm could be heard. It wouldn't reach up this far – maybe third floor – possibly fourth.

It was oddly peaceful up here. Bert felt quiet. His lungs were at last breathing in the clean air after his time in the dusty lift shaft; he wasn't hearing the annoying constant undercurrent noise, bickering and complaining of his companions of the fifth floor and he was conscious of the fact that, though cold, he was actually feeling very excited. Not in a theme park ride – let's go again - sort of way, but just – different from normal routine sort of way. His adrenalin was racing. Bert was a little disgusted with himself.

Adam had stood up having satisfied himself as to how the generator worked. 'We need to go in there!' he said and inched his way back towards Bert.

Bert turned, and lost his footing on the beam. First one foot, then the other straight in the air like a cartoon clown slipping on a banana. He yelled and grabbed for the girder with both hands, his legs swinging like a pendulum beneath him; the torch falling away to rest on the mound of rubble and wreckage below.

Adam had the presence of mind to tug back on the connecting line between them. It was strong enough to hold a man, but he had to be quick – the pressure around his waist could cut him in two. He debated the expanse to the next floor down. Though the distance wasn't far, there was no way he could let this man go before the job was done. Making his decision, he jumped and sat on the beam opposite the troubled detainee, hauling in the line, hand over hand until the slack was taken up and Bert had steadied. He was panting. Reaching up, he whipped his balaclava off and tossed it to the side.

Bert was losing grip. The slippery wet steel girder was not giving him enough purchase. His heart was beating like a jack hammer, the adrenalin definitely pumping now. He deliberately swung twice to try and get a foothold. No good.

Tight lipped, Adam reached a hand towards him. 'Take my hand!' he said almost spitting with the awkwardness of the angles.

It was the first time Bert had heard him speak above a whisper. Looking at him in the poor light, the sweat was glistening on his face. Taking the strain on one arm, he reached his other hand slowly towards him, stretching, extending, elongating. Trying to maintain his balance, he was less than a few centimetres away.

'Jump!' Less than a command – not an instruction. Encouraging. Urging. More of a recommendation.

Bert took the chance. Swinging backwards, he pushed away with his arm and caught Adam's hand with his other hand, the meeting and meshing of limbs a relief for Bert. He had seen Eddie fall earlier, and didn't want the same fate.

Adam grunted as he bore the new weight. Perched on his girder, one fist gripping the rope, the other; Bert. He wished that he had never started this damn fool job. Determined to finish though, he heaved back and hauled Bert up to his level. Bert grasped the girder and felt Adam's hand gripping his belt at his rear, hauling him up to safety.

The two men sat there momentarily, wheezing and regaining composure. Bert had a grudging new respect for his captor. He couldn't be all bad, saving him like that. He looked across and saw Adam's face quite clearly.

'Come on!' It was time to get back to work. Adam stood and motioned that Bert should do the same; indicating the security office. 'You fall again,' he added, 'I'll let you go!'

Tight-lipped, Bert followed the big man to the open doorway and gratefully entered. At least this room had a proper floor – and chairs. Without asking or regarding his captor, Bert sank gratefully into one of the leather swivel chairs and rested his head back in the classic pose of exhaustion.

Adam ignored him and cast his light around the room, looking for the safe. It didn't take long to find; a massive structure taking up a good portion of the room, the opposite side of the wall to the generator. 'Right,' he thought, 'how am I gonna do this?'

Down below, things weren't going too well for the fifth floor survivors. Karl was trying to freak them out with his dubious sense of humour. No one appreciated the contrived effect of the constant twiddling of his beloved gun. If anything, instead of unnerving them, they had become very used to it and it had lost its power of control a little.

The girls had almost stopped blubbering, and Helen had regained consciousness; more than a little embarrassed of her faint earlier. The old dears had wrapped themselves up together and were steadfastly ignoring the annoying young man who kept twirling his gun about like an old Wild West gunslinger or James Bond wannabe. Age had its benefits. Sydney had seen a lot worse atrocities from the Japanese during the tail end of the Second World War, and there was no way some little upstart was going to terrorize him.

The two remaining store employees desperately tried to keep their heads down. Neither Dave nor Philip had the temerity to 'have a go'; the shock of how quickly Sian had been shot lingered in their minds. They had seen the woman in the canteen many times before now. A pleasant girl – never said a bad word about any one. It was a sin that she had gone.

Andy had taken his cue from Bert earlier. 'Can I cover the bodies over?' he asked, 'in deference to the dead! They're upsetting the girls!'

253

Karl thought a moment. His head was screaming to jam the gun into this man's mouth and pull the trigger. He felt a little manic... a lot more wired than ever before. He had killed and loved it at the time – but now – strangely unsatisfied. Mind you, Slater's body was in the way and unusually disturbing to him at the moment. Did he have a conscience perhaps? He smelt bad as well, very bad.

'Yeah, all right – move them... but...' he tapped his gun to make his point as though there was the remotest possibility that Andy could have forgotten it.

Glaring at him in the gloom, Andy started the odious task of removing Sian from the confines of her till area. Respectful, remorseful, and for the first time in his life – with reverence, Andy carried the girl and laid her carefully by Eddie's body. Pausing a second, he returned to collect the dead man. He had no idea who he was, but by his appearance and smell, he must have been extremely unfortunate to wind up with the two men in black.

Knowing that he was being watched, he dragged the second body across the room to join the others. As he did, the wind seemed to drop and the noise of the rain outside began to abate. Maybe now the emergency services will be able to get in – sort this clown out.

He stood and looked at the two new dead faces. He ought to cover them over. That's what Bert had done earlier, but he was unwilling to take his own coat off. It was designer. It was Jasper Conran. Expensive. He'd worked hard for that.

Making a decision, he sat the dead lad up instead, unzipped his coat, and under the watchful and wondering gaze of Karl, awkwardly removed the garment. Pleased at his resourcefulness, he lowered the youth and draped it over both the faces.

Helen watched him and shook her head softly. Only Andy would have done that. He'd never change for as long as he lived. He had once made them walk over a mile out of their way to avoid a small mud pit on a rambling journey and damaging his shoes, and what was it her father once said… never trust a man who spent longer in the bathroom than the woman!

She clutched the mobile phone carefully in the palm of her hand. Modern, it was small enough that their attacker hadn't noticed it. In fact, he was so preoccupied with watching her husband's activities that he had stopped whirling that nasty little toy around his head, and had settled down for a moment. She felt the keypad as it pressed into her lap. She felt for the buttons for recall and pressed them discretely. If only she could get a message out. Her daughter was resourceful. If she could let her know what had happened, then the police would be told… and then they'd come…

The determination she felt ran away with her. Determination that she would step up to the challenge, take the risk of him seeing and shooting her… take down this horrible little man… if only she could get through.

'What you doin'?'

Oh God. He'd seen her.

'I beg your pardon?' she decided to defend through attack.

'What you fiddlin' with?' Karl stood up from the cash desk and made his way over to the pile of boxes on which Helen sat, the gun twisting in his hand, his body language aggressive.

'Nothing!' she lied desperately, staring at his eyes as best she could in the dark.

'Yes you are!' Karl was almost there.

'Hey!' Andy added himself into the conversation. 'What's going on?'

Karl twisted his head to see what the other man was doing. Helen took the opportunity to drop the phone between her legs, where it fell down between two boxes, hit the buckled lid of a box on the next layer down and came to rest out of sight.

'Shut your mouth!' he pointed the gun straight at the advancing Andy, who immediately stopped where he was. Karl turned back to Helen, grabbed her wrist and hauled her forwards off the stock and threw her onto the floor in front of him.

Nothing there. Karl flicked his head back and forth in the waning candle light but couldn't see anything. 'I don' know what you're up to, but that was your las' warning. Next time... *bang*!' He accompanied this last shouted word with a forward jab of the gun to within a hair's breadth of Helen's face.

'Please don't hurt me!' she countered, undaunted, 'I'll do anything you say! Just don't shoot us!'

'Yeah?' smirked Karl, 'well, I just might...' and as Helen started to get up... 'stay where you are!'

Helen sat up properly and crossed her legs. Speaking very clearly, she said, 'the police will come for you! Then you'll pay for those poor people's murder! What are you anyway – a thief?'

'Shut up! It's none of your business.'

Helen decided she had pushed far enough. She bit her tongue and sucked back in her lip. Andy joined her, moving very slowly and deliberately, sitting carefully beside her, his arm around her back.

Karl grunted and spun round to view the activities of his other charges. 'Come on Adam!' he thought. He'd had enough now and wondered how far the authorities had got in their rescue. Their plan had been based on causing enough confusion that no one would realise that a burglary was taking place – a chance to slip in and out without recognition. The tram had made more of a spectacular crash than they had expected. It must have been going faster than Huggins had originally guessed at before the brakes were blown. There must have been people killed. Karl didn't fancy meeting the police or taking any responsibility for his endeavours tonight.

Things were not looking good for Adam and Karl. They were running out of time. No plan ever went exactly to plan, but it was looking less and less likely that they could be in and out of Lexington's before being discovered. It was looking very good for the emergency services competing against the elements outside. The rain had ceased and the third unit were making excellent headway clearing the flooding from the roads around Lexington building – thus making everyone's job a lot easier. Colleen McLaughlin watched gratefully as the water level receded quickly, though was soon dismayed when she saw the remaining filth strewn across the streets that the tide left and realised that she'd eventually have to cross through it to her car.

Behind her, two crane units were now fetching and carrying assorted fire crew to the second and third floors, ferrying survivors down to safety - much to the relief of the Incident Commander, who had promised swift resolution to the presented problems of the evening. Everyone was hoping that the worst of the thunderstorm was now over and the previously hampered efforts could redouble. Other fire crews from across the region were gradually joining the rescue mission

A police investigation team were practically crawling over the distressed tram in an effort to find clues as to the cause of the accident. Colleen was able to report matter-of-factly that foul play was suspected with the discovered residue of an unknown device located on the axle. No further details were as yet forthcoming. The information soon formed part of the never-ending loop played to keep the local viewers up-to-date, dressed up with state-of-the-art computer graphics provided by the station... detailing the extent of the damage through the crumple zone of the trams front end. The crash investigation team had established that the vehicle had been travelling at an approximate speed of forty-five miles an hour at the time of impact, the score marks across the road's tarmac testament to the weight of the tram on unfamiliar ground.

Efforts to clear the ground floor had since proved ineffectual. John Marshall, on Central TV, described the endeavour as similar to clearing the bottom rocks from a landslip – as soon as one is removed, it causes a fresh cascade from the top. The problem this evening was that there were bodies caught up in the rocks; moving them was risking the chance that any were still alive. However, if the stones could be taken from the top of the pile, they could be removed safely without the cascade effect.

National television took the story as a main headline, playing Marshall's report to millions of people. Neither Irene Carlson, nor Colleen McLaughlin managed to make the leap to national prominence; both of their previous contributions being restated by other presenters.

Monk's team was attempting to make entry into each of the lower floors on an individual basis quite successfully. Bodies were gradually being extracted from obvious resting places, but the higher floors were still eluding them except through the newly discovered, quite intact, lift shaft. With much restrained excitement, Hughes, Johnson and Smith were making slow progress towards the fifth floor.

Sandra returned to consciousness hearing a loud banging sound. She stirred in her bonds and wriggled angrily. The banging happened again; a metallic, popping sound – tedious but comforting in equal measure.

'Mmm... mmm!' There was little else that could come from her mouth due to the old sock nestling against her tongue. Indeed, she felt more than a little nauseous and panicky as she opened her eyes and the prior events of the evening flooded back to her.

The banging stopped, but a muffled voice could be heard talking. Oh please... please get me out of here!' She kicked her legs violently, but without much success. She smelt turpentine spirit, paint and glue on the cloth that covered her body. A particularly deep inhalation made her feel queasy again, and her eyelids fluttered again as the conglomerate of smells had a narcotic effect on her vital signs.

Somebody was trying the handles of the van. The noise echoed eerily. Who was it? Those nasty men back again? Or could it be the police?

'Mmmmmm... mmmmm!' More aggravated now. 'Please let them hear me!' she pleaded to her subconscious. She kicked again as hard as she could and tried to move her arms. A stab of pain coursed up her leg from her ankle, reminding her in a flash of excruciating pain that she had twisted it on that step earlier. Her hands were bound together behind her back and she was lying on her front. It brought to her mind an image of a banquet pig lying on a platter with an apple in its mouth.

She tried to roll over.

Sandra made it a little way before slumping back; breathing heavily with the effort. She tried again, bringing her knees to her chest for extra balance. This had the unfortunate effect of banging her head against the toolbox, right on the sore created earlier.

The effort was too much for her at this time, her brain decided to shut down again in an attempt at self-preservation. She fainted where she lay.

Outside, the van had been found by a patrolling police officer. The flood levels had decreased and the rain ceased. This meant that there was a little more desire to venture out from the protection of the cars in order to assist with the operation. The officer in question, PC 5341 Preece, had just begun the ten till six shift. Invigorated by the ongoing incident of national concern, he had arrived at Lexington's with fresh eyes and attitude towards the occurrence. Finding the van sat at the kerb, he walked around it slowly.

No sign of anyone around it. The fire crews had been around here earlier and dismissed the possibility of using the rear of the building due to its architecture. He glanced up at the blank windowless wall that stretched up into the sky.

'5341 to control. PNC check please!'

Static momentarily. 'Control here... go ahead.'

'Yeah, we have a high-top Mercedes van parked illegally. Registration number: Sierra, November, fifty three, Oscar, Bravo, Whisky. Please advise!' Preece bent down and checked the tyres. All good! He banged on the side of the van. Sometimes you got the 'bonkers' in the funniest places – they'd find alleyways and car parks. Sometimes they did it in more public places. To be honest, he never minded the bonkers. Sometimes it was funny – the things he had seen whilst moving them on.

'One moment!'

He banged on the back door and tried to peer in through the window. No good. It had that black film across the glass that reflected and preserved the anonymity of the contents. He tried the door handle. Locked! It pinged back down as he released it. The markings on the floor denoted a loading bay only. It didn't look like it was unloading. Well... it couldn't be to Lexington's. Maybe it was to the Phoenix Centre opposite. He twisted to look around as control came back to him.

'That registration mark is to a grey Mercedes 230L van belonging to a Mr. Ernest Noakes of Perton, Wolverhampton. It was reported stolen late last night after ten pm.'

'Yeah! We've got it. It's been abandoned behind the Lexington building in Wolverhampton.' Result! He'd only been on shift twenty something minutes and already he'd recovered a stolen wagon. Preece wandered around to the side door and tried that handle too.

This time there was the welcoming click as the handle popped outwards, releasing the lock mechanism. Blimey. He heaved on the sliding door which obligingly slid back on its runner. Preece peered inside; plucking his standard issue torch from the belt around his waist. The torch was large, holding four of the bigger batteries. It was designed to be on the big side in case it had to be used as an impromptu cosh for any reason. The added benefit was the powerful beam of light it produced. Immensely pleased with himself, he hummed softly as he flashed it around the inside of the van – picking out the several tool boxes, piping and assorted building supplies. Why oh why did they leave stuff in the back of their van? The sign on the back was supposed to be a deterrent. If they still left their apparatus in there, why would any one take any notice of the signs?

His light picked out a pile of rags directly before him. A fleeting pass of the light up and down, then he was out of the van and sliding the door closed.

Mr. Noakes was having an early night and lying in bed with his wife at his side, eagerly watching the events of the evening on his wall-mounted television, received the knock on the door with a mixture of relief and annoyance. They'd found his van; why couldn't they have just phoned? Why couldn't he just collect it? Apparently it was parked near to a suspected crime scene, and they'd have to check it out before he could recover it. At least he didn't have to find a lift down to Wolverhampton on one of the worst nights for weather he had known for a while, but he could have done with his stuff back. As self-employed, the rental on other transport and tools were metaphorically killing him! He made the officer a cup of tea and made a statement on the time of the theft. He couldn't help them much, but they didn't complain when a thought struck him and he eagerly flicked through the terrestrial channels on the kitchen television in case an alternative broadcast showed his vehicle near the scene of the devastation.

Karl stood at the lift entry on the fifth floor, peering down cautiously. He could hear the sounds of climbing far below him. The flashing of lights betrayed the firemen's progress up the shaft, and despite his outward calm exposure, underneath he was getting more than a little tense. Where was Adam? Come on, man. Get the dough and let's get outta here!

The plan was to retrieve the loot, remove their masks and join the thronging crowd of shoppers leaving the store as innocent bystanders caught up in the melee of noise and confusion. If that was still to happen, they'd have to get out before the fifth floor was reached... unless he started making preparations now.

Adam regarded the safe dubiously. The noise of the generator the other side of the wall was obvious above the gradually lowering howl of the wind. He decided to tell Bert why he had been brought here.

He turned and stared at Bert in the gloom, propping himself on the desk and watching the older man swivelling comfortably in the metal and leather security office chair. 'I need you to do something for me!' he began. 'I need you to shut the generator down outside when I tell you to!'

'Why should I?' Bert was feeling better and more than a little belligerent with his feet on firm ground and now having seen the man's face, he felt more comfortable with him.

'Look...' Adam appreciated his position and contemplated which approach he should take. Should he make threats and promise pain – should he just expect him to help using his own physical intimidation – or should he try reasoning with him... explain the situation and ask him to help with the promise of a quick resolution. He appreciated what Bert could be thinking – he had seen Karl kill two people in cold blood and would be worrying about his own safety. But Adam had already stopped three other killings tonight, and despite the life he had chosen, he didn't really have the stomach for death. Why couldn't people just do what they were told? Life would be so much easier for everyone? 'We're only here for the money. Nothing else. I don't want anyone to get hurt? Especially you!' He thought he'd throw in a menace... it wouldn't hurt to let this man know what could happen!

'What if I don't want to help you?' Bert was feeling angry. 'You killed two people. What's to stop you killing me next?'

'HE killed two people. You don't understand. If it wasn't for me, there'd have been a lot more tonight. Unless you help me, there is no way you're gonna get out of here alive.' This last sentence was delivered an octave quieter than the rest. There was no note of pleading however. Adam had never had to implore before, and wasn't about to start. 'Just do it and we can all go home... I promise!'

Bert considered his options. Shutting the generator down meant that he'd have to be outside the security office and the other side of the wall to this hulk. No doubt shutting this thing down was essential to the plan of attack on this safe, and this man would be busy temporarily with it. It would give him the necessary time to make a head-start on escaping. He reckoned that he could make it down past the fifth floor quite quickly. If he didn't, then this brute would only have to shout and the bastard below would be waiting for him. If he hid, then he'd be saving his own skin, but that nice Lara girl would probably get 'it'. What to do? What to do? If he messed him around and took his time, it would give the rescue services longer to get in and find them! That would mean a hostage stand-off on the floor below, which would again mean problems for those guys! If he helped him, then he might honour the promises and everyone would carry on living quite nicely. Do I have any other real option? No!

'OK!' he returned, 'what do I do? Just switch it off at the main switch!' He righted the chair and took to his feet, much to Adam's relief. He'd wait for his moment later.

'Yeah. Good man. Go back 'round to it and wait for my shout!' Adam detached the rope from between them, then watched the man inching his way back along the cats-cradle of girders with a little apprehension, but a great deal of optimism. Sensible bloke! They should be gone in a few moments. He watched and flashed his torch to illuminate his way, even holding his breath for a second as it looked like he lost balance, and teetered on the edge of falling to the pile of rubble far below them. A bead of moisture formed on his brow regardless of the cool wind now blowing around as he waited for Bert to find his way back around.

Adam returned to the safe as Bert achieved his goal.

'You there, man?' shouted Adam loudly.

A fleeting, 'yeah' came back – carried badly by the wind.

Adam grasped the handle with both hands and hauled himself backwards on it. He didn't know what to expect now. This would have been Slater's job if he'd made it this far. He would have much preferred standing over him, hefting an iron bar for effect, scaring the *bejesus* out of him, rather than doing the task for himself. He braced himself and shouted, 'OK!' as loud as he could.

The other side of the wall, Bert flicked the power switch sat on the control panel. The generator chugged slightly as it registered the sudden loss of power, then ground to a halt, slightly backfiring and spluttering like a small engine, light weight motor scooter that had been immersed in water.

Adam felt the resistance on the handle decrease almost immediately. The lever rotated freely and Adam could hear the braces inside retract. Success. Bloody hell! That was one – very major flaw in the design. He could hear a slight whining noise as the backup circuit came fruitlessly to life and attempt to lock itself down for seven days. Hah! Not this time pal! The extremely heavy steel door wheezed open on its integral hinges and Adam flashed his light to reveal the glorious contents within.

Outside, Bert returned to the office slowly along the girder. He'd done what had been asked of him. Surely to god now - he and his colleagues would be left alone. He gratefully reached the doorframe and regarded Adam on his knees before the safe.

A thin, medium sized leather bag had now been retrieved from the voluminous folds of his jacket. Adam scooped the elastic bound bundles of notes from the many metal shelves in the safe into the bottom of the bag. Piles and piles of them. Twenties and tens mostly. A few piles of fifties and a few of fives. But mostly twenties. All bundled up into five hundred pound wads. Sweet. Sam would be pleased. They splattered down, almost like a waterfall, filling the leather container quite quickly, settling haphazardly in their new dwelling. It seemed like hundreds of them.

Then he looked at the many bags of small change.

All businesses need a float. This was a selection of change that was put into the tills each morning to start the day off. The float value was different in every store. Most stores had a round number of pounds to help the cashier count up, such as twenty, thirty, forty or fifty, depending on the area and type of stock. A shop selling sweets and cigarettes might need a lot of smaller change, whereas a clothing store selling stock of high value would have more notes in the till and less fiddly coins. People shopping in clothing stores would be more likely to pay by credit card than by hard cash. Shopping early morning for a pack of Benson and a Mars Bar, statistically you were more likely to pay by a five pound note and therefore need a handful of change.

A float could never be looked upon as store takings. It was removed from the till on cash up ready for the next day's opening. Only the remaining money was classified as takings. Adam, despite being a youthful twenty-eight, remembered life when credit cards were not the preferred medium of payment. It now meant that robbing a store was not as lucrative as it once was.

Still... the float was cash and possibly worth taking. There were several shelves holding large thick plastic bags, all unopened, full of coinage. He dragged a couple out, looking for the pounds. He found four bags. That was another two grand, and not too heavy to carry either. He ignored the smaller coins and dropped these heavier bags on top of the bundles of notes. He stood up. Not a bad haul. Maybe a hundred and eighty grand in total... possibly a bit more. At least it had made the evening worth while. He felt the weight of the leather holdall. Yeah, no problem! He could manage that OK. Slater wouldn't have been able to carry it. Wimp! Ideally he would have wanted two bags to carry it all surreptitiously. When he got back to Karl, maybe they'd divide it into an extra case?

Okay then. It was time to get out.

Adam strode to the door and past the watching Bert without even a sideways glance. Bert wasn't useful anymore. If he had any sense, he'd stay here and be rescued later. Yes, he had seen his face, but it was dark and Adam had never had a police record. Once he vanished, the only description that the police would have would be... a large black bloke with shaven head. Mmm. Not too many of them around! Hah! He didn't intend breaking his promise though!

Bert watched the larger man work his way back along the beams to the waiting lift entrance with a slight puzzlement. Fair enough. He hadn't been hurt in anyway, but the feeling of outrage was too great. He wanted his chance to pay them back for Sian. As he disappeared into the depths of the shaft, Bert crept after him.

The hostages on the fifth floor had huddled into a group facing away from the lift shaft. The crazy man waving a gun had told them that if he saw them turn, he'd shoot them from where he stood... which was at the lift entrance, watching the progress of the advancing team of firemen. He daren't fire now. There was no way that the services wouldn't hear it – and he didn't want those sort of problems – at least not whilst trapped up here! His victims were totally unaware of this as they sat cuddling their knees, hands held together with an abundance of plastic cable ties taken from the builder's van. The position brought back a few unpleasant memories for Sydney of the Japanese prisoner of war camp in which he languished for two months during 1945.

Lara was not with them. She was currently kneeling on the floor beside Karl, one of his gloved hands covering her mouth, the other; painfully half gripping her hair, the gun barrel pressing harshly into her scalp. Her face was screwed up with pain, but she daren't cry out. The man was agitated and obviously quite psychotic. She hung there – powerless to help herself.

There was a noise from above. Someone was coming. Something was banging and scraping the side walls. Karl hoped it was his friend… if it was; he'd made good time. His fingers tightened on Lara's hair making her yelp.

'Adam. Is that you?' Karl whispered up into the darkness – gun ready in case of problems but confident of the reply.

'Names!' came the curt reply in admonishment. Sod it. They had to get going. 'Are you ready to go?'

'Yup! Did you get it?' Important questions first.

'Yeah!' A grunted answer; the effort of climbing with the bag hanging from his back trying to pull him from the wall was proving a little wearing (though he'd never admit it out loud).

'Did you sort him out… after?' That was the loose end that Karl was most worried about. The rest of the group had been sorted already.

'Don't worry about it!' was the growled reply.

Adam reached Karl at the door. Releasing Lara, the two men gripped hands in greeting, and the bag was held up to the light of a glowing candle. Both smiled. Lara's eyes were squeezed tightly shut as she desperately tried to shrink away from them.

'Let's get the hell outta here! I've one last thing to say to this lot.' Karl swiped Lara on her shoulder blade, knocking her flat to the ground and creating another squeal of pain. Happy, he almost jogged back to the group, his feet squelching slightly on the damp dirty floor and stood behind them.

'We're going now. But just to make you aware… we're taking someone with us. If you move, scream, shout, or do anything else… we're gonna shoot her – and I am sure you know I'm capable. I

271

hope you understand!' He clicked the hammer back again on the weapon. The point had been made. No-one looked up.

Joining Adam at the doorway, he heaved Lara up and almost bodily threw her into the space ahead, watching for a second as she clawed desperately for the frame to save from falling. As she stood there, obviously petrified, Karl leaned over and put his mouth to her ear. 'You're comin' with us. Don't scream, or say a bloody word... otherwise...' He left the implication hanging on his whispered words.

Karl went first, Lara was pushed next, and Adam brought up the rear. They started down the rungs of the ladder; the men a lot happier this time.

Adam was getting used to the bag by now. More than a little proficient at being the normal pack horse for the duo, he hefted the bag quite easily, though began to wish he hadn't packed the coinage.

Lara was making slow progress on the rungs. Her heels were proving cumbersome, but using tiptoes to descend, it wasn't so bad. She had scraped her hands a couple of times and was getting more than a little concerned for her nails; though the magnitude of these thoughts were completely eclipsed by the terror that these two bruisers inspired.

Karl had stuck the gun back into the waist band of his trousers and was clambering down quite easily. He could see the approaching lights of the fire officers working on the fourth floor and was getting himself ready to speak. In preparation, he whipped his balaclava off and pushed it deep into his pockets, rustling his hair to recover his appearance.

'Are you all right up there?' Hughes could hear the approaching noise of people from above whilst stood in the doorway to the fourth floor. The rustling of his protective jacket against the multitude of equipment as he moved was quite deafening together with the conversation of his men with the inhabitants important, but he could definitely hear the sound of feet on the rungs and heavy breathing.

'Yeah!' Karl spoke up in reply. 'There's three of us. Are you the police? Or fire? Oh thank god. We thought we'd be up here for ever! We were so scared. We didn't know what to do!'

'Don't worry, son!' returned Hughes. 'You'll be all right!'

'I've got my sister here. She's petrified and I think she's gonna be sick.' Karl reached the fourth floor access and stepped off to fill the doorway. Hughes took a small step backwards to accommodate him. 'Can we keep going down, we've gotta get out!'

Adam motioned that Lara should keep moving. Petrified, she did as she was told with Adam silently urging her on; his feet on rungs only just vacated by her hands an encouragement.

Karl kept one hand on the gun grip just in case of problems as Hughes tried to peer around his frame.

'Thanks, man! She's gotta get out. We were on the stockroom floor and got caught. Boy, the mess up there!' Karl continued to gabble, almost hopping from one foot to another as though in panic. 'Managed to get the lift doors open... and come down! Boy, were we scared. Thank god you guys are here! Which floor would be best to get out from?'

273

'Yeah...' Hughes shook his head. His work colleagues were helping assist the injured behind him, and there was a chance to possibly save a wounded woman trapped between the remnants of the escalator and a particularly large piece of masonry. He hadn't the time for this conversation. 'Err... yeah... second floor.' His mind was on too many things at once; his head twisting like a Meer cat to keep his eye on his colleagues; the bunch of downcast shoppers; an obvious dead body and now this able bodied lad from a higher floor. 'Second floor! There's an evacuation slide bein' set up from there... keep goin' down if you're all right with the ladder... you'll see the exit. Hey...'

Behind him, a dubiously supported beam was teetering precariously above Johnson as he hefted another lintel. Shouting over his shoulder, 'just keep going if you can!' he scrambled to help his friends free the injured woman.

Karl watched him with a rye smile. Excellent! Looking left, he saw the top of Adam's head disappearing from view. He released the gun and jumped back to the ladder, confidence overflowing like too much water in a cup. He clambered down, passing Adam who swung to one side to allow his descent and came to Lara.

Hands clawing, gloriously happy, he scaled down past her and continued as fast as he could to the second floor. There was no further resistance. A quick check on his watch; it was nearly half past ten. They'd be out in time for last orders. Ditch the broad in a moment when they knew they were clear and they'd be gone.

CHAPTER 19 *Valour*

Despite the recommendations to the contrary, Bert had not stayed where he was. Breathing deeply, and knowing deep in his heart that it was a very bad idea, he followed the larger man down the lift shaft – desperate not to be seen. Shivering, and wishing he had retained his coat, he crept down the shaft as quickly as he dared, watching all the time for the weak light of the torch that could possibly be looking for him. Though his hands were painfully cold, he knew he couldn't just stay on the top floor and wait for the services. The feeling of hate for the gunman welled within him like a geyser. He felt guilty – thinking he could have done more to prevent the murders earlier. He'd make sure that they were both arrested.

As he neared the fifth floor, he heard the men climbing back onto the rungs. He pressed himself into the wall as far as he could, desperate not to be seen. The wind howled above him across the lift opening at the roof, making a noise like a child blowing across the top of a glass bottle – only more frightening.

His feet grazed the breezeblock surface of the wall causing a little cascade of dust and particles which clattered on the metal rungs and disappeared down the shaft. Bert held his breath and pressed himself into the wall, hugging the ladder for all he was worth, praying fervently for luck.

Bert was lucky. They were only looking down the shaft now. A cautious glance down proved he had got away with it. No evidence of searchlights being directed upwards. Who was that with them? It looked like a girl – he could see long hair glinting vaguely in the poor light. Was it… was it Lara? Bastards! No! No way are you two getting away now. He considered shouting (instinctive obscenities coming to mind) and making his move… No! Better not. They might throw the girl from the ladder, and he himself was almost a sitting duck up here – neither of them would stand a chance.

From his vantage point he watched them climbing down quickly, and followed discretely taking the utmost care to be as quiet as possible. Passing the fifth floor, he quickly glanced in to see what he could. He could distinguish the group huddled around a candle as though cowboys around a campfire. Best leave them for the moment. They were safe enough without the gun being waved around their heads. Lara was more important now.

Passing the fourth floor, a quick look through the damaged lift doors confirmed that the rescue services had got that far up the building – the yellow hats obvious even from this distance. He scrambled down past the opening quickly. He could hear his quarry below him. They had reached the lift… heavy thuds as the first man landed on the roof… then a vague clip clop of heels a few moments later. Was that a scream from a woman? It didn't sound like Lara's voice! After waiting a frustratingly reasonable amount of time, Bert landed more quietly on the same roof and peered cautiously in through the trap door opening. In the gloom he could make out a body lying on the floor and a softly wailing woman in the corner… but no one else. He dropped silently into the compartment next to the man's body much to the surprise of the woman who became instantly silent. He wobbled on the edge of the trap in the floor, suddenly aware of it and his heart beating even more rapidly than before.

'Shhh,' hissed Bert softly. 'Don't worry! Stay where you are… and stay quiet!'

He knelt as low as he could to the man's body. Feeling around he found a damp pool around the man… an odd smell assaulted his nostrils. It took him a moment to identify that the odour was blood. Brushing his fingers further, he felt the naked chest – trailed his fingers up to the neck and found the pulse still throbbing faintly. Relief. At least he wasn't dead – needed medical attention though. He wouldn't have put it past that one bloke to have killed him… a bit 'gun happy' he was. 'You OK?' he asked as softly as he could.

'Yes!' She replied in an extremely small and timid voice. She could tell that this man wasn't there to hurt her – maybe even help her. Not like the other two who had just passed through dragging that girl – she wondered briefly who she was and why she was being forced to climb down… they had practically dragged her though the lift with little regard for her health and ability.

Her main concern, however, was her almost naked beau who hadn't moved for the last half an hour, regardless of her cuddling him tight and shaking him softly – though this was more in loving fear for her own safety than anything else. 'Is he all right?' she motioned unseen in the darkness.

'He's fine! Stay quiet. I'll send someone for you!' Turning away, Bert knelt on the edge of the second hole and again peered down to check if he could proceed. Below him he could see the bobbing lights of the torches, and just about make out the vaguely audible whimpering cries of Lara.

Despite being extremely aware of the pitch black shaft below him, the draft whipping around his neck and the rising panic he felt in his chest, Bert had the courage to continue. He hung his legs through the hole – twisted and gripped the lip before breathing deeply and launching himself down. Swinging slightly from the effort, he felt around for the ladder with one hand... his second grasp finding the steel He pulled himself to safety with a sense of extreme relief.

No rest. Got to keep going!

Hugging the ladder appreciatively and counting his blessings in silence, he followed on again at a safe distance. They were just reaching the ground below him. He hung still for a moment and stared into the gloom, trying to make out the shapes below him.

Adam had a grudging respect for the girl. All right, they were going down which was easier than up, but she had coped better with the distance than Slater had... and in heels. She had made the descent in record time. She was still crying though. He couldn't wait to get rid of her.

He dropped the bag on the floor and reached for the mini crank handle high up on the wall to retract the roller shutter. Karl was darting about quite happily like a big kid given ice cream, hefting the

278

weight of the bag and feeling the sides. Conversation was minimal; they didn't know who was outside yet.

With a yielding crunch, the shutters began their slow trip back up. Lara sank to the dirty ground and prayed for salvation. Her hands were aching, as were her calf muscles – emotionally a complete wreck, she wanted the peace of her family home instead being sat here, frantic with concern.

The shutters reached half way and gradually revealed the handles held by the cable ties. Adam pulled out his pocket knife and slit the plastic to free them. He eased the doors slightly open and peered through the gap, looking for anyone beyond.

'Shall we take her?' Karl hissed from behind him.

'There's a copper out here. He's stood over there by the van. He's on his own and talking on the radio.' Adam tried to alter his perspective, eager not to mess things up now at this late stage.

'What do you reckon then?' Karl peered over his shoulder, desperate to make his own decision, but needing the comfort of Adams's concurrence. Privately he found solace and reassurance in the big man's company – never let on to him though – and actually over compensated with his attitude sometimes.

Option one. Stagger out and pretend to be confused and dazed customers who had found a way out of the store through the back. Hopefully, they could bluster their way into the confusion at the front of the building and away. Option two. Fling open the doors and leg it as fast as they could before he realised what had happened.

They'd have to be quick whatever they chose. Where there was one copper, others were sure to follow.

Option three. Surprise the single constable with a blow to the head and then leg it. Leave the van where it was and forget about it... it had served its purpose. Sizing him up, Adam didn't expect much of a fight from him. The guy looked miserable enough to collapse in a stiff wind. All he had to do was get close enough...

Either way, the girl could either be a nuisance and in the way or a possible reason for a quick exit in the same manner as before on the fourth floor.

'We'll go out calmly!' Adam had made up his mind. Carrying this bag would have prevented him running easily, but running could always stay a possibility. He knew the alleyways and streets of Wolverhampton better than anyone. Once he was out and with a little head start, he could disappear completely. Apart from the constable, the street looked deserted. That was good!

Karl nodded agreeably and turned back to Lara. 'You're coming with us, babe! But quietly! Any screaming... I'll shoot you... and then... I'll shoot him out there! D'yer understand that'd be your fault?'

Lara nodded her head, tears still streaming down her face, though feeling a little cried out by now. She felt punch drunk by the events of evening and the effort of climbing with the constant fear of falling or being shot for her troubles. She had noticed his features now that the balaclava was off and was disgusted that he was only a youngish lad – not much older than she was. She hadn't really known what to expect from his earlier characteristic behaviour, but hoped that his face would give her an insight into his psyche. All she got though was that she wouldn't trust him – what was it her mother had once said...? Never trust a man with his eyes too close together! Rubbish at the time... but...never a truer word spoken – and all that!

Adam was taking his black sweater off showing that beneath was a shoulder pocket pouch hanging down the side of his torso. He slipped that off also and pushed both into his money bag. His grey shirt below was stretched tautly across his powerfully built chest prompting a quick double take from Lara. The new appearance was now a lot less threatening however. He wanted to remove the look of the criminal, plus, if he had to run, he'd feel cooler without the thick jumper. He had to cater for contingencies.

Blowing his cheeks out momentarily, Adam swung the heavy steel door open and faked a mild limp as he exited. 'Officer... officer...' he called loudly in a needy voice, his normal dulcet tones raising a few octaves to feign distress.

PC Preece had just completed a slow walk to the front of the building and back. Mildly bored now and under instructions to monitor the van for a few moments until more crime investigation could be mobilised, he was feeling the cold and unfortunately had just stepped in one of the remaining puddles down the side street, which had uncomfortably soaked his left foot and annoyed him considerably. He heard the cry and turned towards the noise.

'Please officer...help us!' Adam neared his target, closing the gap between them quickly despite the false limp. Behind him, Karl pushed the unresisting Lara out, his gun pushed painfully into the small of her back; mimicking his partners approach.

Preece didn't know where to look, but made a couple of steps forward in his confusion before twisting the radio that was hanging on his shoulder, to his mouth... 'PC 5341 Preece to control... over!'

The limping Adam was a step away from him. Karl and Lara were cowed a few steps behind, huddled together as though supporting each other. Lara was aware of her captor's increased and erratic breathing pattern. Shit! No! He was hyperventilating! His hand was shaking against her back. Adam was aware of the change in his friend and twisted to see what was going on.

Preece stopped talking and looked curiously at the second man. Was he all right? What was he doing? Was he holding something behind that girl? He flicked his gaze back to the first man who he now noticed carrying a ballooning bag. Had he brought his shopping out with him? That was unusual. He had seen people come out of situations like this barely carrying their coat, let alone their luggage.

'Control here. Go ahead!' The metallic voice was crystal clear in the quiet of the street, but didn't quite mask the sound of Karl's irregular breathing.

The girl looked haggard and dirty in the light of the street lamps, her face glistening from tears but man behind her was very clean by comparison; almost composed except for the heavy sound of his breathing. What was going on here? Who were these people?

Could they have something to do with the van? He instantly realised he needed back up; things weren't right!

'Control... I need assistance... we've got...'

Karl completely lost it. He pushed Lara to one side where she staggered and fell - then drew his gun to the horizontal in front of him, half lining the sight to his eye.

Adam frowned.

Preece's eyes opened wide as he realised what was happening before him. Instinctively, he tried to drop to his knees; his hand released the radio and tried to cover his face, his second reaching pointlessly for the baton clipped to his belt; his silent mouth spelling an 'O'.

Karl pulled the trigger; the cruel streak of sadistic pleasure blossoming in his heart; his lips a pitiless crack.

The explosion of noise had no sound deadening in the street. The noise carried up and around the edifice, echoing loudly and ricocheting back and forth between the buildings. Monk, talking loudly with his team across the poor reception on the force radios at the front, stopped still and cocked an ear, puzzled as to where the sound had emanated from.

Colleen McLaughlin stopped talking to camera, ignored her latest interviewee, and twisted in an effort to isolate the direction the sound of the explosion had come from; the cameraman and producer swinging to follow her gaze.

Crime Investigation looked up from their attentions to the wrecked tram in amazement. That had sounded like a gun going off.

The bullet flew from the muzzle and pierced Preece barely a centimetre above his standard issue bullet proof vest. It cleared his lungs and other major organs easily but embedded itself in his gullet, causing him to choke, his mouth filling instantly with blood; his airways blocking. He collapsed to the ground beside the van, the dampness and soaking wet left foot forgotten in his effort to breathe.

Karl calmed instantly. His breathing returned to normal and Lara was forgotten as he sauntered with a confrontational swagger towards the stricken policeman, passing his friend without even a sideways look. Blowing easily on the barrel like he'd seen the black hat baddies in the cowboy films do, he struck a gunslingers pose with one hand on his hip then re-aimed it downwards – directly at the frightened man's forehead.

Preece gagged with fear and clawed at his neck with desperation and extreme anxiety. Was this it? He instantly felt the regret his of short life. Why haven't I done more? I should've married and had kids. Jesus. No! Don't kill me! Please! His eyes widened; the whites of his eyes strangely exciting to Karl.

The dawning realisation struck Adam right at that moment. His friend had lost it and he wanted no part of it, no matter how good a friendship they had… it wasn't about to survive this. He clenched and unclenched his hands and his head shook softly with sorrow – unwilling to get involved.

Bert appeared at the doorway behind the small group. It was time to act and he prayed he wasn't too late. He'd heard the first shot as he jumped from the foot of the ladder, and now he was witnessing the pre-meditated murder of yet another person.

'NOOOO!' he shouted as he broke instantly into a run towards the group – thoughts of his own safety oddly pushed from his mind. The sound of the word trailed on as he hared the few metres towards them. Both the men turned to look with astonishment.

The surprise had prevented Karl from firing the gun, Uncertain; the barrel waving unfocused, he twisted to watch the oncoming yelling fool. Ignoring the police officer, he brought the gun around to centre the sights on Bert who was closing the distance quickly.

Bert passed the tiring Adam before he could do anything, and launched himself onto the younger man in a classic rugby tackle; arms out stretched; his face a mask of hatred. The surprise element was enough to prevent Karl from getting off a shot. The moment of impact threw the warm weapon from his grip and it flew in a long arc to hit the tarmac and skitter underneath the van still parked at the kerb, leaving the two men to fall to the ground locked in each other's grip - tumbling painfully over and over on the ground, each searching for the upper hand. Karl was furious his beloved weapon had gone and anxious to punish.

Lara watched in quiet fascination from her vantage point in the gutter, before the over-whelming desire for self-preservation over took her and she slid backwards – away from the three men, searching for a hiding spot.

Adam was struggling with his conscience. His friend was out of control and beyond help… and what the hell was that bloke doing here? He thought he'd left him on the roof? He didn't fancy sticking around but his feeling of duty towards his partner obscured everything else – even the weight of the bag still dragging on his back. Looking up at the sound of a 'hey' he saw the group of running police rounding the corner towards them.

'You – stop! Stop right now. Police!' Bellowing shouts.

'Come on, Karl!' he yelled at his friend who had by now rolled on top of Bert and managed to strike him once powerfully across the face. 'We need to get outta here!'

Bert lay there panting, his nose streaming with blood; his arms now limply at his side as Karl looked up and saw what his friend had seen.

Jumping up, he aimed a kick at the fallen man's ribs before joining Adam in running down the road away from the newcomers.

Bert wasn't beaten yet. Despite the explosion of pain, he clawed himself up and followed the fleeing duo, splashing in the puddles when he didn't pick his feet up; creating washes of water to cascade across the pavement. He gave a relieved glance and weak smile at Lara as he staggered past her, then built up a little speed to chase the couple.

From the other direction came another two constables who instantly assessed the situation in the dim light and heard their partners calling out to them. Seeing the two men approaching, they decided to tackle the larger of the two. He looked slower and more ungainly with a large bag bouncing on his back, though a lot more beefy than the other one. The three collided and stumbled to the ground.

Karl side-stepped them then paused and jigged nervously on the spot, uncertain what to do now. He looked up and saw Bert bearing down on him, then back down at his friend wrestling helplessly with the two officers, the bag of money crushed irretrievably under them.

Decision made. He turned and ran.

Bert was after him and more determined than ever. He wasn't going to get away with what he'd done.

Lara was being tended to. Appreciating that she was safe for the first time for two hours, she tried to blurt out everything that she had seen. She had witnessed murders and been dragged down the lift shaft by her hair... and...

Preece was receiving emergency first aid by paramedics drafted quickly from their other duties. They reckoned he would live, but not be back at work for a while. Swathes of bandages were clutched to his throat in an effort to stymie the flow of life force.

The excitement of the ambulances passing the court house on their passage through the maze of side streets to the rear of the store proved too much for Colleen McLaughlin who was now giving a report like a formula one commentator as though they were competing for first place.

CHAPTER 20

Karl dashed down the glistening wet streets, his once careful measured breathing changing progressively to hacking wheezing. He passed a shuttered department store and skidded to a halt at a pointless sign post denoting the fact that the area was for taxis and buses only. Leaning and gripping the pole, he desperately tried to collect his thoughts whilst gasping to regain composure.

He whipped his head around to survey the immediate area, frantically searching for a way out. It had all gone wrong. He'd lost the money, lost his friend, and why was that annoying bloke still chasing him? He heard the oncoming footsteps pounding noisily in the puddles eerily in the quiet of the street.

Bert was catching up quickly. He had one desire and one desire only now: catch the murderer. He felt more anger in his gut than ever. This shit was not going to get away. That poor girl dragged down the lift... that pitiable store assistant murdered... his blood boiled at the recent events practically burned to the rear of his retinas.

Apprehension! What was going to happen next? Did the lad have another weapon? Would he himself be the next victim to die this evening? What would Sandra say?

Sandra! What would Sandra say? She wouldn't care. She had cared less and less as the months went on about anything to do with him. She started stupid arguments. She moaned about stupid things. I know she doesn't love me anymore! The signs were all there that she had someone else. I'm trying to deny them, but they're all there... the secret conversations on the phone... the late night returns to the marital home... the sudden change in clothing style for a much more tarty image. Bah! What does it matter anymore? Lara had cared more for him in the few minutes they had spent together than Sandra had done for the last year – and this bastard had hurt her.

It crucified Bert that he had opened the lift shaft door and let him into their lives. If only he had left them shut...stayed sitting down!

And there he was!

Karl looked directly down the street and saw the looming figure of his pursuer. It was the last thing he needed and Bert looked angry. Cock-sure confidence was almost a distant memory as the sudden realisation that he'd have to sort this problem without his gun crashed into his mind. A quick decision made, and Karl took off again, crossing the small raised traffic island at full pace, jumping the kerb and trampling the central small planted area without care. He slipped and slid slightly on the damp earth, dropping to his knee fleetingly as he lost his footing, regaining his balance and continuing now with a dark brown patch of damp soil pressing uncomfortably against his leg. Bert took the opportunity to close the gap considerably, following the same path with a little more success.

Karl quickly looked left and right. He could hear the distant yells of approaching police and the closing breath of his pursuer immediately behind. The church loomed ahead of him, minimal up lighting around the building signifying that it was still open. Karl leapt over the short stone wall and almost stumbled on the uneven grave stones behind. Hastily he regained his footing and sprinted to the heavy front doors, throwing his weight against the metalwork adornments on the right hand one to open it as rapidly as possible.

It crashed open into the foyer to surprise a small group of elderly ladies readying themselves for the elements outside. Plastic hair coverings and tightly buttoned coats were already in place; the last remnants of vital gossip imparted. Over large brown hand bags and unwieldy umbrellas were brandished in shock as Karl interrupted their conversations with his sudden entrance. They gasped behind their glasses and muttered, 'well I nevers' to each other as he almost bowled one of them over in his haste to get past and through the inner door. As soon as he was through, the front door crashed open again – another howl of wind playing at their plaid skirts – Bert was hastening through, though this time with a quick mumbled apology.

Karl ran down the central aisle, skidding a little because of his wet shoes on the stone floor. Losing his balance, he crashed painfully to the floor, but had the presence of mind to shuffle hastily between two pews as he heard the inner door open for the second time. He lay there trying to control his breathing, staring at the huge cavernous ceiling above him; beautiful wooden beams crossing the building and into the apex, black metal pins securing the joints that were over a hundred years old, and more than aware of the damp trousers pressing uncomfortably against his knee whilst listening for the approaching man.

Bert came abruptly to a halt as he realised that he was at the back of the church and surveyed the empty hall before him. Deserted. No one evident inside. The air was heavily scented with the stale smell of burnt incense and pungent flowers.

The vast space still echoed from the door banging on the door stop before closing discretely. Casting his eyes around, searching for his quarry, he failed to appreciate the beautiful architecture – the stone carvings and ornate stained glass windows depicting religious figureheads and biblical occurrences. From where he stood, his gaze searched the rows and rows of ancient wooden seating eventually taking in the pulpit at the far end and the choir stalls beyond. There was no sign of the man he was chasing.

To his left there was a secondary aisle – narrower than the main, central one. These aisles had the effect of splitting the width of the space into three distinct seating areas, like the layout in a large airplane. The pulpit arose from the front of the centre section of seating; an attractive wooden lectern and ornate gold coloured candlestick holders each side as the main features; the church organ obvious beside that to the far left. There were plenty of places to hide for a fleeing murderer.

Decision made, Bert started a slow walk down the central aisle, checking left and right between each row of pews. He'd have to be here somewhere, he had been right behind him and the only other door was at the far end leading to the vestry... but he wouldn't have had time to reach that far.

First, second and third rows. Nothing! Fourth row now. In the second aisle there was a wide stone column reaching into the higher echelons of the roof... chipped and showing the distinct wear and tear of a hundred years of people pushing past it, it was still wide enough to hide someone behind it. Bert hesitated and craned his neck to check it out. Confident that he wasn't hiding there, another deep breath and he continued to the fifth and sixth rows. Still nothing!

Measured paces; arms bent at the elbows; fists clenched. Bert tried desperately to ignore the cold draft on his poorly covered body through the ill-fitting windows and loose tiled roof of the church. These places were so cold! His coat had been lovely and warm despite its poor condition!

Seventh row. Bert looked right and a split second too late, he looked left. Karl hurled himself from the space between the pews – arms outstretched like a missile from a launcher; his right fist catching Bert on the side of the face, reopening the wound above his eye, and knocking him to the right so as he fell over the pew armrest and crashed to the ground. Karl took the momentary opportunity to continue his flight down towards the pulpit, scampering like a scared jack rabbit.

Bert was soon up again and after him.

His quarry had scooted around the large oblong communion table and chairs, his steadying hand knocking the chalice, heavily embroidered velvet runner and bible from their usual home to the floor, avoided an elaborately carved wooden stand holding a forgotten music score, leapt up the few steps to the choir stalls and was now frantically trying to open the door to the vestry.

The door was obviously locked. Karl was furiously banging the arched wooden entry, but without success. The heavy metal locks and hinges rattled enticingly but held firm. It had been strongly built and withstood worse than Karl in its day.

Karl turned to face the oncoming tracker – fists raised like a pugilist – face twisted in a condescending sneer. He had no choice now but to fight – there was no where else to go. His back was against the wall and otherwise trapped. He tried to change his mindset and decided to attack now instead of defend. He was positive that he had the upper hand; much younger and therefore much more agile.

Bert approached more slowly. He was angry and his heart was pumping loudly. He had to make amends for letting this man onto the fifth floor. He was determined to see justice done. Determination!

'You don't stand a chance, old man!' Karl mocked; false bravado keeping his adrenalin pumping feverishly through his veins.

'The youth of today!' Bert derided in return. 'I always blame the parents!'

This hit a raw nerve. Karl was furious. He practically growled an inarticulate reply. His blood boiled and hate coursed through his body. How dare he say that?

A flurry of blows and the two men proved an even match. Both winded from connecting punches, kidneys aching, they eyed each other with mutual disdain. Bert wiped the steadily flowing drip of blood from across his eye with the back of his hand. Oblivious to the pain, he thought only of vengeance.

Unexpectedly, Karl kicked out at Bert's midriff. It connected, but Bert had the presence of mind to grab hold of the foot and twist viciously, causing Karl to lose his footing and fall to the left. A follow-up step and Bert's own foot connected with Karl's groin causing a loud howl of pain as he curled up and rolled quickly out of range.

Encouraged by his success, Bert leapt after him, but strode too far. He was off balance – his feet too far apart. Karl kicked again and caught Bert's knee. It gave way and once again he found himself on the dusty floor.

Karl was up and obviously taking the steps to kick him in the head. Hands up immediately across his face and he deflected the attempt.

Undaunted, Karl hurled himself at the man on the floor, and they rolled, clamped together – each desperate to get the upper hand and be on top. Endeavours at blows failed in the close proximity, merely futile tussling as they grabbed at each other's clothing and tried to find enough clear air to backswing. Bert's shirt was ripped a little more. Ineffectual kicks from each caused bruising but no other damage.

With Karl on top, Bert's wildly snaking elbow caught the other's chin, creating a window of opportunity. A raised knee between them, and Karl was flung off, banging his head against the solid oak communion table as he came to a halt.

Both rose to their feet, eyeing each other contemptuously. Karl had his back to the table. Much to Bert's chagrin, his steadying hand found a solid metal candlestick holder on the table and he produced it dramatically, brandishing it before him like a sword.

'Shit!' murmured Bert to himself as he watched the item swing dangerously before him; whooshing back and forth. It looked heavy and quite lethal. Karl's lips curled into a smile.

Karl darted forward and swung it again. Bert ducked just in time; the swishing sound painfully close to his head. Off balance, all Bert could do was drop down onto one knee. The candlestick was now on the backswing. It caught him soundly on his ribcage; the fire of pain projected through his lungs and he gasped helplessly, instinctively awaiting the completing blow of death.

Fortunately the surprise of making contact had loosened Karl's grip. The candlestick shot from his hand and skidded underneath a choir stall where it joined a discarded and overlooked black bound bible.

Bert was panting, desperately drawing breath deep into his lungs – tasting blood.

Karl took the opportunity. He turned and ran down the length of the main aisle in a bid for freedom, his footsteps and heavy faltering breathing the sign of a tired and worried man. Bert was up and after him as Karl skidded again on the damp floor at the welcome table by the door, sending a vase of flowers and collection plate crashing noisily to the floor. He wrenched the door open and disappeared through it with a last glance at the gap he had created between himself and Bert.

Fresh air again as Bert passed an elderly couple on the flagstone path outside; a large ancient mobile phone clamped to the man's ear as he struggled to hear the voice of the 999 operator asking about the episode at the church on which they were reporting. He saw that Karl was clearing the stone wall once more and summoned the energy to continue the chase.

As he ran around the bank, Karl slapped the stone walls either side of the cash-point to keep himself upright as he stumbled across the wet pavement in his haste. Shadows. Shadows were good. Were they enough to hide in? He splashed through the gutter. The drains were still trying to cope with the torrential rain fall of earlier and though the water was going, it wasn't disappearing quickly enough. Karl ignored his soaking feet as he checked out his location.

No police yet. That was a good sign! He still had a chance of escape. Just keep going.

Where to go? Where was safe? He could hear the sound of Bert's approaching feet running. Why wouldn't this guy knock off? What was with him? A little respect for him though? He was a determined bugger!

Running across the rest of the tarmac now towards the pedestrian entrance to the Phoenix Centre multi-storey car park at full tilt, Karl slammed into the peeling pale blue wooden door. It yielded immediately against the broken spring and slammed against the wall behind. He stumbled over the concrete step and continued in, his hands slapping the graffiti written wall to maintain his momentum en route to the first flight of stairs, which he then took two at a time.

The sound below was similar as Bert made his entrance through the broken door and found the bottom of the stairs.

One floor up, Karl looked over the rails to see if he could spot the following man. Twisting against the bar he desperately tried to see down in the weak glow of the municipal building lights. He could see that Bert was making good progress.

Karl looked at the exit door to the first storey parking area, and decided against it. Continuing up, he passed the second and third floor signs. The graffiti here was getting more offensive, far beyond the usual BAZ WOZ ERE type writing that today's unimaginative youth think they have the been the first to utilize. There were various gang tags and unintelligible bubble writing that would look more in place on the front of a teenage girl's diary than on the once white wall of a car park stairwell. The smell of urine was a little overpowering, and the tiny CCTV camera lenses high in the corners of each landing had been sprayed over with a selection of different colours. It was not a friendly atmosphere and though Karl had spent many happy days in previous years adding to the colours on the walls here, he would have given anything to be elsewhere right now. He imagined the police were catching up by now and wondered if he had been right in dashing in here.

Bert listened carefully for the sounds of his quarry ahead of him. He hadn't heard another door bang yet. He followed a little faster, gripping the handrails each side of the steps and heaving himself forward to aid his complaining leg muscles. Leaning out, he caught sight of Karl leaning to do the same.

Both men stopped and their gazes fixed upon each other. Bert took in the frightened look on the blond man's face; the unkempt messy hair a shockwave over his eyes; the stubbly chin more than a little threadbare in too many places. His eyes were the same eyes as he remembered earlier from the fifth floor. The only thing visible through the slit in the balaclava had been the drooping sides with dark shadows beneath – the features he now picked out again in the moment of eye contact. Karl recognised now the crazed look of mania on Bert's blooded face... a man possessed... a man on a mission.

Karl dodged back away from the edge and hauled open the heavy fourth floor door. The restraint was working on this one and the hinges screamed loudly from years of neglect. He dodged through and found himself sharing the same place with a handful of cars parked in the vast space. He looked around in panic, before running to the side to look over the parapet. He could hear the shouts of police. Two of their cars were circling the traffic island; the flashing blue lights oscillating viciously on the roofs; headlights flashing in turn like beacons; the sound of shrieking tyres on the damp surface as they searched for direction.

He looked up and down the street. The visible dual carriageway running across further down the one way, still carried a full load of vehicles despite the late hour; the distant sound of horns carrying across the strange stillness of the night following the storm. From a pub a short way down the opposite side of the road there pounded heavy rock music that changed in volume as the front door was opened and closed. The other way he could see the church from which he had just come; the spire dark against the night sky; a clock face glowing white. A police vehicle was now parked against the front wall that separated the short garden from the road; two wheels propped on the pavement to allow others past while the officers illuminated within checked their radios for information. He felt lucky to have got away just in time!

He turned and scouted the parking space. The exit ramps were further down, an aging grey Rover Montego estate parked opposite as though waiting to pounce; missing wheel trims and a red undercoated rear wheel arch giving the vehicle an abandoned, unwanted look.

Bert came through the doorway at full pelt, his grimy t-shirt hanging off his sweating body and scalp shiny from the endeavour. He pulled up when he saw the object of his chase standing before him.

The two men stood looking at each other across the concrete. Bert was desperate to get his breath. Karl shot glances left and right looking for a way out.

'You're not going anywhere!' Bert spoke with the harshness of hatred. He forced himself to calm down. His head and especially his ribs were throbbing and his nose now felt like it was broken.

'And what you gonna do abou' it?'

'Not so tough without your gun, are you, you little shit?'

'I took you before, an' I'll take you again!' Karl kept the wall to his back, but inched down towards one of the many supporting pillars in an act of unconscious self-defence.

Bert advanced once more. He was the taller man and he had the general fitness of his occupation to count on. Not a weight lifter, his strength was wirier than Karl's, his sinews used to the repetitive tedium of mauling machinery, climbing scaffolding and unloading vans. His back gave a warning twinge as though it knew what was coming.

Karl had always had Adam to sort this sort of thing out and had never bothered to actually develop any muscles... but he had the conniving cunning and wits of jackal which usually solved his created situations. He had the age advantage. The older bugger was going down. Tiring after the altercation in the church, he punched the air between them as a prelude to show him what to expect and to demonstrate his superior stamina.

A returned right hand powerhouse blow struck Karl on the jaw, snapped his head back with a crack. He staggered slightly but recovered his balance in record time. There was no way this balding prat was going to take him. He darted forward and jabbed his fist to Bert's stomach, trying to find the ribcage, before following an upper cut to his chin.

Bert went over backwards; his back throbbed again in agony. As he desperately tried to ignore it, he rolled sideways on the ground across wet oily tyre tracks, more than aware that the other man was closing on him.

Karl advanced and aimed a kick at his head, but Bert was too quick. He rolled again away from the passing foot and twisted to kick Karl's other leg from under him; his foot connecting nicely with the ankle.

There was a satisfying cracking sound (hopefully of bone) and this time Karl went down with a yelp of pain.

Both men slid themselves away from each other and returned to their feet, both rubbing themselves in their aching places, a small stream of blood now dripping from Bert's lip.

They closed again, more wary of each other this time.

Karl's sweeping fist found clear air as Bert bent out of the way. Both men were breathing hard, fists now held up in typical boxer's stance; small shuffling steps.

'Bastard!' cursed Bert softly hoping that the other one was wearing himself out. He himself was waiting for the most opportune moment to attack.

'Yeah... bring it on!'

A flurry of blows from Bert caught Karl several times on his torso, winding him slightly before he recovered and dealt a return punch which knocked Bert's head back with its force and opened the lip cut even further. More blood around his teeth, he could taste it with disgust.

He spat to the ground and returned his fists to the space before his face; a tongue searching his cheek and gums for possible broken teeth. Self preservation. Sandra wouldn't look at him if he had broken teeth. It was a pet hate of hers – people with bad teeth. What would it matter though, she never looks at me anyway? Extreme high emotion and rage coursed again through his body. Pent up passions and hatreds filled his brain, disabling any defence instinct and he suddenly launched forward.

The sheer ferocity of his attack took Karl by surprise, and in staggering back, he banged against the pillar before taking several blows to the face and chest. Karl sagged to the ground, and Bert relented in surprise while he watched the younger man panting on his knees. 'Please... no!' he whimpered. A hand was held before him, the other clutched his belly in a futile attempt to ease his ribs.

Bert felt the flush of pride. If only Lara was here to watch. Lara? He had thought of Lara; not Sandra. Hmm! He backed away as Karl crouched there with no attempt to follow, and looked over the balustrade to the road below.

A last quick glance at his obviously defeated opponent, he lent on the concrete surround and shouted down to the milling police. 'Up here! He's up here!' Shouting louder as they didn't register the direction of his voice. 'Hey... the car park.' Bert leaned up on the surround to project his voice. He could see one of the men look up followed by a couple of others. A welcome effect on them. He waved to help them understand.

Behind him Karl had got his second wind. Jumping to his feet, he scampered as fast as his ankle would allow towards the Montego and the ramp to the lower floor. It was no good being up here with bloody coppers around the building. He had to get out.

Bert heard him move and twisted away from his shouting to watch him running. A split second later, he was hot on his heels. 'You're not gettin' away!'

The fleeing Karl reached the ramp and swung himself around on the handrail; his ankle was aching unbearably from the kick earlier. He tried to put it from his mind.

Bert was there a moment later. Following down the ramp, he launched himself at the fleeing youth once again; catching him on his back in a bizarre piggyback and bringing him collapsing on to the bonnet of silver green Toyota Avensis as Karl's legs buckled. The supple plastic bonnet distorted under their combined weight as Bert tried to mash the other man's face into the paint. The warmth of the recently used engine warmed their bodies.

Karl kicked back but missed his aim, giving Bert the chance to gain the upper hand as he slithered on the slippery surface.

Bert held his shoulders and smacked his head onto the windscreen with enough force that a small hole appeared – followed by a splintering sound and a spider's web of cracks meandering from the hole across the screen. He did it again – receiving a rewarding cry of pain from the obnoxious youth.

Karl found the energy to kick again, finding Bert's shin and causing a long scratch down the centre of the bonnet into the bargain; Bert yelled and slid from the car, accidentally kneeing the headlamp unit and making him stagger as he hit the floor, his face perilously close to the front grill. Another kick found his jaw, and he was down on the ground with a thump.

The younger man sat up and shook his head, a hand feeling the back of his head for the newly created damage and drawing back his fingers full of blood. He growled with displeasure as he regarded the man now sat on a right turn white painted direction arrow, panting; groggy from the blow.

As they watched each other with distrust, they could hear the squeal of tyres in the lower floors. Distant indecipherable shouts of approaching police made Bert smile as they neared through the levels.

Karl slid from the bonnet of the Avensis, leaving a large dent in his wake. He found his feet and stood between Bert and the car, wobbling slightly on his one damaged foot, a hand propping himself and maintaining verticality.

The exertion had spent both of the men. Evenly matched, Karl would have had a slight upper hand – had he been able to trust his damaged ankle – due to his position above his seated adversary. It had been a long evening for both of them.

'They're comin' for you!' said Bert with satisfaction. 'You're not going anywhere. You may as well give up!' He turned to the direction of the approaching police and jabbed a thumb towards them. 'See...there's no way out...they're all around you!'

'What's it to you anyway?' Karl couldn't believe the effort this troublesome man had gone to. 'Why couldn't you have just sat still and let us leave?' His eyes glared with hatred, disgust at Bert's mocking smile and the perceptive 'knowing' expression on his blooded face. A lifetime of abusing unresisting and helpless victims had left a false impression of how they dealt with it – no one had ever stood up to him before.

'You'll never understand decent people!' Disgust. Repugnance! Bert shook his head to convey his abhorrence and small splatters of blood covered his t-shirt like a spray can. The damage his nose had suffered earlier had left wide track of congealed blood down his chin and neck. The new cut was now adding an extra layer and his teeth shone brightly through the mess – like pearls. Shock and adrenalin was quenching the numbness and pain in his face but nevertheless, his smile widened. 'You don't murder innocent girls without going to jail. They'll like you in jail. You'll be *very* popular...very!'

Karl's eyes flicked back and forth again and saw that a bullet proof vested police officer was rounding the distant up-ramp; his bowed head talking into his radio. Karl was sweating. He was nervous. He didn't want capture... he wanted options...he was missing his previous confidence. What to do? What to do?

More police were finding the correct floor. One had arrived through the stairwell door and they had all slowed to a walk; shouting something which echoed far too much in the mostly empty floor to be understood, but sounded like 'down on the ground'.

'They'll love you in jail!' repeated Bert again, goading the younger man with delirious enjoyment. 'Do me the favour of remembering that poor girl you killed!'

Karl made an instant decision. He couldn't be caught. Adam had been taken down and didn't want the same fate. He turned and ran down the side of the Toyota and quickly climbed onto the broad concrete balustrade at its rear. Looking out, it was pitch black beyond, the poor fluorescent lighting of the car park not enough to project out. There was no street-lighting this side of the multi-storey – no obvious shops – nothing…just darkness. He couldn't make out the ground below…didn't know how far it was down…maybe it was for the best. He snatched a glance towards the approaching police.

The police had broken into a run towards them now. Bert didn't bother to move from his vantage point watching the unfolding events and prodded his damaged lip gingerly with a moist tongue; his hands flat on the ground to keep him upright. From his viewpoint, the damaged front of the late registration Toyota seemed to smile at him with a certain knowing.

Karl crouched on his perch and looked back at Bert with fearful eyes. The bags beneath them looked a little fuller, and for the first time he looked older than his years. Not a word spoken, his expression spoke volumes: relief perhaps. The linking gaze down the length of the car maintained a communication. Karl wasn't left with a preferred choice of action.

The first officer reached the parking space and got to him a second too late; his outstretched hand groped futilely for the youth; unheard words and commands shouting unheeded for response.

Karl pitched forward and out of view.

His final cry of uncontrollable fear through his descent terminated abruptly with the tinkling sound of glass and the immediate commencement of the high pitched whistling wail of a cheap car alarm and the accompanying car horn's harsh intermittent blaring.

Bert closed his eyes and wished for sleep.

'I want to see him…is he all right? Please! I'm OK…I'm all right. Where is he? Where's Bert?' Lara was receiving the full response from a helpful medic who was desperately trying to cover her with a shiny thermal coat to keep her warm and check the dilation of her pupils and head for damage. She was trying to push the poor green jacketed girl away with protestations and lies of good health.

Monk had assigned another crew to make entrance to the building now through the opened rear doors with the advance knowledge that there were two people (one badly injured) trapped in the motionless lift a floor or so up the shaft.

The Incident Commander was brought up to date and decided to find the local television crew again to make a statement. He wandered off making notes in his little black bound book.

Lara was on her feet and staring down the street. She had no idea of the current time and didn't care. Though the hour was late, adrenalin was still pumping through her veins as the recent events of the evening still haunted and consumed her thoughts. She could see the larger of the two men being arrested further down. He was going quietly now after the initial fruitless struggle. Handcuffs were clasping his hands behind his back and he was being walked back towards Lexington's – a warning hand on his shoulder to remind him of his predicament. One of the young constables who had made the arrest was dragging the confiscated bag behind him. The black man looked dejected and trailed his feet awkwardly.

'His friend killed two people!' Lara screeched as he approached – an accusatory finger pointing and jabbing in his direction. 'The other one!' she reiterated, 'the other one is a murderer!'

'Yeah,' spoke one sergeant, pulling momentarily from another, more important conversation with his staff, 'we know. Calm down... come on, love!' A placating hand was placed on the agitated girl's arm.

Lara pulled away from the condescending man, and drew the coverall closely around her shoulders against the cold wind that was beginning to stir again. Damp, she shivered and moved to the side of the van for a little shelter, where she leaned with her arms folded. She alternated staring up the street looking for her new friend and checking the progress of the injured policeman resting on the ground as a paramedic worked on him.

An ambulance had pulled around and parked in the road with its back doors open. The bright fluorescent green and yellow stripes and logos glared in the harsh light of other headlamps; the flashing roof lights bathing the back of the building in intermittent colours. She watched as a stretcher was assembled beside the incapacitated man before he was moved carefully to the mattress; a plethora of tubes, bottles and pouches accessing his body through syringes and needles fixed into his arms and mouth.

She looked at his frightened face bound with bandages and neck guards as he was lifted across; his staring eyes fixed on her with a strange expression of wonder and bewilderment. Lara instantly recalled a similar expression on Sian's face as she faced the oncoming bullet and choked back another sob. Come on…be strong now.

The policeman was in the back of the ambulance and the doors were slammed loudly. An accompanying wail of the siren, and it was off to the nearest hospital. – the diesel engine clattering loudly.

Everywhere she looked now was filled with emergency services. Yellow hats; black garments; strange machinery; people bustling everywhere. A fire tender had joined them at the back of the store and cutting equipment was being hauled from the lockers on either side.

THUMP! The noise of fevered activity around her was getting louder in the more enclosed area between the buildings, but she could definitely hear a kicking sound against metal.

Lara twisted around and observed the van beside her. THUMP! There it was again! It sounded like a metal panel was being banged in and out…a popping noise coupled with a grunt. She placed her hand against the van and was rewarded with a definite vibration. Dawning realisation! Someone was inside. 'Hey!' She shouted for assistance. 'Hey help me! Over here! I think there's someone in here trying to get out!'

As two or three officers looked up to respond, Lara was testing handles to gain entry to the vehicle. The front door was locked, but the side door reacted and slid sideways out of the aperture. She blinked against the gloom inside as her eyes adjusted to the change in light level.

Louder now; the separating baulk head between drivers seat and load space was kicked again by someone within the folds of a bundle of cloth and covers; the lump vaguely alarming when united with a muted groan of pain. Lara spotted a bare knee sticking from amongst the creases. It looked like a woman's leg.

She reached in – tentatively grasped the nearest piece of cloth; took a deep breath and pulled it, exposing the hidden person beneath. Yet another frightened face; more obvious tears; more personal trauma. But all this (this time) on someone who was tied up with what looked like plastic string.

'My God...are you all right? Shit...stay still...I'm here to help you!' Calmly. 'A LITTLE HELP HERE...PLEASE!' Louder. Now she was shouting to any one who was listening in the vicinity.

As another policeman joined her, Lara was in the process of climbing in to the van in order to pull the taped cloth from the poor girl's mouth. She herself almost gagged in concurrent understanding and empathy as the relief was obvious on the newly discovered woman, before the responding attempt at gratitude from a dry and sore mouth. A bright flashlight was flicked across her features as the officer reached for his pocket knife in order to release her.

'Come on, let's sit you up. Are you hurt?'

Together, they sat her up in the open doorway and faced her outwards. Sandra responded slowly and delicately. Her head was throbbing and her legs felt numb. She eased herself carefully and winced as the cuts made by the plastic ties on her ankles found the cool wind. The one ankle was almost black with the bruise and twice the normal size.

Lara sat down next to her. 'What happened to you?' she asked propping the other girl from falling over and dragging the insulated cover from her own shoulders to around Sandra's. The officer requested extra assistance – more medical help was needed.

'Mmm…I was…' Sandra had problems talking following her ordeal. She felt groggy and tried to concentrate on breathing the clean air, a little part of her brain trying to comprehend the busy action around her and recall the strange sequence of events leading up to her enclosure in the temporary prison.

'I was looking for my husband. I got dragged in…by…there were two or three of them!' Sandra tried shaking her head to regain her composure. 'Masks and…' She descended into gasping wails of self pity, leaning heavily on the younger girl for female support. Other medics were arriving at a run to check her out.

She pressed her face into Lara's shoulder and sobbed freely.

Bert was helped to his feet and escorted slowly to the waiting police Volvo 760 Estate which had climbed to the fourth storey after it had found the main route into the car park. He had refused immediate medical assistance and now just wanted to return to the Lexington's building. The effort of the evening was taking its toll pretty badly by now. He felt physically drained and a little close to tears… though he wouldn't admit it, and tried to maintain his dignity with composure he didn't really feel.

Would Lara still be there? He wanted a hug. The time delayed shock of his quarry's demise had started to affect him and now he just wanted someone to tell him that everything was going to be all right. He needed the closeness of someone who cared. Lara!

Muttered protestations about his health and the fact that there was others trapped in the lift needing more assistance were met with 'yes sir...don't worry...everything is in hand' style responses. He felt heartened slightly, and more than a little pleased that there had been other witnesses to the lad's leap from the building and that he hadn't been hauled into handcuffs and the back of a waiting van.

The car rounded the traffic island and returned to the rear of Lexington's; Bert's throbbing head was making him feel extremely nauseous. He could see the abandoned builder's van ahead and make out Lara sat in the open side doorway, the visual picture of her bare legs and heels a little irresistible regardless of the current situation. Who was that sitting with her? Whoever it was looked pretty battered as well?

The Volvo pulled to a halt alongside the van and the rear door was opened for him. Bert climbed slowly out, helped more than a little by a helpful policeman who was calling for medical attention; worried by the layers of dried blood coating his face, neck and visible down his front through the damaged t-shirt.

Bert stood there, barely erect with the agony in his back and ribs. He looked at Lara; the power of his feelings was running into overtime. The latent desire that had long been quelled and forced into remission was surfacing. He felt like he'd been to hell and back and all he could remember was her tender touch and comforting presence whilst up on the fifth floor.

She gazed back with pleasure, happy beyond words that he had returned to her. The intense worry that she had felt, since the moment he had been made to disappear into the lift with the threat of her own demise, disappeared instantly. She wanted to run to him and hold him. Kiss him at last; show her true feelings to the man. She tried to ease the other girl from her shoulder – she was in the way now.

Sandra pulled her face up out of Lara's blouse and stifled her sobs, desperately trying to focus on the familiar man stood before her; arms held up as though ready for an embrace.

Bert's eyes widened with astonishment; he couldn't believe what he was seeing. The incomprehension was evident in his voice now. 'Sandra?' he said, the pitch of his voice rising slightly. 'What on earth are you doing here?'

'Bert?' croaked Sandra in return, 'is that you?' She blinked feverishly, desperate to return full 20:20 vision as quickly as possible and confirm the identity.

'You two… you two know each other?' Lara struggled with the concept. 'Bert… who is this? Do you know her?'

The three regarded each other with the shock of the situation. Bert looked between the two girl's faces. 'My wife!' he almost whispered in dismay, 'my wife!'

Lara was returning a look of puzzlement but concealed desire. The pleading in her eyes melted his heart. She hadn't realised that he was married. Her heart pounded anxiously; her breathing deepened and the quiver in her shoulders was evident as the gravity of the predicament struck her.

Sandra returned a similar look of confusion and although the trauma of the evening had affected her deeply, she recognized the mutual desire between the two... one that she once had had with her husband. Anger! This was her husband. How dare she? Her face creased into resentment as she glared at her new rival.

Bert's face dropped noticeably as he saw the choice he had to make. It was too much for him now. His body wanted to give up. Eyes glazing over, he slumped back against the rear quarter of the Volvo and allowed the oncoming medics to help him onto a stretcher.

'Now on the evening news we have the latest report now from Wolverhampton. Colleen McLaughlin is still at the scene and reporting LIVE!' Irene Carlson smiled to camera one and swivelled slightly in her fancy chair to face the desk mounted monitor screen again whilst shuffling papers. The viewers saw the picture of Colleen above and to the right of Irene's head as picture in picture. 'Colleen, I can see that the weather is returning to normal there. Could you bring us up to date on the latest developments there?'

The picture of Colleen, looking immaculate again with her hair glossy and sleek with a lock hanging seductively across the top of one eye, expanded to fill the entire screen. The close up demonstrated that her 'Chanel' jacket had managed to avoid any water damage, and the white lace topped blouse was still pristine.

She smiled through a slightly down-turned face and up turned eyes; the barely visible eyebrow lifted clearly and her top row of teeth gleamed in the dim back light once more. 'Yes, Irene. There has been a lot happening in the past few minutes, coinciding with the passing over of the thunderstorm. Gun shots were heard not long ago at the rear of Lexington's, causing many of the police services to leave the area behind me, and disappear down that alleyway... over there.'

The camera panned to her left and picked out the barely visible street to the side of the building beside the parked fire tender and still hardworking fire officers. Colleen's face turned with it, then back again as it returned to centre.

'It is reported that an arrest was then made. Allegedly there were two individuals who had organised an attack on the cash office on the top floor. As yet we don't know if they were successful, but we have confirmation that one police officer has been badly wounded.'

The picture of Colleen returned to the corner of the screen as Irene Carlson coughed slightly, a thin pale hand waving at her lips. 'So, Colleen, is there any link between the accident caused by the tram and this possible theft? Or is it more of an opportunistic event by people already in the store at the time of the incident?'

'That has not yet been ascertained, but we do know that the two or three men entered the store through the rear doors *after* the tram had hit and attacked several people on their way up.'

'Has anything more come from the reports of a shooting on one of the floors?' Irene checked down her list, her manicured nails professionally running down the points that needed clarification from an agenda put together by the show's producers and research assistants.

'It has been confirmed that a phone call was made to a central police station detailing certain events that were taking place on the fifth floor of Lexington's. The caller had been contacted by someone inside the building, but at this time, no further information has been forthcoming from the police.' Colleen stopped and tilted her head slightly to one side as though a friendly puppy, her practiced smile ready again on her lips as she dreamt of the ultimate prize. Anchor position. She was cold and more than a little hungry by now. A limp packaged garage forecourt tuna sandwich and packet of cheese and onion crisps had not constituted much of a meal earlier on, though the producer had kept her plied with over sugared canteen coffee during the evening. Oh for a hot bath, soft music and a low fat chicken salad washed down with a glass of wine whilst snuggling into her new white towelling robe. Bliss. But. Work first. She waited for the next question with eyes glinting. Does this mean I can have a lie in tomorrow or up early to file another report?

'And how about the tram? Do we yet know why it left its tracks or how it managed the speed it had?' Irene checked her notes again. 'We heard mention of it being over forty-five miles per hour at impact! Is that possible?'

317

'Yes Irene, forty-five miles an hour is more than possible on this modern public transport. Most of their route is tram dedicated, though they generally slow down when following main roads. Police Forensics have been crawling over the vehicle for the past hour or so now. We now know that there was a simple incendiary device placed on the main brake servo mechanism, but as yet we don't know how it was detonated. Speaking to one of the officers earlier, he told me that it was a fairly simple device, possibly operated by a mobile phone signal. If that is true, then there must have been someone on board the tram to be close enough to detonate it. A hallmark of a suicide bomber or maybe someone who didn't know what was going to happen.'

'An accident if you like?' Irene shook her nut brown hair indiscernibly, more than aware that she was still on main screen and subconsciously trying to compete with the younger woman's faultless locks.

'Well, that is a possibility. The police, at the current time, are ruling out a terrorist attack due to the nature of the incident. A public place, yes, but not the ideal location or time of day. To make the massive political statement, it would be unlikely that al-Qaeda or any other terrorist network cell would use a Wolverhampton department store at eight thirty on a Thursday night to make their point. It would be more likely that this act was organised and executed as a diversion for the other events... In which case it is unlikely that it was a willing person who would have sacrificed themselves for the distraction.'

Irene Carlson nodded her head thoughtfully. The image of Colleen was replaced with footage taken earlier of rescue attempts. No pedestrians had yet been allowed around the rear of the building; the monitored cordons extended to the new crime scene, so no shots were yet available to show the events there. Producers contented themselves with showing images of the cranes working overtime to ship out bedraggled survivors and William Monkham shouting orders to his extremely weary crew.

Alison had never stood a chance. From the moment she had met the two men that afternoon, her fate had been sealed. Overwhelming self confidence that the obvious desirable condition of her body and patent assertive attitude were enough to keep her safe were the main equipment she carried as defence against the nastier elements of society. Today, Thursday, they had been her undoing. Adam's testimonial just past midnight at Wolverhampton Central Police Station was an eye opener for the attending Crime Investigation Department.

With the promise of a more relaxed criminal processing, coupled with the fact that eye witnesses had cleared him of any observed murders, he had been invigorated to share the details of the afternoon. His solicitor advised him against the declaration, but Adam knew that he was now juggling his life doing twenty-five to thirty at her majesty's pleasure, and Birmingham's Winson Green Prison had a reputation that he didn't fancy living for any longer than necessary.

Knowing that the bespectacled pinhead solicitor did most of his work for Big Sam meant that he kept that name omitted from the tapes in the interview room. Big Sam had fingers in many pies and

Adam wanted to be able to sleep soundly in which ever cell he languished without the threat of retribution. He knew which side his bread was buttered. Be cool... say enough to please the cops... do the stretch and be out ready to start again.

The solicitor removed his rectangular framed glasses to the desk before him, stroked his thinly covering black beard with one hand and twisted his red and blue striped tie between the thumb and forefinger on his other – listening intently to every word. Adam was more than aware that his 'now former' boss would soon know everything that was said tonight and had assured his solicitor in a discrete whispered aside that he needn't be concerned.

Nevertheless, it was with barely disguised fascination that the three other men in the little room listened to Adam's relation of his version of events.

Adam insisted that when they had blown the brakes and operating system on the tram, they hadn't expected a simultaneous fork of lightning to hit the power cable. Adam denied prior planning beyond anticipating the tram to hit the station with enough speed that it would have caused a big enough headache and spectacle for emergency services. The idea that it could have jumped the track and caused the devastation that it did was beyond expectations. The explosive device that he had attached to the underside of the unit was not powerful enough to do anything more.

His deadpan expression and deliberate and eloquent language failed to fully convince his interviewers, though they continued to take his testimony in relative silence. They didn't need to come on strong with him – he was talking enough for the moment. By Adam's words, it had been a plan that had just worked a little too well.

The whole (and true) version would never be told.

The ambulances carrying the injured police officer and Bert left without being noticed through another exit on to the dual carriage way ring road that circled the town, bound for the hospital through the residual surface water in the much quieter streets.

On board the second ambulance was the exhausted Robert Simmonds. Seated in silence beside him on a plastic drop down bench were his wife and Lara. The onboard paramedic looked between the three soundless people and measured a small dose of morphine for the man on the stretcher into a newly opened, vacuum-packed plastic syringe.

Lara held her head in her hands, playing compulsively with her fringe, twisting the strands between her first and second fingers, the other hand fiddling with the shiny thermal coat. It had all become too much for her. Legs crossed, she had balled her thin form into an inadvertent fortress.

Sandra had her damaged leg propped on the end of her husband's bed; the bright and varied colours of her leg glowing warmly; her head tilted back and eyes were closed as she thought through the revelations of the evening.

What was she going to do now? She'd pushed him hard enough away, and now been rewarded for it – he had lost interest in her. The man lying before her was not the same person she had left that morning for work – this man had passion and the results of obsessive determination covering his body. She'd heard one police officer talk of him chasing down one of the men who had hurt her in the van. He looked like hell.

Frankly, he had never looked more desirable.

CHAPTER 22

Harmony

Halloween was a better day for weather. It opened bright and sunny, though with a distinct chill in the air that proved reluctant to leave throughout the day's duration. Typical British weather. When we need it sunny; it rains... when we need it snowing; full sunshine. When the day's mood was dark and miserable, the weather was beautiful!

It was never appropriate.

The national newspapers had since stopped paying attention to the tragedy in Wolverhampton, though the local ones continued to keep running backgrounds. They found as much information as possible on the disaster. Twenty six were dead and five injured in the Lexington building and their biographies were given in glorious detail. Hopes – dreams – occupations! It was the biggest thing to happen to the West Midlands since a freak tornado wrecked a street of housing in Birmingham and it was going to be milked for all it was worth.

Local television continued to give screen time to the latest developments. Crash investigation teams were looking into the reasons for the complete collapse of the upper floors at the Lexington building. Architects, surveyors and construction engineers were coming under scrutiny for the part they had played in its initial creation. Insurance companies and lawyers were either sweating or rubbing their hands in glee. Lawsuits were plentiful.

But national television had moved onto other important news. Another downed airplane in Athens through suspicious circumstances and immigration problems through an ineffectual government stance had taken public attention from the Midlands. The time in the limelight was fleeting. The only people still interested in the disaster beyond those caught up in it were those who stood to make or lose money.

A documentary team had staked out the site to take footage of the recovery for a documentary. There was always extra money to be made on the back of these things. A few interviews from key personnel – repeated footage from the news that night and a small number of extra computer graphics demonstrating in tedious detail the implosion of the top floors and a whole hour of television could be created for minimal expense and maximum payoff.

The police were tight-lipped as to their findings on the alleged criminal activities. Nominal statements and the promise of an on-going investigation had sated the public thirst for a whole day – the news of one of the perpetrators demise raising questions as to the police's heavy handling of the situation. Did they chase him over the parapet to his death? This was yet another death at the Phoenix Centre car park… should the architect for that particular building face prosecution for negligent construction? Voiced concerns about the dead youth's family and whether it was a lawful death disgusted those actually there at the time. The twenty six dead and five injured were almost forgotten in the police bashing.

The press loved to stir up trouble because it was good for sales. A good story was a live story; one which encouraged lively debate and opposing views of the same situation. They had at least another good month of added paper sections and in-depth compulsive reading interviews left from this.

Today it was the day for the memorial service at 'West Park' opposite the town's beloved football stadium. It was a day for the necessary people to pay homage to those who died whilst going mindfully about their own business on that fateful night.

Bert awoke that morning with the usual hesitation. The period of time between sleep and consciousness blurred for a moment before he found full vision and realised he was home in bed. Racked with nightmares again, it was always a relief to open his eyes on even the minimal sunlight through his bedroom window. The horror of the dead on the top floor still tormented him, as did those hours he spent in the dark – climbing up and down a lift shaft 'wind tunnel'. He turned and looked at the woman lying beside him. She looked peaceful and quiet; her hair cascading across the pillow. He checked the luminescent figures on the clock radio beside the bed. 7:55. why did he always wake a few moments before it was due to go off with the cheerful chatting of the early morning disc jockey? He rubbed both hands briskly across his face in an effort to bring full consciousness then flicked the 'off' button on the alarm... now not required.

Slipping from the bed leaving the covers undisturbed, he padded through the bedroom door to the bathroom. Behind him he heard the sleeping murmurs of the girl and the soft rumbling snoring of Tyrone, curled up in his bedroom basket; ears drooping across his eyes.

Brushing his teeth furiously, he stared at his reflection in the false light above the mirror. A grim and hard faced man stared back – a cruel scar evident below his hair line – a nose not quite central – a wound not yet quite healed on his top lip.

His usual morning depression had not changed, though he did now have a little appreciation of life. The sight of Sian's murder had altered perceptions. He was still sad, though not as self absorbed as perhaps he once was. No one should ever take the choice on another's life.

He spat once into the sink, the rushing of the cold water swirling the paste down the plughole.

'You all right baby?' The soft and loving voice came from the doorway. Tired, yet worried. 'I love you, you know!'

Bert grunted his affirmation, and suddenly found her hands encircling his body, stroking his chest. Her soft naked breasts pushed hard and desirably (comfortably) against his lower back; her cheek and warm breath rubbing his shoulder blade; a smooth hairless leg caressing his, her foot soft on his shin.

She was like a cat against his skin; almost purring with affection. He couldn't help but smile; a mouth full of foam as he heard her sigh; fingers now tweaking a nipple then twirling through his plentiful chest hair as she blindly searched his body. Pleasure.

He finished at the sink and turned to face her... her arms now around his neck, they kissed passionately... his arms holding her tight. She couldn't get enough of him. There they stayed until Tyrone appeared, yawning and stretching with a little whimper, and Bert had to move on. Jobs to do. The dog to be walked.

It was going to be a big day. The memorial service was to be held at the park for the Lexington deceased. Survivors. Relatives of the departed. A selected few from the emergency services. Lexington himself would be attending as well as VIPs and assorted others from Wolverhampton council. The Salvation Army Brass Band was to be playing in the old bandstand; wreaths were to be laid; important words of wisdom, sorrow and appreciation spoken. Colleen McLaughlin had begged her producers to be allowed to cover the all-morning event.

Bert wasn't looking forward to it; wasn't going to go to it, but he had been in almost constant communication with Helen for the last week or so, and she had managed to convince him that he should go. Resolution. Closure. A sharing moment to put it all behind him.

She had kept in contact with the others from the fifth floor.

Sydney and Doreen had proved more resilient than anyone had expected. Instead of being completely distraught by the affair, they had seen it as a moment of excitement in their usually very repetitive lives. Doreen had surprised her husband with her positive attitude. It was a story to tell the grandchildren!

Sophie had apparently dumped her bloke; new confidence and a desire to live her life to the full had eclipsed her usual personality as a testament to Sian, whom she would never forget. She had decided never to be a 'push-over' ever again. You never knew how long you had left in this world!

'Bert,' Helen had beseeched, 'you've got to go.'

He knew she was right.

It was with a heavy heart he pulled on his one and only dark suit and tie in readiness for the day, and left the house to walk Tyrone to the local park. He was not in the mood today to carry him over the massive amount of broken glass and litter that was strewn across the tarmac paths from the previous night's bored underage drinkers, but did so anyway with the customary groan of routine. For the umpteenth time, he wondered who on earth sold them the 'alchopops' in the first place, and why the purchasers felt the need to smash the emptied bottles. Privately he hoped that they cut themselves doing it… fatally maybe?

Bert released Tyrone from his leash and watched as he sniffed happily through the shrubbery on his morning quest for the invisible; oblivious to his master's private torment.

Across town, Helen and Andy were readying themselves for the occasion. Claire had the day off school and was dressing appropriately for once. It had been a strange few days for the family who all had seen each other in different lights and ways. Andy was quieter and more attentive; Claire less belligerent.

Helen had been eager that Bert attend. Much to her husband's unspoken disgust, she held him in high esteem for his selfless actions. She intended to go and doubted the support Andy would give her; she needed him to go – disagreeing entirely with Bert's viewpoint on the Thursday's events; she had spent many hours on the phone to him.

Bert walked around the park in a daze and for the hundredth time replayed the incidents in his head. If only he hadn't opened those lift doors… he wouldn't have let those men enter the floor – and Sian would still be alive. Her death was his fault! He hated how he felt. He choked back a welling sob.

He couldn't blame Andy, even though he had been there. Andy had been right to say 'sit back and do nothing. Sit and wait for rescue'. Andy had helped open the doors. Shit… why did they have to open the doors? Sentenced that poor girl to death!

He had tried to make amends by chasing down that lad and there was some sense of justice in that death, but it hadn't taken the pain from him… of distrusting his own actions… and he didn't feel absolved of blame for Sian. The thought of the unnecessary death plagued him mercilessly.

If only he had left well alone.

Helen had the opposite view. Hindsight was a wonderful thing, but when you hear shouting for help, a real man steps up. How would he know what was going to happen? How long was he going to blame himself for? If he was going to be that foolish, then, was it Lexington's fault instead for opening so late? Wake up Bert – you didn't pull the trigger!

Bert let them into their home; Tyrone padded off for a drink of water from his circular metal kitchen bowl and he sank into his favourite armchair – the culmination of conflicting emotions and bad memories giving him yet another quickly emerging thumping headache and a dull pain behind his eyes.

Suddenly she was there again, slinking in through the lounge door and propping herself on one of the chair's arms. Dressed appropriately in black, she wore a black blouse, skirt and stockings and high heeled shoes. She hugged him close and felt his pain… understood his pain…disagreed with his reasons for angst but trying to be a good wife at last – again.

Sandra was a changed woman. She knew she had come close to losing him, and it had taken that eventful night to realise how much she needed him as a constant companion and life partner. She hadn't needed to plead. Marriage was a strong enough bond that Bert had never wanted to break. She was disappointed that she had let down her side and glad that he was willing to forgive. They had made new promises to each other – held each other tightly – walked Tyrone together – reviewed their relationship and established that they both had to move on and put the last year or so behind them.

Bert had no doubts now. He knew that they would be together forever… hadn't wanted anyone else to take her place! They weren't young any more and both now realised that they had taken their relationship for granted for too long. It needed working at; both needed frequent friendly words of encouragement and mutual understanding and interest. Sandra thought that she had found once more the man she had fallen in love with, and Bert knew he had changed irreparably. Some things would never be the same.

As long as they could get through this day. A chance to see Lara again and wish her luck. He hoped that she was coping all right. Helen hadn't mentioned her in their conversations. He felt for her – as a father figure would.

He kissed his wife tenderly again and winced a little as her weight shifted against his damaged rib. The hospital had recommended a chiropractor and a lot of rest and recuperation but both Bert and Sandra doubted he would follow their advice.

His hand stroked up her leg and found the bare thigh above her stocking top. She caught his soft intake of breath and beamed with pleasure as he smiled up at her. There was more healing to be had there than in any hospital bed.

Enough words had been already spoken and thoughts shared. 'Come on, love!' she encouraged, 'let's have a nice cuppa before we go. I'll make it. Come and sit with me!'

She took his hand, and without reluctance he followed her.